Written Off

Written Off

E. J. Copperman

NEW YORK

This is a work of fiction. All of the names, characters, organizations, places and events portrayed in this novel are either products of the author's imagination or are used fictitiously. Any resemblance to real or actual events, locales, or persons, living or dead, is entirely coincidental.

Published in the United States by Crooked Lane Books, an imprint of The Quick Brown Fox & Company LLC.

Crooked Lane Books and its logo are trademarks of The Quick Brown Fox & Company LLC.

Library of Congress Catalog-in-Publication data available upon request.

ISBN (paperback): 978-1-68331-199-7
ISBN (hardcover): 978-1-62953-599-9
ISBN (ePub): 978-1-62953-600-2
ISBN (Kindle): 978-1-62953-664-4
ISBN (ePDF): 978-1-62953-675-0

Cover design by Louis Malcangi
Cover illustrated by Robert Crawford
Book design by Jennifer Canzone

Printed in the United States.

www.crookedlanebooks.com

Crooked Lane Books
34 West 27th St., 10th Floor
New York, NY 10001

Hardcover Edition: June 2016
Paperback Edition: April 2017

10 9 8 7 6 5 4 3 2 1

Chapter 1

It was the way the grass had been mowed that made the difference for Duffy Madison.

He stopped dead in his tracks and shouted, "Here! Dig here! *Now*!"

The six FBI agents scouring the field behind the convenience store halted in their tracks and pointed to the uniformed police officers, who were the ones holding the digging implements. The uniforms were quickly on the spot and began frantically planting their shovels in the precise spot where Duffy was pointing.

Almost immediately, Lt. Antonio was by his side. "What did you see?" she asked, breathless from rushing to Duffy.

"A difference in the pattern," he answered. He turned toward the men, who had already dug down more than two feet. "Hurry, please!" he shouted. "She only has a minute and twenty seconds of air left!"

The officers did not look up but did seem to pick up the pace of their digging.

"What pattern?" Antonio asked.

"The pattern of the mowing," Duffy told her, intent on watching the effort. "The grass was mowed within the past two days, and it has not rained since. Harold Magaden managed to replace the sod over the grave he dug, but he didn't take the mowing pattern into account. The grass over this spot looks different. I can't believe I didn't see it sooner. Oh, just let me," he shouted, and grabbed a shovel from one of the officers, who deferred to him.

Duffy launched himself into the shallow grave and furiously clawed at the earth, making dirt fly everywhere. One especially vicious thrust flung soil onto Lt. Antonio, but she didn't react other than to brush herself off.

"Forty seconds," Duffy muttered.

And then there was the sound of a shovel hitting something hard.

"Here!" he shouted. Duffy cleared off the edges of the makeshift coffin and leapt out of the hole, allowing the six officers to pull it up quickly. Within seconds the lid was off and there was the sound of someone gasping desperately for air.

Danielle Bancroft lay in the pine box with plastic insulation—really the bubble wrap that online shippers use in packaging—wrapped around her from her neck to her toes. As soon as she sucked in enough air to permit it, she began to sob.

Antonio took a step toward the sobbing girl, but Duffy grabbed her arm firmly and gently. "Let her cry," he said. "She's earned it."

The End

I let out a long breath, as I always do after I finish a first draft. The novel was far from finished—there would be a rewrite starting tomorrow and then revisions once my editor Sol Rosterman had read it over and found all the inconsistencies I didn't see and mistakes I'd swear I didn't make—but the heavy lifting, the creating-something-from-nothing, was over. People compare writing a book to giving birth, and I don't know about that, but while I'm sure writing is less painful physically, it usually takes months of exhaustive work, so there is a certain feeling of relief, coupled with crippling weariness and a type of postpartum depression. But that would take a little while to sink in.

Looking around my office, the former mudroom of the two-bedroom house I'd bought a year ago in Adamstown, New Jersey, I realized that this book might have taken a little bit more out of me than previous ones. There were papers everywhere, which wasn't terribly unusual (remember the "paperless society" we were promised?), but there were also a couple of sweaters, unopened mail, three stress balls, copies of six books I'd been sure I wanted to read, information about a dinner in Manhattan I had once wanted to attend, and in one corner, a bottle of diet soda that I was fairly sure I'd opened in early spring. Today was July 21.

I'm not even going to begin telling you about the dust. It was depressing to think there were that many dead cells in the one room. I wondered how I had any live ones left.

So maybe the long breath was coming out more like a sigh.

"Paula!" I called out. Paula Sessions, my indispensable assistant, was in the next room, the second bedroom, which was her office. The fact that her office was larger than mine was my own fault: Paula had more office furniture than me and needed more room for filing and being efficient, which I was unquestionably not. Paula works only two days a week and regularly gets about six times as much done as I do. Someday, Paula is going to take over the world. Trust me, the world will be better for it.

She appeared in the doorway almost immediately. "What do you need, Rachel?" she asked.

"A good man, a bottle of champagne, and a month to prepare," I said. "But I'll settle for cookie dough ice cream."

Paula's eyes lit up. "It's done?" she asked.

I nodded. "Time for our ritual. The first draft is finished, and we get to celebrate. And Paula, make it two scoops."

"This was a tough one, huh?"

"It's getting harder to find stuff for Duffy to do without repeating myself," I admitted. The manuscript file on my MacBook represented the fifth Duffy Madison mystery. I loved Duffy and his world, but repetition was becoming my most feared nemesis.

"I'm sure it's great," Paula said. "You're too hard on yourself."

"Not as hard as Sol's gonna be."

"Sol loves your writing. You get this way every time you finish one."

I spun my finger, pointed down, to indicate she should get moving. "That's what the ice cream is for. It's a restorative," I told Paula.

"I'm off," she said, turning in the doorway.

"I know, but I love you anyway."

Paula didn't even turn around. She had heard that joke more than once. I saw her recede into her office and heard her grab the keys off her desk. She'd be heading for the local ice cream shop, the Cold Cow, and be back in about a half hour.

I decided to take the time to begin—and it would be a rough estimate at best—straightening up my office. I got a roll of paper towels and a spray bottle of furniture polish from the kitchen and headed in feeling righteous.

That didn't last long. I had barely cleaned off one shelf of books, with no new resting place for them in sight, when I had lost interest, thinking instead about how I'd started out to be a newspaper reporter and ended up writing mystery novels.

Graduating from William Paterson University in Wayne with a degree in print journalism had oddly not prepared me for the situation I found: Newspapers were being slaughtered by television news and especially Internet sources. I had one contact after spending a summer interning at the *Record* in Hackensack, and Jim Wolpert was anything but encouraging when I arranged to have lunch with him after graduation.

"Carve out a niche and get on the web," he told me solemnly over "rippers," deep-fried hot dogs found only at Rutt's Hut in Clifton. "Newspapers won't be here in twenty years. Hell, they might not be here in ten. You're young. Don't tie yourself to a dying industry."

He did spring for our rippers, though, although he had to ask me for an extra single to make the tip.

I tried to take his advice and establish myself in one coverage area—a beat—to exploit on websites and managed to get some articles on women's sports and real estate posted on New Jersey–based blogs. But the web wasn't paying for content, so I ended up taking a job in corporate communications for a paint company in Montvale writing press releases about new colors and openings of new company-owned retail outlets.

I hated it.

The company itself was fine, but I wasn't using any of the mental muscles I had hoped to exercise when I'd graduated college. I was, finally, six years out of school, living in a one-bedroom garden apartment, working in a job I didn't like, without much of a social life. Occasionally, my friend Brian Coltrane—we are, believe me, just friends—and I would go out for a beer or two. I went to a lot of movies by myself. I didn't really mind that so much; it was easier to concentrate on the film.

My parents had divorced when I was in high school. My mother was living in Denver, exploring her freedom in ways that she felt no compunction about describing to me on the phone once a week. My father was in Claremont, New York, near Woodstock, having given up his corporate job at a Wall Street firm to take up carpentry, which he did in a workshop he'd built in his barn.

My father had a barn.

He was the one who had turned me into a reader when I was little. My mother had always been more interested in television and music, but my father rarely spent his evenings joining her (perhaps a harbinger of things to come) and often told me that a good book "never steals hours away from you; it always helps make the hours feel like they were spent doing something special. It's like you get extra time, Rachel—the hours you spend reading and the hours your mind spends in that place, that's time that the author gives to you."

Mostly, though, he read to me. When I was a tiny girl, it was Dr. Seuss—my favorite was *The Lorax*, who spoke for the trees. Later, he read me the adventure stories he loved like *Kidnapped* and *The Three Musketeers*. When I complained, at the age of six, that the girls in these books didn't have much to do, he moved on to *Ivanhoe*, which I didn't understand (and which was still all about some guy). Out of frustration, he took me to the local bookstore to pick out something for him to read to me at night.

I spent quite some time scouring the stacks in the children's section and eventually picked out a book whose cover featured a blonde girl (I am not blonde but wanted to be at that age) and the word "secret," which I could make out, having learned to read on my own by then.

Daddy looked the book over and nodded approvingly. "Nancy Drew," he said. "She might be just the thing for you."

As it turned out, *The Secret of the Old Clock* opened up a world to me, but in a very indirect way. I liked Nancy and I adored the idea of snooping around and uncovering secrets, but she seemed to live in a world that wasn't really very much like the one I knew in northern New Jersey, decades after the book had been written. But I "read" three more Nancy Drew books with Daddy before I asked him if we could try another book. "One like that, but different," I said.

And that was when I was introduced, through my father, to Encyclopedia Brown.

Even though Encyclopedia was a boy—there was nothing that could be done about that—he did always have at his side Sally Kimball, the girl who had tried to trick him but found out how smart Leroy (Encyclopedia's real name) was and thereafter acted as his bodyguard. The girl rescued the boy—and he solved the problem with his brain! After Daddy explained what an "encyclopedia" was and why Leroy might want to use that as his nickname, I was hooked.

It started a love of mystery stories that had persisted from grade school into high school (when I discovered Agatha Christie and Arthur Conan Doyle) and then college (Robert B. Parker and Elizabeth Peters). Years out of college and alone in my apartment, I was reading Julia Spencer-Fleming when a story idea occurred to me out of nowhere.

Actually, the idea came to me in the shower, but I'd been reading the night before. Getting ready to go to work and write more about paint, I was consumed with the possibility of creating a character of my own, one who would be as fascinating as the people I'd met through all the authors from Dr. Seuss (I still have a soft spot for the Lorax) until today.

The train of thought that led me to Duffy Madison was not a straight one; the tracks took many a turn and more than one switch was thrown along the way. If I tried to map it all out for you now, I'm not sure I could manage to do so accurately. Suffice it to say that I flashed on the idea of a consultant to the police, a very specific kind of genius who would be able to find lost things and, more important, lost people when the authorities could not.

Duffy had some of the Holmesian qualities many fictional sleuths have—he noticed things that most people don't and is not always the most charming of people to hang around with—but he added (and this was all instinctive; I did not tailor Duffy so much as he came to me with all his cuffs hemmed) an emotional level that Sherlock somehow lacked. Holmes believed emotion got in the way of an investigation, becoming the Mr. Spock of detectives; Duffy had to empathize with the victims of kidnappings in order to understand their plight and find them. He was driven by compassion, not by the thrill of the hunt.

With that first rush of inspiration, I barreled through my first Duffy Madison novel, *Olly Olly Oxen Free*, in less than two months. And then I didn't know what to do with it, so I sent the file to my father in upstate New York because I wanted some encouragement and to my mother in Denver because I needed to know what a tough critic would say.

Neither disappointed. Mom sent back an e-mail after three days saying she had "gotten through" about half my book and thought Duffy "would be cute if they made a movie out of it." She suggested several actors she thought could play him, then wondered if I knew how to write a screenplay.

Dad was a little more constructive. He actually called the day after I sent the file cold, saying how impressed he was that I'd written a book. He then offered specific notes with page citations—many of which I should have caught and some of which were simply nitpicking—and asked me what my plans were for the manuscript.

"I have no idea," I told him honestly. "I've never even met anyone in the publishing business, but I think it's pretty good."

"I know a few," he said. "Let me see what I can do."

Now, there are those who would say that a book should be considered for publication on its own merits and not on the basis of a personal connection between an editor and the author's father. To these people, I say, please feel free to submit your work blindly on its own merits. Though I agree with you, I think an author needs to use every possible advantage just to be read.

The bottom line was, if Dwight Levinson had not thought *Olly Olly* was a novel worth publishing, it would not have mattered that my father had once been his investment counselor and had made him the money on which he would, eventually, retire.

But not before buying my book for Stockton Publishing.

It took another year and a half, but eventually, having learned a little about book promotion online (which is the only way an author can afford to do anything on a paint publicity salary), I saw my first novel sitting proudly on the mystery shelf at BooksBooksBooks, the local independent bookstore in Adamstown. Of course, by then I had written *Little Boy Lost*—which Sol (having taken over for Dwight, who did in fact retire about a month after buying *Olly Olly*) now had for revisions—and was about to begin the first draft of *Misplaced*, the third book in the Duffy series.

Sales on *Olly Olly* were good if not great. The publisher was happy enough, Sol assured me, to go ahead with the other two books (not a huge surprise, as the initial contract was for three) and possibly, if sales on the second book held firm, to do more.

And so it was the fifth in the series, which I was now calling *Alive and Buried*, that I had just backed up on an external hard drive when my "cleaning" was interrupted by the ringing of the phone. The landline. That didn't happen very often. I figured it was a telemarketer calling, but caller ID showed a cell phone number but no name. I toyed with the idea of letting it go through to voice mail, but I had promoted tomorrow night's signing at BooksBooksBooks and was concerned that Rita Mendham, the store's owner, might be calling with a problem. I picked up.

"Hello?" The voice on the other end of the line was male, slightly tentative, but not the just-out-of-high-school or really-in-another-country type of voice that shows up when your caller is trying to sell you insurance or tell you about "your credit card account" despite not knowing which credit card might be in question.

"Yes?" I said. It might be a reader—it's really not that hard for them to find out your hometown and look up the phone number—so I had to be polite, at least. "What the hell do you want?" would probably have been a little too aggressive.

"Is this Rachel Goldman?" the voice asked.

You can't be too careful. "Who may I say is calling?" I asked in my best impression of Paula. She provides a great role model. And mentally, I decided that no matter who this person was, I wasn't spending more than twenty dollars on whatever he was selling.

"Um . . . this is Duffy Madison," the voice said.

Okay, maybe twenty-five.

Chapter 2

Now, it's not absolutely out of the question to get a phone call from someone claiming to be your books' protagonist. Authors—even lesser known ones like me—are sort of public figures, and there will always be some nut who wants to connect with you or just wants to play a joke. It happens every once in a great while, although usually via e-mail. There are also probably just a few people in the country whose parents were cruel enough to name them Duffy Madison. I've heard from one or two, usually with the flattering comment, "I've never heard of you, but my friend says you have a character with my name."

So I breathed in a little, wondered exactly why I still have a landline that appears in the phone book, and said, "Can I help you?"

"*Is* this Ms. Goldman?" the man asked again. I had not, after all, admitted to being me.

"It is," I allowed. "What can I do for you, Mr. Madison?"

There was a noticeable hesitation on his part. "I believe . . . that is, I think I might be . . ." His voice trailed off and then came back, with a more authoritative, professional tone to it. The kind of voice I've always heard when I write Duffy's dialogue for him. "I'm consulting with the Bergen County Prosecutor's Office and have a matter of some importance I'd like to ask you about. Is it possible we could meet?"

Well, that was a new approach. Usually, they just want an autographed bookplate. "That's very nice," I said, my tone suggesting some admiration. "But you know, in the books, Duffy consults with the *Morris* County prosecutor."

"I wouldn't know," he said. "I've never read any of your novels."

Huh?

"Duffy" didn't give me any time to consider that idea. "This matter is of some considerable urgency, Ms. Goldman. Can we meet?"

Paula walked in carrying a bag marked "Cold Cow" with the logo of hoofprints leading to a frosty sundae (hey, it's a local independent store; give them a break) and saw I was on the phone. Before I could gesture to her that I had a nut on the line, she turned around and headed toward the kitchen, presumably to stash our treats in the freezer until I could ditch the call and get to what was really important.

So I was, at least theoretically, alone with this guy.

"I'm really not at liberty to meet," I said, not really sure where "at liberty" had come from. This was a problem, as I use words for a living. "In fact, I really should be going now."

I made a mental note to get the landline deactivated, or at least to change to an unpublished number.

"Ms. Goldman," the man said, "I'm aware that you write novels in which a character with my name is a consultant on missing persons cases. I'm aware that my calling you must sound incredibly odd. But I assure you, my business truly is terribly important."

Okay, now I was sure this guy was crazy. Or worse, wily: Sometimes people think they can get an author's attention by showing their devotion to the author's work. That's almost always extremely touching and welcome. Other times, like when the person in question thinks he can pretend to be the author's character (and do a damned fine imitation—this guy was good!), it's a sign that either the caller is an aspiring author who thinks (mistakenly) that a published writer can help his career or, worse, the caller really thinks he's a crimestopper, which borders on the terrifying.

Paula walked back in, noticed the shift in dust and clutter, nodded approvingly, and sat down on an unoccupied few inches of futon. She narrowed her eyes when she looked at me, trying to determine what that odd expression on my face might indicate.

"I'm sorry, *Mr. Madison*," I said, pointing to the phone for Paula's benefit. She curled her lip in amusement. I shook my head—this was no laughing matter. "I make it a policy never to meet with fans."

"I'm *not* a fan," "Duffy" replied. "As I said, I haven't ever read any of your novels. I'm sorry if that is a slight; I don't intend it to be. But I do need to see you."

That was the tell: "I need to *see* you" rather than "I need to *talk to* you." I reminded myself that I was a professional and he was a consumer (even if he insisted he was not one of my readers). Getting snarky would be unproductive. "If you have a warrant, feel free to drop by," I told him. "Can you give me the name of your contact at the Bergen County Prosecutor's Office?"

The fictional imposter on my phone didn't answer for a long moment. "I work with Chief Investigator William Petrosky," he said.

"Nice try," I answered, forgetting my pledge of four seconds ago not to be snarky. "But Duffy always works with Lieutenant Isabel Antonio."

"That's a *novel*," the man said. You could hear his teeth clench. "This is *real life*."

"Mr. . . . whoever you are," I began.

"Madison. Duffy Madison. And a woman's life is in danger. Please!"

I hung up on him and turned to Paula. "Call Verizon and get them to disconnect the landline," I said.

She pulled a pen from behind her ear and wrote a note on the scrap of paper closest to her.

The phone rang. "Wait," I told Paula. I reached over and unplugged the line coming in. The ringing stopped immediately. "Now, let's have some ice cream."

Chapter 3

"I love Duffy Madison!" The woman standing in front of me looked positively enthralled. Usually, that's good; this was a little unsettling.

One day after Paula and I had polished off a good deal of ice cream, BooksBooksBooks was looking its best and the evening sun was just about giving up the ghost, but I was having some trouble concentrating on the event. Normally there are few things as nourishing for an author as a book signing—when people show up. I've been at both kinds, and people showing up is definitely the better option. Because the people who show up are those who have read and (almost always) liked your book, and that can put a glow into an author that, under the right circumstances, can last for a week. I love going to book signings these days.

When *Olly Olly Oxen Free* was first being published, I knew nothing about signings, so I called Rita Mendham at BooksBooksBooks and asked her if I could come to the store a few weeks before the publication and at least let people know that I had a novel on its way. Rita, who is among the best people on the planet (I adore booksellers!), said to wait until the publication date, when she would have copies in stock, and we could have a "launch party." Who knew there was such a thing?

Rita did, luckily, and she turned BooksBooksBooks into a one-title store for the night. She had banners and posters made—something I'd never imagined—and invited her most loyal customers for weeks in advance. I invited pretty much everyone I'd ever known (my parents had each sent regrets), since having your first book published is not exactly a small milestone in a life.

With something Rita called "hand selling," which means that she told customers whom she thought would be interested all about *Olly Olly,* she sold more copies out of her little independent store than a lot of the large chain stores and maybe some online retailers, although I'm really not sure about that. Authors don't know nearly as much about our book sales as people think we do (and we're not responsible for the covers, either).

Tonight, Rita had ordered bagel sandwiches and soft drinks from the Adamstown Deli (I'd paid) and had store staff members, of whom there were two, dressed in semiformal attire to hand them out from trays. The food and drink were excellent, of course, and while the store didn't have lines out the door and around the block, there was a nice turnout of about twenty-five people. (Okay, so there were twenty-seven. I counted. And yes, I always do.)

I read a portion of the latest published Duffy book, *How to Vanish Without a Trace*, after a lovely introduction from Rita. I don't care for reading from my books, but only because I think I don't do a very good job. I get nervous and read too fast, eventually mumbling into my own chest. Then it gets bad.

So I had kept tonight's reading brief, gave a short talk on how this particular episode had occurred, and answered a few questions from the group, who luckily had been offered some wine from Rita's private stock in addition to the soft drinks. That loosens up people who might be nervous about speaking and helps open a few wallets when Rita says I'll be signing only books people purchase at her store that night. This is, I'm quick to point out, Rita's rule and not mine. On my own, I'll pretty much sign the back of your dry cleaning receipt if you show the least bit of interest in my books.

"I'm so glad you enjoy the character," I said to the enthusiastic fan. There wasn't a huge line left (to be honest, there had never been a *huge* line, but it had been representative for sure). "It's always fun to meet people who get him."

"No, I mean I *really love him*," the woman, who was wearing a wedding ring, said. I noticed a man standing near the new fiction stack, out of the line, glancing nervously in the direction of the table where I was signing. Maybe her husband. No wonder he was nervous; she was declaring her love for another man—admittedly one who didn't exist, depending on who you talked to.

Duffy's readers are most often women, and some of them have a really interesting relationship with the character. I've received marriage proposals in e-mails . . . for Duffy. There was one woman who was, let's say, explicit in her special interest in him. On occasion, they'll send photographs of themselves, presumably for the fictional character to peruse. I try not to whenever I can avoid it. But sometimes Paula can't resist showing me.

"Well, I hope you'll keep reading. How would you like the book signed?" I asked Duffy's enthusiastic fan. The man in the back—the only male left in the store besides my pal Brian Coltrane, who was helping Rita clean up after the party—glanced over again, saw me looking at him, and looked away. Her husband, for sure.

"Sign it, 'To Liddy, who I dream about at night, Duffy Madison,'" she sighed. I stifled an impulse to look around for Paula, then remembered this was not a night she was working. I'd have to do crowd control on my own. Unless I could get Brian to walk over and look threatening.

"Well, I'm not Duffy Madison," I said with what I hoped was a reassuring smile.

"I know," she said, not without a touch of sorrow.

What the hell; she'd paid for the book. I wrote the inscription as she'd asked, obstinately signed my name under Duffy's, and handed it back to her.

"Oh, *thank* you," she gushed. She clutched the book to her chest and headed hastily for the door.

On her way, she passed the man who'd been watching us and never gave him so much as a glance. Lucky guy; he'd dodged a bullet not being her spouse. Imagine having to compete with someone who wasn't real!

I signed four more books, bringing the total to sixteen (I count those, too) before the last person in line was satisfied. Fortunately, I'd been able to sign all the other copies with my own name. It saves a lot of mental energy when you don't have to remember to be someone other than you.

I stood up, shaking the hand of the last woman in the line, who grinned and nodded again and again, and watched her go to the door. Rita came over as I stretched my arms straight up. Signing really doesn't take all that much out of you physically, but there's always a certain level of tension, so when the event is over, I release it by stretching out my shoulders and legs.

"Not a bad night," Rita said, smiling. "I think we did better than with the last book."

"Nope," I corrected her. "With the last book, we sold seventeen copies. We're one short this time."

She pointed to the remaining copies of *How to Vanish* on the signing table. "You can sign those five for stock," she said. "I'll sell them by Friday."

"You're the best," I told Rita, and it was true. I sat down to sign the five books for her. Next week, I'd be sure to drop by again; Rita would have more copies, and I would sign them for her. Then she'd sell those and order more. Rita could, I sincerely believe, sell *me* a copy of my own book.

Rita headed for the back room to make sure there weren't copies of my previous novels she wanted signed, and I was on book number three of the ones on the table when I noticed a shadow fall over the page I was autographing. I looked up.

The man who had been loitering at the back of the signing line was standing over me. His face, thin but with character, had almost no expression. He didn't say anything.

In my best author-here-to-please-you voice (which is actually pretty natural, since I really *do* want to please my readers), I asked, "Would you like your book signed or inscribed?" I reached for one of the unsigned copies left on the table.

"I don't want a book," the man said. The voice was almost familiar. "I would like to talk to you, Ms. Goldman."

The guy from the phone call.

I decided to play it without showing that I really wanted Brian to come back and offer me protection. "You called yesterday," I said in a nonthreatening tone.

"Yes. I am Duffy Madison." There was no hesitation, and yet the eyes betrayed no madness. He wasn't a raving lunatic; he was just a lunatic. I supposed that was a positive, of sorts.

Maybe I could reason with him. "You realize that's not possible," I said.

He let out an audible breath and closed his eyes briefly. "And yet, here I am," he answered.

"Can you explain it?" It might be possible to lead him to the realization that he was indeed not a fictional character and instead someone else entirely. The upside would be that he was real; that was something to aspire to, no doubt.

"I can't," the man said. "But you must believe me that I am not pretending, Ms. Goldman. I *am* Duffy Madison, I *do* missing persons consultations for the Bergen County Prosecutor's Office, and I *am* asking for your help in the disappearance of a woman from Upper Saddle River. Will you please take the time to help me?"

"Look, Mr. . . ."

"Madison. Duffy . . ."

"Yeah, I get that. You seem like a pretty rational guy. You must know what it sounds like for an author to be approached by someone who says he has the same name as her lead character. I'm sort of used to that, but you also have the same job, and you're asking me to act like that isn't odd."

I saw Rita coming from the back room carrying an armful of books and breathed an inward sigh of relief. Then she headed for the cash register at the front, no doubt thinking "Duffy" was going to buy a book and would need assistance, and my inward sigh almost turned into an outward groan.

"I'm not happy about it," the man said. "Believe me, before yesterday, I had no idea you existed. But having done some research, I must tell you that it's not as simple as it seems."

It didn't seem simple at all, so that was very little comfort. "It's not?" I asked. I'm not sure why. That's not really a question. But there was a gap in the conversation and I filled it.

The man shook his head a little. "I am not someone with the same name and profession as your fictional character," he said. He looked a bit sad, and I thought that was odd. A person shouldn't be saddened simply because he was making no sense at all.

"But you just said you were," I pointed out. Rationality, although it was clearly not working here, still seemed to be my best course of action. Mostly because I couldn't think of any other course of action short of running for the door, and in order to get there, I'd have to get past the crazy man in front of me.

"No," he said. "*You* suggested that I claim to have his name and his job. I'm saying that's not a coincidence and it's not a pretense. I really am Duffy Madison, and after gathering all the facts about your work that I could find, I believe that, somehow, you created me."

Chapter 4

My eyes must have narrowed, because I felt like I was looking at him from very far away. The villains in my books have tended to be people who seem quite reasonable and then are revealed to be dangerously deranged and violent. Now my writing was coming to life—literally, if you believed this guy—and I was as defenseless as a character sent up to the dark attic with nothing more than a flashlight with a shaky battery. In the business we call such characters TSTL, for "Too Stupid to Live."

"I . . . *created* you?" I echoed back at him. I usually pride myself on being a good conversationalist, but now I was impressed that I could come up with something above the level of "gaaaaaahh."

"I can't explain it," responded the man who called himself Duffy. "I have no memories before four years ago."

"When my first book was published," I said. Probably to myself.

"Yes," he agreed. "And all I know is that my name has always been Duffy Madison, and I have always done this work. If you'll just take the time to discuss it—"

"Is there something we can do to help you, sir?" Rita had appeared at my side, like a loyal sidekick and protector. She's not a sidekick by any means, but I suddenly did feel considerably more protected.

It didn't hurt that Brian was now standing to the man's right, his arms folded casually. Brian had been on the wrestling team in high school. He wasn't great, and it was fifteen years ago, but he had a better chance of dealing with this crackpot than I did if things got out of hand.

"I'm simply trying to persuade Ms. Goldman to cooperate in a serious investigation being done by the Bergen County prosecutor," the man said, cool as a cucumber. I have had, I feel I should point out, dishes in which the cucumber was hot, but this guy was completely calm as far as I could tell. Idioms.

"Let me introduce you," I said as I stood up. You can run better when you're standing up. "Rita Mendham, this is Duffy Madison."

Brian unfolded his arms.

Rita, however, has been working in retail for a long time, so nothing on Earth can faze her. She stuck out her hand. "Nice to meet you, Mr. Madison," she said. Not a flicker. Not a glance in my direction. Nothing. She knew she was meeting a massively deranged person, but from her manner, you'd think he was claiming to be a shoe salesman from Dubuque, Iowa.

The crazy man took her hand in a professional manner. "Ms. Mendham," he said.

"Are you interested in buying one of Rachel's books?" Rita asked. "I don't want to pressure you or anything, but I do want to clear the register." She pointed toward the counter.

"Duffy" probably considered the idea that Rita had mentioned my books without noting that he was in them. Brian took the opportunity to move closer to my table, positioning himself between me and the lunatic on the left side, so I'd have a clear path on the right if I had to bolt. Brian was a very nice guy and a large one; if he had to place himself in harm's way to protect me, I would make sure to tell his mother about it the next time I saw her.

"I don't think I'll be buying a book tonight, Ms. Mendham," the allegedly fictional character said. "Please feel free to clear out your system."

"In that case, Mr. Madison, I don't want to be rude, but we were planning on closing the store." Rita feinted slightly to her right side, toward the front of the store, indicating a direction in which the man might want to walk. Now.

"I appreciate that, ma'am," he answered. "But I am here on official business, and I am trying to persuade Ms. Goldman to cooperate in an investigation, a very urgent one. A woman's life is at stake."

"Oh dear," Rita said. "And Rachel has some information about it?" Wait. Whose side was she on?

"Perhaps," the fake Duffy said. "But it is of a somewhat confidential nature, and I will need to speak to her alone. I'm sure you understand."

"*I* don't understand," I volunteered. "Why should I believe a word you say? You walk in here and tell me you're my fictional creation, that I made you up and so you exist, and you need to take me somewhere alone so we can talk it over? Exactly how stupid do you think I am, pal?" Well, *somebody* had to say it.

"I don't think you're stupid. But you *don't understand*."

Somewhere around the part where I said that Duffy believed I'd created him, Rita's eyes had widened and her mouth opened slightly. Brian took a step directly in front of the determined nut job and said, "Rita said we were closing."

The man who claimed I had conjured him up took a step back, then looked at each of us in turn. He seemed to be assessing his situation. Much like Duffy Madison would do in one of my books. Damn, he was good!

"Yes, she did," he said to Brian. "I believe you've been more than polite about it." He reached into his inside jacket pocket, and I saw the muscles in Brian's upper arms tense. But the imposter slowed his movement and pulled out his hand slowly, then showed Brian that it held only a business card. He moved slowly toward me, noted Brian's proximity again, and placed the card on the edge of the table.

"Please think it over," he said with an edge in his voice. "There is very little time."

Then he turned, nodded his head in farewell to Rita and Brian, and walked out the front door. Back straight, head held high. A purposeful stride.

Like I'd noted on page sixty-seven of *Olly Olly Oxen Free*.

The collective sigh of relief from Rita and me once the door closed and Brian locked it was not just audible but palpable. The level of carbon dioxide from our exhaled breath probably fed the six plants Rita had brought in to spruce the place up (almost literally).

"What was *that* all about?" Rita finally asked.

"Just what I said. The guy called yesterday, said he was Duffy, and he needs me to work on a case with him. Then tonight he tells me he really *is* Duffy, and that I created him when I started writing the books four years ago."

Brian kept his eye on the front window, to be sure the guy had left, but he still was listening to us. "That's eight different kinds of crazy," he said.

"Newsflash," I said.

"Do you think we should call the police?" Rita asked.

"And tell them what?" Brian responded. "He didn't break any laws."

I picked up the business card on the table and examined it. "He said he worked in consultation with the Bergen County prosecutor," I said, mostly to myself.

"But Duffy works in Morris County in the books," Rita pointed out, as if I wasn't aware of that.

"All true. I know people in Morris. I did a few ride-alongs when I was researching the first two books, and I got to know a couple of the investigators there. And I know the chief of police in Morristown. This guy couldn't claim to be working for them because it would be too easy for me to prove that he was lying."

"But in Bergen?" Brian asked.

"In Bergen I don't know anybody," I admitted. "But I get the feeling I'm going to be doing some checking tomorrow."

"How can you check if you don't know who to ask?" Brian said.

I smiled. "I do research on all the books, Brian. I make cold phone calls all the time. Believe me, I know how to do it. And now I have a brand-new contact at the Bergen County Prosecutor's Office."

I handed him the business card "Duffy" had left on the table. He glanced at it and looked puzzled. "I thought this was his card," he said.

"So did I, at first," I answered. "And for all we know, that might be his real name. I'll check in the morning."

Brian handed the business card to Rita. She read it and looked at me. "Chief Investigator William Petrosky?" she asked. "Who's that?"

"According to him, that's Duffy Madison's boss."

Chapter 5

"Bill Petrosky is a real investigator with the real Bergen County Prosecutor's Office." Martin Dugan, who held a similar position with the equally nonfictitious Morris County prosecutor, grinned a little at me as he spoke. Marty thinks I'm a riot, trying to find out what it's like to be a "real cop," even while cooking up my preposterous (his opinion) little stories. "Are you writing about a guy who pretends to be an investigator?"

"This is not for a book," I told him. I sat drinking an iced coffee from Dunkin' Donuts. I'd brought one for Marty, too, knowing that his office didn't have a coffee pot and he had a serious caffeine habit. The poor guy had to get up from his desk six or seven times a day and trudge all the way down the street to a bodega just to keep himself right.

It's a dirty, rotten job, but somebody's got to do it.

I practically had to take a solemn oath to be careful before Brian had let me out of his sight the night before. I think he would have insisted on spending the night at my house, but his girlfriend Cathy back at his place would have thought that was odd. I had indeed kept watching for cars following me on the way to Marty's office this morning.

"If it's not for a book, why are you asking about whether Petrosky is a real guy?" Marty said, draining the large drink I'd gotten him (mine was a medium, and I was about a third of the way through it). "Why not call him up and ask him if he's real?"

Marty's cubicle was less messy than some but still messier than others. He was not like those cops who speak like they're in the military, always call you "ma'am" (which can be a little disconcerting), have flattop haircuts, and crack a smile once a year on J. Edgar Hoover's birthday. He was a real person, and when I was researching the first Duffy book, he had welcomed me in, even if he couldn't resist the urge to needle me about my complete ignorance of police procedures.

"I got this business card from a man I met last night," I said, and showed him the specimen, which was none the worse for the sixteen hours of wear it had endured in my purse.

"Got picked up in a bar by a Bergen County investigator?" Marty's eyes twinkled joyfully. He thinks the fact that I'm female is hilarious. Cops.

"That's a riot, Marty. Truly. I'm going to write it down when I get home and repeat it the next time I get together with my girlfriends."

"Ooh, touchy." Marty's eyes got a little more serious. "So you got a business card from a cop. If you met Petrosky last night, you know he's real. Do you have some reason to believe the guy you met wasn't Bill Petrosky?"

"I know for a fact he wasn't; he didn't claim to be," I answered. "He said he was Duffy Madison."

Bill sucked a little on the straw in his iced coffee, which couldn't have given him more than a few droplets of melted ice at this point. He was thinking. I half expected smoke to waft out of his ears. "So you met a nut case last night, and he gave you Petrosky's business card. Why?"

"He says that he's the *real* Duffy Madison, that he's investigating a disappearance for the Bergen prosecutor, and that your pal Bill is his supervisor. He wants me to call to verify, and I figured I'd check with you before I did."

"Why? Why not just call Petrosky?"

It's scary that some people with "investigator" in their job titles ask questions Encyclopedia Brown could answer without blinking. "Anybody can pick up a phone and say they work for Bergen County," I said. "I wanted to be sure William Petrosky was an actual employee of the government. You'd know."

"So would the Internet," Marty pointed out.

"The Internet will tell you that a zombie apocalypse has already begun," I said. "Besides, you're so much more personable, and I can't buy the Internet iced coffee."

"All true." He leaned back in his chair. "So you have your confirmation. Do you want me to call Bill and check this guy out?"

I considered that but shook my head. "I think I want to hear his voice when he answers and maybe have a few follow-up questions depending on what he says. The man I met last night—and it was at a book signing, before you say anything else—was really kind of disturbing."

Marty looked concerned. "Scary?" he asked.

"No. Exactly not. And that's what was unsettling about him—he seemed so *reasonable*. And he acted, I swear, Marty, just like the Duffy Madison I've been writing for four years."

Marty shrugged. "He's studied the books."

"He says he's never read them."

"And I say I'm a captain when I meet a woman in the supermarket," he answered. "Guys say things, Rachel."

"It wasn't like that."

"It's never like that. Especially when it's like that."

I looked at him, living somewhere between rumpled and elegant, in his cubicle, being a cop who wasn't exactly a cop. "You always think everything's about sex," I said.

"Name something that's not." He gave another pull on the straw and got that "Hey, I'm empty" sound that a cup makes when you've done all the damage you can do.

"Iced coffee," I said.

Marty leaned back and closed his eyes, smiling. "That's more about sex than sex," he said.

* * *

The next logical step would be to call William Petrosky from my office. So I didn't do that. I drove from Marty's office in Morristown to Caffeinated, the local coffee bar in Adamstown. Having just had coffee, I ordered a piece of Ruthie's crumb cake, which is better than anyone else's, and a glass of milk. Ruthie smiled with the left side of her mouth, acknowledging the nuttiness of the local author, and said she'd bring my order out to me once I had set up.

I took a seat on a stuffed (not overstuffed) chair in the corner and placed my computer bag on the ottoman in front of it. By the time Ruthie brought over my order, I had gotten the laptop out of the bag and was ready to start revising the book I had been sure was completely finished two days before.

Revisions, you should know, are an absolute necessity. I break into a cold sweat at the very notion that a first draft of anything I wrote would ever be seen by anyone who can actually read. Paula doesn't get to read my first drafts. Neither of my parents gets to read my first drafts. If I had a husband, he probably wouldn't get a look until about the third draft. Revisions are the process through which the drivel that falls out of my brain becomes a coherent piece of work that I am proud to call my own when someone sends me an e-mail or meets me at a book conference.

The other thing you should know is that I hate doing my revisions. Hate, hate, hate. With every fiber in my being. It is a tedious, brain-aching, emotionally crippling process that makes me believe I should certainly have gone into the bagel business rather than take up a word processing program and try to express myself. I would rather clean my entire house, do six loads of laundry, and actually reorganize my linen closet than do revisions.

So you can imagine my intense relief when I opened the file for the new book and my cell phone immediately rang. Even if this were someone who wanted to connect me personally with the world's most long-winded insurance salesperson, I would listen to every word and ask questions to keep the conversation going for the longest possible amount of time.

Instead, it was my agent. Win-win. I get to procrastinate *and* feel like I'm doing something related to my work at the same time. Just to reward myself, I took a sip of milk before hitting the "talk" button.

"Hey, Adam! What's shakin', dude?"

There was a chuckle on the other end of the line. "Doing revisions, Rachel?" Adam Resnick asked.

"How could you tell?"

"You sounded positively giddy to hear from me," Adam answered. "I know you love me, but you never sound that happy to hear from *anybody* unless the call is taking you away from a first draft."

"Revisions kill pieces of my soul, Adam." Downside to the call: I couldn't eat any crumb cake while talking on the phone. It sounds disgusting to the other person, and I didn't hate Adam nearly enough to subject him to that.

"I know, Rach. I know. Just think how proud you'll be when the book is ten times better."

"You think the book is bad now? Who have you been talking to?" I was kidding. Mostly. You hear about hackers. I'm just saying.

A man and a woman seated at a far table, possibly in a close and personal relationship, shared some beverage or another together yet were both so engrossed on their smart phones that they never made eye contact or spoke a word to each other. For this they left the house and came here.

"Easy, tiger," Adam said. "I'm calling about movie rights."

That got my attention. Getting your book sold is the Holy Grail for a midlist author like me. It can catapult your sales into the stratosphere and give your work the kind of exposure that is truly mind-boggling—and best of all, you get lots of money without having to do anything at all.

Adam had been doing the usual rounds of production companies (we call them "prodcos" in the business, except that we really don't) since *Olly Olly* came out four years ago and had been roundly rejected at every turn for various reasons: people didn't want to deal with kidnapping stories; Duffy wasn't a believable character (although I could contradict that one now!); there was no sexual tension between him and Lt. Antonio; it was too soon after 9/11 (it was more than eleven years later, and what did *that* have to do with Duffy?); and so on.

So news of possible interest in Duffy on the big screen shot me full of adrenaline much faster than the coffee I didn't order.

"What's going on, Adam?" I asked. Agents usually call only when they have some news to report, that there's been some interest if not an offer.

"I'm not sure yet," he answered. "I don't want to get your hopes up too high. But Hugh Ventnor wants to see it, and he wants to see it right away." Adam thinks I remember the name of producers in Hollywood as well as every editor at every publishing house in the world. I'm lucky I remember Sol's name, and he's edited all the books I've published to this day.

"Which one is Hugh Ventnor, Adam?" I asked.

There was something of a sigh from my agent. He believes I'm a terrible businesswoman, a sentiment I share, by the way, and I think he's the one who's supposed to keep track of all this stuff, a sentiment I'm willing to believe he shares. He just likes to put on a show.

"He's the executive producer at Monarch, Rachel," he said in a tone clearly intended to make me feel stupid. "And he called me, out of the blue, to ask about *Little Boy Lost*."

That sounded strange. "Not the first book in the series? And he called *you*? You hadn't submitted it to him?"

"I never submit to Hugh," Adam said. "I submit to one of the readers in his acquisitions area, and they pass on the ones they like to him. I submitted it to Sheila York, but it was just yesterday. There's no way she read through it and recommended it to Hugh that fast."

I was really considering that crumb cake. If I could get Adam to talk for a long time, I might be able to get a bite in, anyway. And since I really am not one to buy in on his dramatic crescendos, I had only been moderately interested, not enthralled, at what he'd been saying. "So what does that mean?" I asked. That should get a lengthy response. I grabbed the crumb cake and took a mammoth bite.

"I'm not sure what it means," Adam said. And then he stopped talking.

Dammit! Now he expected me to say something, and I had enough delicious carbohydrate in my mouth to keep me chewing for a good—no, a *fantastic*—half minute. Maybe if I just kept chewing . . .

Sure enough. Adam must have thought I was putting him to the test, so he went on. "I mean, if he's just calling because he's heard about you and wants to see if there's something there, that's *great*," Adam said, speaking a little too quickly while I concentrated on chewing. "Maybe he's checked your sales numbers and thinks you have a chance at the list next time out, which would help justify an option at least with his partners."

The "list" is the *New York Times* Best Sellers list, and my chances of making it are roughly equivalent to my being declared queen of the Netherlands. But Adam, a good agent, likes to think that my star is constantly on the rise and that the next step in my career is a trip to the list. I let him think it.

I also let him continue to talk; it wouldn't take long for me to get to the "wash it down with milk" step in the process, which my mother taught me when I was three.

"Anyway, I think it's an amazingly good sign that Hugh is asking for the book, Rachel. I can't guarantee he'll go for it—he's not always open to anything but graphic novels—but him asking for it without being solicited can't be seen as anything but encouraging."

Finally! I got a sip of milk in, cleared my mouth (realizing that all the stress on getting to swallow had pretty much destroyed my enjoyment of the snack), and considered. "How do you think he found out about it if Sheila York" (whoever she was) "didn't give it to him?" I asked.

"Well, he had a story, but you have to take it with a grain of salt," Adam said. "No. A whole *shaker* of salt."

Okay, it worked: I was intrigued. "What does that mean?"

"Keep in mind that he doesn't consider mystery most of the time," my agent told me in a tone that indicated I shouldn't be insulted. "So he's probably never heard your name before and certainly doesn't know anything specific about what you've written."

"So obviously he's going to jump right on an unknown book in the middle of a series from an author he's never heard of before," I said. "How the hell does that work?"

"I told you all that because you need to understand that he has no point of reference," Adam explained. "So he didn't know that what he told me about *Little Boy Lost* was crazy."

Crazy was a word that had popped into my mind far too often for the past couple of days, and I didn't like what it was doing to my stomach. Although that could have been the effect of eating crumb cake too quickly. "What did he tell you?" I asked.

"He said he'd gotten a call about an author whose name was unknown to him. That he'd asked around his office and found out that there was a manuscript in house by that author. That's you, you know."

"No kidding. Who was calling about me?"

And somehow I knew the answer before Adam had the opportunity to say it. I can't say it made my stomach feel any better.

"He said he'd gotten the call from someone in a county prosecutor's office and the guy's name was Duffy Madison."

Chapter 6

After spending twenty minutes (unsuccessfully) trying to convince my agent that I was, in fact, *not* paying some guy to pretend to be a law enforcement official and call publishers on my behalf (why would a producer read a book because a county investigator told him to?), I forgot about my revisions, got into my car, and drove, with the help of my very reliable GPS device, to the Bergen County Prosecutor's Office.

Hackensack, New Jersey, is not all it's cracked up to be. On the other hand, when you start out with a name like "Hackensack," you're not exactly shooting for the stars to begin with. It's the seat of a county that includes some of the richest real estate in the country within its borders, and yet the city itself is a little tired, a little rundown, and frankly, mostly forgotten by Bergen County's wealthier residents except when they have to find a way to get out of jury duty.

My purpose was considerably less hypocritical (I thought). I asked very nicely for Chief Investigator William Petrosky's office and was told I couldn't see him.

That was something of a problem. You'd think that a woman of my accomplishments (which were up to about five now) would have thought to call ahead, but I'm more of a take-the-bull-by-the-horns kind of girl, and besides, it had never occurred to me that Petrosky wouldn't drop everything on his to-do list just to converse with a woman from a county he didn't represent and of whom he had almost certainly never heard.

But I decided to persevere. "It'll only take a minute of his time," I said. "I promise. Did I mention I'm a mystery author doing research?"

"He doesn't have any time today." The receptionist, whose expression indicated she had expected to marry out of her job by now, wasn't exactly looking at me. She was glaring into an iPhone, which was situated in such a way that I couldn't tell exactly which *Candy Crush* game was giving her trouble. "You want to make an appointment for next month?"

"I'm afraid it can't wait."

"Sorry. There's nothing I can do." She slammed the phone down on her desk. "Dammit!"

"I appreciate your frustration," I told her. "Couldn't you just ask him?"

The woman looked up, apparently startled that I was still there. "I told you, he's booked."

Defeated, I started for the office door. Then completely on an impulse, I turned back and blurted out, "Duffy Madison."

She looked dumbfounded. "What did you say?"

"I want to talk to him about Duffy Madison." I had no idea what this conversation was about, but it was working.

"Hang on," she said, and walked to the door six feet to my left. If I'd had any indication that was where Petrosky was located, I'd probably have tried to barge in, but the door wasn't marked with anything but the numeral *4*. The receptionist knocked, walked in, and shut the door behind her. I waited perhaps ten seconds before she walked back out, smoothed her hair (which did not need smoothing), and said, "He says to go right in."

Petrosky turned out to be a man of about fifty, was an inch or two shorter than me, and wore a white shirt and navy-blue tie. The jacket from his navy-blue suit hung over the back of his chair, which was behind his desk.

"I'm sorry," he said, "I didn't get your name." He reached out to take my hand in a businesslike manner. I gave it to him, but just for a loan. I was going to need it again later.

"I'm Rachel Goldman," I said, mostly because I am. I could have added that I write a series of novels about a guy who claimed to be working for him, but I wanted to gauge Petrosky's sudden interest. It was clear Duffy's name had gotten me in. Maybe not talking was a better way to find out something about what was going on.

"You're the woman Duffy's been talking about," Petrosky said, sitting back down and gesturing for me to sit on a county-issued chair in front of his county-issued desk. Okay, that indicated that there in fact *was* a Duffy Madison, or at least someone using that name, and that Petrosky had heard of him—and me. This keeping quiet thing was working out, so I did it some more.

Sure enough, more information came my way. "Duffy says you write novels and that you use his name for a character you write," Petrosky went on. "How did you find out about Duffy?"

Clearly, I couldn't stay silent after that, since I'd probably set a personal best just in those twenty seconds. "Wait," I said, "this guy really *is* Duffy Madison? And he says I stole his name from *him*?"

Petrosky smiled in an avuncular manner and spread his hands in a gesture of calm and reconciliation. "Oh, don't worry," he said soothingly. "Nobody's going to sue you."

Sue me? For using my imagination and creating a fictional character? What world was this? Still, I had to maintain my composure. I was talking to a man who came to work in a navy-blue suit. Some sense of professionalism was called for, clearly.

I couldn't get my jaw to open the whole way, so through the tiny space my teeth would allow, I said, "Well, I'd hardly think I was going to get sued, but I don't understand." The jaw loosened up a little. Soon Petrosky would be able to recognize vowel sounds I made. I barreled on through before he could ask me for the name of my translator. "You see, I created Duffy Madison, my character, from scratch four years ago. I had no idea there was someone going around using that name. I made him a consultant with the Morris County prosecutor. I took two whole days to settle on the name Duffy Madison after using baby name books, death registries, and a random search of the Morristown phone book."

Petrosky's smile had dimmed, and he leaned forward in his chair, resting his elbows on his desk. "So you're saying that you'd never heard of Duffy Madison before you wrote his name down?"

"That's exactly what I'm saying. How long have you known *your* Duffy Madison?" I asked.

"Just over four years," the chief investigator said, staring at a point about two feet above my head.

"And how did you meet him?"

Petrosky didn't focus so much as he simply answered the question from memory. "We were working a missing person case in Lodi," he said. "Woman left her bed in the middle of the night and vanished. We had no trail at all. This guy walks up to one of my investigators at the woman's home while it was still a crime scene, says he specializes in this stuff. We looked at him hard as the possible kidnapper, but nothing pointed to him ever having met her before."

"And that was the guy who calls himself Duffy Madison," I said.

Suddenly, Petrosky's face was completely attentive and focused directly on me. "Look, lady, we didn't just take him in off the street and ask him to start looking into crimes. I checked into his background personally. Saw his ID—Social Security number, Selective Service registration, driver's license. Had him fingerprinted, no matches. We took samples of his DNA to use when we thought he might be a suspect. Nothing. He's clean as a whistle."

"How is that possible?" I asked. "The guy's claiming to be a fictional character."

"And *you're* claiming you'd never heard of him when you started writing your books," the chief investigator snapped back.

That got me—he was looking at me like *I* was a suspect in . . . something. "What's that supposed to mean?" I said.

"It's supposed to mean, who should I trust—a guy who's helped us solve eight missing persons cases or a woman who makes stuff up for a living?" Petrosky waved a hand to dismiss that. "No. I'm not saying I think you're lying. I'm saying that what you're telling me doesn't add up."

"Imagine how I feel."

He caught my eye a moment and studied my gaze. "Yeah. I'll bet. Look. I know Duffy. I've worked with him. He's never told me anything that was the least bit questionable. Tell me what he said to you."

I could have; maybe I should have. But something in the back of my mind was insisting that I refrain from outing "Duffy Madison" as a raving lunatic, and I didn't know why. I simply couldn't tell Petrosky that he'd said I had created him from whole cloth and that the grown man in his thirties who came to my book signing had claimed he hadn't existed before I'd started writing a character with his name.

"Besides his name? He said that he worked with you on missing persons cases. He said that he had a case he thought I would be able to help with and that it was a matter of life and death."

Petrosky, as good investigators will, had been watching my face as I spoke. He'd been paying excellent attention. "There's something you're not saying," he suggested. "What did he tell you that you don't want to say?" Far too excellent attention.

I looked away as if I were embarrassed. "He said he'd never read any of my books," I said. Then I sniffed a little, not as if I were stifling tears, but as if I were terribly offended and wished the subject to go away.

Petrosky smiled. "Well, I'll tell you what. After this conversation, I'm going to make a point of going to a bookstore on my way home and buying copies of all your books. I want to see if your Duffy bears any resemblance to mine."

Good; he'd bought the act. "Yeah, I'd kind of like to find that out myself. I'm even more confused now than I was when I got here. That's not what I was hoping would happen," I said. I stood to leave.

Petrosky held up a hand like he was directing traffic and wanted me to clear the crosswalk for an old lady. "Maybe you can get your chance," he said.

"To do what?" I didn't know what he was getting at, but the odds were that I wouldn't like it.

"To find out if our two Duffys match and to get less confused," he answered. "I'd really appreciate it if you would talk to Duffy about the case he's working."

I *knew* I wouldn't like it. "Why?" I asked.

"Two reasons: First, because I don't understand what's going on with him and your books. I need to know if one of my best consultants is a nut job."

"And second?"

"Second, because what Duffy told you is true. The case he's working really *is* a matter of life and death."

Chapter 7

"Her name is Julia," said the man who called himself Duffy Madison. "Julia Bledsoe. She is forty-seven years old, divorced, no children. She lives in Upper Saddle River, and her sister called three days ago saying she was concerned because she couldn't contact Julia. Her phone was going directly to voice mail, and the box was full. Her house was locked; the sister has no key. When police arrived to check out the scene, there was no sign of Ms. Bledsoe."

We were sitting in a conference room that Petrosky called "Duffy's office." It was bare except for the standard oblong table in the center of the room. No windows. A plain, light-brown textured wallpaper. Refreshingly, incandescent rather than fluorescent light. Duffy (I'll just call him that in an effort to simplify matters) sat in the center of the table on the right side.

I was opposite him on the left.

Petrosky had insisted that I meet with the imposter, simply because the case of Julia Bledsoe was still active and the police felt time was short to bring it to a favorable conclusion. I had agreed because I am easily bullied and, to be honest, because I was intrigued by this strange creature on the other side of the table.

Duffy Madison was not exactly how I'd always pictured him; I don't think of my characters in specific physical terms because I prefer to let the reader decide what they look like. This is especially enjoyable when readers insist they know a character is blond, or tall, or has green eyes. It's a real ego boost to know they can picture my people so vividly.

In this case, though, the man was in front of me and clearly visible. He was tall without being imposing and a little thin for his height with unruly brown hair that had some wave to it but couldn't be classified as curly. He had brown eyes that were large and seemed to be able to bore into a person (me, for example). He was the kind of man who, although he was not doing so at the moment, looked like he should be wearing tweed.

"She lives by herself and now she's not answering her phone," I summed up. "That's a matter of life and death?"

"It's the pattern that's the problem," Duffy answered. "This is something I've seen happen to three other women in the Northeast in the past two years."

I didn't like the sound of that. "How did the other three women get found?" I asked.

Duffy looked away. "They were not found alive," he said quietly.

In the books, Duffy would be driven by guilt. "Were they your cases?"

"No. None of them was in New Jersey. But they are all dead."

It took a moment to sink in. I felt something like a trap close around me; now I had to be committed to do whatever this weirdo wanted me to do because there really was a life at stake. "I'm guessing they didn't all die of natural causes by coincidence," I said.

"Sadly, no."

"So there's a serial killer targeting upscale divorced women in the Northeast?" I asked.

"No," Duffy said. He stood, looking restless, like he really wanted to leap out of the window, if there had been a window, and go rescue Lois Lane. Instead, he was stuck in this room explaining the details of an odd missing person case to a mystery novelist. That didn't make any sense, and I started to raise an objection, but he went on. "That's not the pattern. One of the other three women was married, another was single, not long out of high school, and without much of an income. The third was divorced, it's true, but she did not have the same economic advantage as Julia Bledsoe."

I write dialogue for a lot of characters—more so for Duffy Madison than others. I know his speech patterns because I have made them up; they are not even second nature to me; they're first-and-a-half nature. I don't have to conjure up Duffy's conversation when I need it. I know exactly how he talks; that's the easiest part of writing the character.

So the way he was talking now was especially worrisome, because I could tell there was a gap in it, but I didn't know where. "There's something you're not telling me," I said to him, and he avoided eye contact, so I knew I was right. "You're either withholding something that's confidential about the case, or you're trying to lead me into an area of conversation I don't want to bring up. Which is it?"

"I'm sure I don't know what you mean," he said. "I'm simply telling you the facts of the case so you can help me find Julia Bledsoe."

"No, that's not it." I stood, too. I write best when I glue my butt to the chair and force myself (writers spend years, sometimes decades, trying to become full-time authors, and once they do, they'll do anything to avoid writing), but I *think* best on my feet, pacing. "There are questions I should be asking, and I haven't stumbled onto them yet. You just want to tell me in your own way, and I'm not giving you the opportunity."

He stared at me.

I ignored that; there was no way *I* was going to be the crazy person in this conversation, and I had to remember that. Duffy hadn't anticipated my ability to think his thoughts—he was a talented imposter, but I was the character's creator—and he could probably feel the tables turning on him.

"Let's break this down," I said, talking mostly to myself and pacing back and forth on my side of the table. It was a decent-sized room, so there was plenty of pacing space. "Three women have been murdered in the past two years. There's a pattern to the victims, you said so yourself, but it's not marital or economic status. And the wild card is that for some reason you think I can help you find the latest woman to disappear, this Julia Bledsoe, even though I've never actually heard of her before. So given that I have no knowledge of the victim but you're intent on talking to me, there has to be some common ground. How am I doing so far?"

Duffy tried to regain his dignity by drawing himself to full height and lacing his fingers behind his back, as if he had been given the order to be at ease. "Your reasoning isn't bad," he said. "But you must be careful. Jumping to conclusions in a case like this is extremely dangerous. We have to stay—"

"—one step ahead of the kidnapper. Yes, I've heard that before. In fact, I wrote it." I stopped pacing and faced him directly. "Cards on the table, Duffy. You truly believe that you're a manifestation of the fictional character I created four years and now five manuscripts ago?"

He nodded. "I confess, I can't come up with another scenario that fits the facts. What's that got to do with the case?"

"You have to know that I think you're a nut. But you're a smart nut. You act exactly like the character I write, and he's brilliant. You can't do anything stupid. You can't step out of character, not even once, especially when I'm around. And that gives me an advantage—I know your moves better than you do. I know them before you do them."

"This is not a competition, Ms. Goldman." But the tightness in his mouth betrayed his real feelings.

"You aren't capable of dodging the question. I know that. So I'll ask it: why are you so intent on talking to me about this case?" I put my palms on the conference table and leaned toward him. "Why do you need me?"

"I think you know something about the victim," he answered. I thought there'd be more, but there wasn't.

"No, I don't. I've never heard of Julia Bledsoe."

In my books, Duffy Madison has a flair for the dramatic; he uses it to his advantage to get kidnappers to confess or witnesses to talk. So I fully expected to see him use it here, and he didn't disappoint. "Yes, you have," he said. "But you know her as Sunny Maugham."

I felt my eyes widen and drew a sharp intake of breath. Damn, he was good. "Julia Bledsoe is Sunny Maugham?"

Duffy nodded. "Her pen name."

I knew Sunny Maugham. I didn't know her well; we'd met at mystery conferences once or twice, and I was fairly sure we'd both been on a panel at the New York Public Library a couple of years before. She was a lot higher up on the literary food chain than I was. "You brought me in because the victim is a mystery author."

"That's the pattern," he almost whispered.

I stared into his eyes. "The pattern? The other victims? They were all mystery authors?"

"I'm afraid so," Duffy said.

It was too much to take in all at once. Sunny Maugham, an author of light, paper-thin mysteries, was missing. But that wasn't all—Duffy believed that she was the fourth in a series of such abductions, and the other three women who had been taken had been found murdered. All three of them mystery authors.

Like me.

"I don't mean to alarm you," Duffy said, although he had done exactly that. "I thought you might have known Ms. Bledsoe."

"I know Sunny. Not well, though. We've met a few times and really only talked once." At a convention in Bethesda, Maryland, Sunny and I had closed the bar one night when my first book was just on the shelves and her twelfth novel had just reached the *New York Times* Best Sellers list. We toasted each other until we were thoroughly toasted, and she gave me some advice about using social media to help people find your work. Mostly, it was about not being a pain and sounding like a commercial. She hadn't had to do that. She had gone out of her way for me, strictly as a way of "paying it forward," and I appreciated it.

"What did you talk about?" Duffy asked, suddenly intent on the question.

I left my reverie and looked at him. "Who are you, really?" I asked.

"Duffy Madison. What did you talk to Sunny Maugham about?"

"Nothing. Books. Publishing. Twitter. It wasn't significant."

Duffy gave me a look, and I knew before he said it that he was going to tell me, "Until we hear all the facts, we don't know what will be significant." I was pretty sure I'd written that one for him. "Is there anything you can think of that might point us in a direction? A place she liked to go? A lover or a relative she'd visit? Something like that?" He said "lover" like it was something he'd heard about but didn't really understand.

"She didn't tell me anything like that. I told you, we weren't close." Then, of course, just to prove that he was right and I was wrong, I remembered something. "Wait. She said she had a place down the shore. In Spring Lake, I think. She liked to go there when she got blocked writing or when she just needed to clear her head. She called it her bungalow."

Duffy's eyes lit up. "Why wouldn't her sister know about it?" he asked. "Was it a secret?"

"I honestly have no idea," I told him.

He pulled a laptop computer from a bag he had on the floor and opened it on the conference table. "There must be some way to get the address," he said to himself, because clearly there was no reason I needed to hear it. "Yes! Looking under Sunny Maugham, there's a deed to a small house in Ocean Grove, not Spring Lake." He couldn't resist letting me know where I'd been mistaken. "She might have gone there or been taken there. It's worth checking." He grabbed a jacket off the chair he'd been standing near and threw it on in a dramatic gesture. "Let's go."

Go? "What do you mean, 'let's go'?" I asked. "Isn't this police work? What do you need me for?"

Halfway to the door, he stopped to give me an incredulous look. "Don't you want to know if your information helped solve the case?"

"Not especially. I hope Sunny's all right, and I'd appreciate it if you'd call me later and let me know. But I'm going home. I've got revisions to do." I picked up my purse. Now, I surely wasn't going to do any revisions when I got home, but it sounded important enough. "After all, if I don't fix my book, how will you know who to be tomorrow?" Maybe that was mean.

"I'm not fictional, Ms. Goldman, I assure you. And I must insist that you accompany me to Ocean Grove."

It wasn't until I noticed the room getting alternately dark and light that I realized I must have been blinking a mile a minute. "Ocean Grove? Now?" It was an hour and a half drive, and that was without traffic. Even if he hadn't been pretending to be a figment of my imagination, now I would be sure this guy was nuts.

"Yes, please. You see, you lend a perspective that I can't hope to understand, never having written fiction. You can empathize with the victim, put yourself in her shoes. You can be invaluable."

"Why not just call the Ocean Grove cops and ask them to check in on her house?" I asked.

"I will do that, but I think it's imperative that you and I be on the scene as well," the fake almost-a-cop answered. "If Ms. Bledsoe is not there, you might be able to spot clues to her next destination. If she is there, you might be able to draw her out and determine the reason for her behavior."

Something didn't add up. "That doesn't fit your assessment of the situation," I told Duffy. "You practically told me before that you think Sunny might be the latest in a series of murders. You think she's dead."

"I don't think anything yet. I need facts. And you are keeping me from getting them as we speak."

I folded my arms. "I'm not keeping you from anything. You want to schlep down to Ocean Grove, enjoy yourself. The beach is lovely—and crowded—this time of year. But there's no logical reason for me to go, and I am definitely not going."

He regarded me without a readable expression on his face for a long moment. "If the situation were reversed and I asked Julia Bledsoe to help me find you, would she do it?" he asked.

Well, there went my day.

Chapter 8

In fact, it took almost two hours for us to reach Sunny Maugham's little beach house. Duffy had indeed notified the Ocean Grove police, who reported no sign of activity in the area and no car parked in front of the bungalow. There was no garage and no driveway.

An Ocean Grove police car was already in front of the place when we got there, and I saw a few neighbors standing out on their doorsteps wondering what the cops were doing in the area. Ocean Grove is one of the quieter shore towns, even during the height of the season.

We hadn't spoken much on the long drive down. I had pretty much plastered myself against the passenger side door, trying to stay as far away from this odd manifestation of a fictional character as possible. He, probably sensing my apprehension, stared straight ahead. Maybe he thought I was worried about his driving, which was so safety conscious I gave some thought to hiring him as my chauffeur.

My cell phone rang halfway down and I saw it was Brian calling. I don't know why, but it seemed rude to take the call in the car. That was weird. Duffy Madison, or whoever he really was, made me act weird. That couldn't be good.

There was one moment, right around Holmdel, when Duffy blurted out, "I'm concerned that Ms. Bledsoe might not be in her house alone. The Ocean Grove police aren't hearing anything, but they don't want to break the door down without a warrant or some indication of wrongdoing inside."

I considered thanking him for the lovely images now bouncing around in my brain—a crime fiction writer's mind is no place for the faint of heart—but didn't respond. Words have always been my best weapons and my tools of choice. Now I was incapable of finding any that would help make sense of the situation.

Let's recap, shall we? A man claiming to be the physical embodiment of my own fictional creation had invaded my life, insisting that he had come to being at the exact moment I'd started writing about the character with his name. He had the same job, under different circumstances, as my character. He looked roughly like I'd pictured my character. He spoke like my character. His demeanor was . . . you get the idea. And yet, he insisted he'd never read a word I'd ever written.

This guy wasn't just disturbing every notion I had of reality; he was a really bad consumer.

"How can you be Duffy Madison?" I demanded of him in lieu of a response to his worries. "There *is* no Duffy Madison. I made him up completely from scratch."

Not a flicker on his face, not a second when his eyes left the road. "Don't ask me to explain it. I've never known anything else. It's who I am."

"But you have identification. Mr. Petrosky told me. Voter registration. Fingerprint files. A driver's license. You have records with the Selective Service, for Chrissakes. If I just started writing Duffy four years ago, you can't be more than four years old. How can you have any official paper trail at all?"

Duffy was driving at three miles over the posted speed limit; he must have been really worried about Sunny Maugham. "Wouldn't your Duffy Madison have all those pieces of ID?" he asked.

"Yes, but he's a man in his thirties."

"So am I."

"You don't remember a childhood? High school? College? I gave Duffy all those things, but you don't remember anything before I started writing four years ago?" Duffy—my Duffy—was a logical man. If I could prove objectively that he was not who he believed himself to be, maybe we could figure out who he actually was.

"That's about right, yes."

We didn't talk again until we reached Ocean Grove, and then it was just about directions to the house.

It was, as advertised, a small structure, one of four raised a few feet higher than they had probably been before the shore was ravaged by winds and rain. More or less a clapboard version of a tent home, it had a triangular roof and one or two rooms—it was hard to tell from the outside—with three steps up to the front door. The four homes were surrounded on either side by much larger homes, clearly rental properties that leased by the apartment, as many as four flats in each house. Sunny's little bungalow looked like it was the baby some of the bigger houses had spawned.

At the moment, it had police officers at its door and, I was certain, more in the rear, where there was a tiny yard with no fence. The cops didn't have their weapons drawn, but I saw one rest his hand on his holster in anticipation.

"What happens now?" I asked Duffy. I opened my door because the air conditioning had gone off; I really wasn't interested in getting out of the car and becoming involved in this scene.

"I'll check in with the local police. I have no jurisdiction here or anywhere; I'm just a consultant." Duffy got out of the car, then looked inside. "Come on."

Dammit! I couldn't look cowardly around this guy; he wouldn't let me write about him being heroic anymore. Yeah, I know it's crazy. What about this situation *wasn't* crazy? I got out of the car, feeling like the biggest sucker on the planet.

Duffy started to close his door but stopped, looked inside, and reached in. "Your phone," he said. I didn't think I'd need it, but I didn't want it to feel like molten plastic when I got back in. Duffy leaned in, said, "Oops," when he dropped it—"Oops"? Really?—and after a few seconds, handed me my phone, which was only the temperature of a freshly baked bagel. I shoved it into my pocket and felt it warm my leg, which didn't need warming.

Without any further words or a look in my direction, he strode directly across the street to the house and spoke to the first officer he reached. I couldn't hear what was said, but the officer pointed at the front door. I followed at a discreet distance (I wasn't even a consultant) and stopped at the curb.

Duffy shook hands with one of the officers at the door who was wearing sergeant's stripes. They spoke briefly, and Duffy nodded, pointed at me, and nodded again. The cop acknowledged his nod, then turned back toward the door and said something into the comm link on his shoulder. Duffy walked down the three stairs and came to stand next to me.

"They haven't seen any sign of life," he reported. "But they also have a decent view of most of the inside; it's a small place. They don't see anything disturbing or dangerous, or they would have gone inside already."

"So what are they going to do?" I asked.

"They're trying Julia Bledsoe's cell phone again because there is no landline in the bungalow," Duffy answered. "They want to see if they can hear the ringtone."

"Doesn't seem likely," I suggested. "If she's there, they'd probably see her, and if she's . . . if something happened, her cell phone is either gone, out of power, or holding enough messages that the call will be sent straight to voice mail. What happens if they don't hear anything?"

Duffy looked dubious. "They could try to get a judge to sign a warrant, but I don't think there's enough evidence to merit one." He stopped talking and looked intently at the officers at Sunny Maugham's front door.

One of them was punching numbers into a cell phone. He waited, phone away from his ear. The two other cops leaned in toward the front windows, one looking in, the other two with their ears to the glass.

All of a sudden, the two listening both stood up straight with a jolt. They looked at the sergeant with whom Duffy had been talking, who nodded and pointed at the front door. Then the officer who'd been looking through the front window positioned himself at the door, got his balance, and kicked. Hard.

"I guess they heard the phone ring," Duffy said, not necessarily to me.

"No shit, Sherlock." He gave me a quick reproving look; I'd forgotten that Duffy doesn't care for profanity. My publisher's idea. Get more women to read the books. Hey, it's a living.

The cops, led by the sergeant, rushed into the tiny structure and then . . . nothing. We didn't see anything through the front window but police officers walking around in a nondescript sort of pattern, and we didn't hear anything through the open front door, which looked like it would require a decent amount of repair if Sunny was going to close and lock it again.

Neither of us said anything; it was becoming a learned behavior. We avoided eye contact and didn't speak to each other. A stranger passing by would have thought we'd been married for fifteen years.

Finally, the sergeant appeared in the front door again and beckoned. "Mr. Madison?"

Duffy started toward the house and then turned and looked at me. “Come along,” he said.

I had the strangest urge to look around for the person he was summoning, but I resisted it and did not ask, “Me?” I’d like it noted that when given the opportunity, I avoided the cliché. “You sure it’s all right?” I asked him. Any excuse to not go into that house, if something had been found, would do.

“If it’s safe for me, it’s safe for you,” he said impatiently. “Let’s go.”

Because—and only because—I couldn’t think of a plausible reason not to, I started toward the house. Duffy, already on the front steps, stopped and waited again when he saw I was clearly not relishing the amazing opportunity I was being given and was lagging behind. But he didn’t say anything.

Eventually, I reached his position on the top step and waited for him to enter the house. But he, gallant as ever, waved an arm toward the interior. “After you,” he said.

Finally, I meet a man with some manners, and he’s an idea I got in the shower. There was almost something poetically ironic about that.

The inside was one room, and it was not large. There was no television, no sofa. To the right, there was a tiny galley kitchen that included a microwave oven, a minifridge, and a two-burner cook top. In the center of the room was a fold-up card table with one chair (also collapsible) next to it. There was a folding beach chair leaning against the wall near the table. A thin line of sand led from the folding chair to the door in the back. Toward the back were towels hung on a line that ran across the room and flip-flops by the back door, which led to a tiny porch. The back door was open, showing a small yard that had probably once been grass and was now mostly sand.

This is what upscale New Jerseyans can afford when they want to own a home down the shore.

The sergeant approached and looked at me, then at Duffy. "Who's this?" he asked.

"My assistant," Duffy said with no hint of irony. *Without me, there'd be no you, pal, and don't you forget it.* Now in my own head, I was starting to sound like his mother. "Ms. Goldman is here to catch anything I miss and to chronicle anything we see. I assume that's all right."

The sergeant looked me up and down, which did not make me more comfortable. "If you say so," he said. Then he looked at me. "Don't touch anything."

Resisting the impulse to thank him for the vote of confidence, I nodded.

"Come on," Duffy said.

I reached into my back pocket for a reporter's notebook, which Duffy had undoubtedly seen. I always have something to write on in case an idea comes when it's not convenient. I don't own a smart phone, and I don't much care for voice recorders; they are not as reliable as paper. Paper never runs out of battery power. In my side pocket was a pen, so I got that out as well.

"Fire away, Duffy," I said. He'd want to detail everything he saw that he considered relevant, and that meant everything. Luckily, I knew his method. I had invented his method.

He walked to the center of the room, next to the card table, and began revolving, very slowly, to take in every area of the room. "No sign of a struggle. No blood on any surface. No overturned furniture. No broken glass in the kitchen. No indications that any large furniture or rugs have been removed." I wrote down the list in my own shorthand, which only I would be able to decipher later. Good penmanship is not the same as writing well.

Duffy often says that what an investigator doesn't see is at least as important as what he does see. I don't know if it's true or not, but it sounds good when I write it.

"Why would someone have removed a rug?" the sergeant asked. I knew why, but I let Duffy have his moment.

"It's one of the safer ways to remove a body without being noticed," he answered. "Quite often blood and DNA evidence go with the rug. Even a live victim being transported could be carried in a rug once sedated."

The sergeant looked impressed and maybe a little concerned.

"What *is* in the room that's relevant?" I asked Duffy, to get him going a little quicker. Even though I didn't see any evidence of foul play—and it seemed Duffy didn't, either—I wasn't crazy about being here and wanted to begin the interminable journey back to Adamstown, where I was absolutely itching to get to those revisions.

Duffy redirected his attention to the room. "The room is used mostly as a staging area for days at the beach," he said. "There is an usual amount of sand near the back door where people would leave and return, and a line of sand from the back door to the folding chair by the card table indicates that it had been taken there after a trip to the beach. There is a futon near the back for those times when Ms. Bledsoe might want to spend the night. The kitchen does not appear to be fully stocked, although we will have to check the cabinets." One of the officers, hearing that, immediately opened some doors and looked inside.

"Nothing special," he said. Duffy walked over to him to see for himself, but the cop kept talking. "Cereal boxes, some dishes, some spaghetti. Not much."

Duffy gave me a glance as he got a vantage point. "Enough food for one person who wasn't planning to stay long or two who were only staying overnight," he said, and watched me write it down. "Cooking implements for the most basic functions. Cleaning supplies under the sink, again very limited. Just kitchen surface wipes, dishwashing detergent, and glass cleaner. This was not set up to be a long-term residence for anyone."

"That's not a huge surprise," the sergeant said. "These are beach houses. People come down for weekends, mostly. If you're using it as a summer rental, you're probably in one of the bigger houses, renting an apartment."

"True," Duffy noted. "But Ms. Bledsoe came down here on occasion for a purpose other than recreation. The only piece of furniture in the room that doesn't have a coat of dust on it is the card table in the center, yet there are no dishes in the drainer. It's unlikely Ms. Bledsoe, or anyone else, ate dinner here recently. No dust on the table means it was being used for some other purpose."

"It's a card table," the uniformed officer said with a hopeful voice. "Maybe she came down to play cards?"

"With no garbage, no empty bottles or glasses obviously used, and no deck of cards anywhere, I would say not," Duffy answered him. He wasn't trying to dash the kid's hopes of becoming a plainclothes detective anytime soon, but his tone probably had that effect anyway.

"The table isn't entirely dusted," I pointed out. "Just the side by the one chair. There's nothing on the other side at all *except* dust. And the seat of the chair has just about the same look to it, a little dust but not as much as everything else."

"So Ms. Bledsoe used the table, but not for eating, since that doesn't seem to have happened here recently." Duffy knew I was on to something, but he didn't know what yet. To me, it seemed obvious.

"This is Sunny's writer's retreat," I told him. "She comes down here when she gets stuck, maybe, or just needs a change of scenery to keep the work coming. She uses that table, but she probably goes out for dinner instead of cooking. She wouldn't want to take the time to cook dinner, and if she's down here alone, there's no reason to cook when there are plenty of restaurants in the area. Any excuse to get up from the table and move around is probably welcome. She works here. Probably not all the time because the house isn't winterized, but she definitely works here."

Duffy smiled an enigmatic smile. The sergeant and the uniformed cop who had looked in the kitchen appeared perplexed by my explanation, but Duffy pointed at the table and waved his finger a bit.

"There are no indications there were notes, paper files, index cards," he said. "No scratches from paper clips, no pens or pencils, no note pads."

"Welcome to the computer age," I said.

"There is no desktop computer."

"Okay, welcome to the laptop computer age. I haven't written anything out on paper for years. My desk doesn't even have enough open space for me to consider writing on it. No flat surface that isn't taken up with something. The only reason I think this isn't Sunny's primary workspace is that there's no visible modem, no Wi-Fi server. There's no printer. She only uses this place when she needs to be away from her usual office because she's reached maximum density there."

"Writer's block?" Duffy suggested.

I waved a hand dismissively. "There's no such thing. Writers made that up so they could procrastinate better. We love to make up excuses not to write, and we're great at making things up. Writers are the best procrastinators on the planet."

"Still, no indication there ever were notes. Is that all on her laptop?" Duffy seemed genuinely intrigued by my explanation of the process; it was like he was asking me how he'd been born. I got a little nauseous but fought that feeling off.

"Not necessarily. From what I can see, Sunny's probably a pantser."

The two cops indulged in a shared look, and Duffy's eyes widened a bit. "A *pantser*?" he asked.

"Sure. There are two kinds of writers: plotters and pantsers. Plotters work out every detail before they ever commit a word to their hard drives. They outline. They take notes on the backs of napkins and pull them out of their pockets at the end of the night. They have charts and graphs and three-by-five file cards that tell them the whole story they're about to write before they dare try to write it.

"But pantsers fly by the seat of their pants. They start with a premise, maybe have a scene or two in their heads that will serve as landmarks along the way, and that's it. They know who their characters are and what their stories are generally about, but they don't have any idea what the connective tissue will be. How they get from point A to point Z is a complete mystery. For pantsers, that makes the writing process more fun, if something that difficult and painful can be considered fun."

"And you?" Duffy asked.

"Pantser. From day one."

"You frown on those who plan ahead?" Duffy is meticulous and plodding; he rarely takes a wild chance. He was asking me for some sign of acceptance—or not.

"No, of course not," I assured him. "Writing's too hard to exclude people whose style is not the same as mine. Whatever process works is the one people should use."

He grinned. "That's very understanding of you," he said.

"But it doesn't get us any closer to what happened here," the sergeant pointed out, no doubt anxious for the writing seminar to be over. "It looks like the owner of the house was here pretty recently, but it doesn't look like there's any sign of a crime. If she's missing now, she probably isn't missing from here."

"I must disagree," Duffy said. "Ms. Bledsoe was definitely taken from this bungalow."

"How do you figure?" The sergeant might not have been pleased with this civilian tutoring him on the fine points of crime investigation, and he certainly wasn't crazy about the "assistant" to the consultant going on about the creative writing life.

Duffy, unfortunately, was blind to the muffled disdain in the sergeant's voice. "It's simple. What led us into this house?"

Oh, boy. He was going to hold a symposium. I instinctively backed up a step away from the sergeant, if for no other reason than to give him a visual separation between myself and Duffy, a quick "Hey, that's him, not me" indicator.

"You called our department and said that a missing woman might be found here," the sergeant answered through thin lips. "And I'll report that we didn't find her."

"That's not what I'm asking," Duffy insisted, the tough-but-fair professor trying to point his clever-but-limited student back to the right path. "What gave us the impetus to enter the house?"

I worried momentarily that the sergeant would stumble on the word "impetus," but he went straight through. "When we called her cell phone, it rang inside this house," he said, squinting as if the answer to the puzzle were far away and he couldn't quite make out the lettering.

"Exactly," Duffy said. "Very good." It was a miracle he didn't try to feed the sergeant a liver treat. "And did we find the mobile?" There are times he uses words that make him sound British; that's unintentional on my part. Sometimes I think he bleeds a little into Sherlock Holmes in my head. I should work harder on that.

"Yeah," the uniformed cop said, producing the phone in his latex-gloved hand. "It was right there on the floor next to the table."

"Excellent!" Duffy gushed. "You're doing very well indeed." You see what I mean about the British thing?

"So how does that lead to her being taken from the house?" the sergeant wanted to know.

"Ms. Bledsoe comes down here to work on her latest novel," Duffy began. "She might be floundering at home and decides she needs a change of scene, or maybe she just wants to go to the beach. That doesn't matter at this point.

"Once she's here, she encounters another person who might show some interest in her work or simply strike up a conversation at the beach or at dinner in a restaurant one night. A person dining out alone is not impossible but certainly not standard. It draws attention to her, and maybe she is happy for the company."

"You're getting this from a cell phone on the floor?" the officer asked.

"I'm not sure about the details," Duffy said. "What I know is that Ms. Bledsoe and another person—because that folding chair must have been stored in the back of the house and then brought here for a guest, based on the trail of sand—came back here, and from here they made a very hasty exit. That, given the fact that her sister called the police concerned—because this is a serious break in Ms. Bledsoe's routine—leads me to believe that she was taken."

"How does the cell phone lead to abduction?" I asked, finally. *Somebody* had to get him to the reveal or we'd be here all night, and I wanted to get home. To revise. No, really.

"A writer without a cellular phone is unthinkable," Duffy said. "To be out of touch with an editor, an agent, a publicist? Never. Am I correct about that?" he asked me.

Considering that I'd talked to my agent today and had to e-mail my editor as soon as I got home, I nodded.

"So she forgot her phone," the sergeant said. "It happens to everybody."

"Yes, but then everybody comes back to get it," Duffy said. "Ms. Bledsoe's sister confirms there is no second cell number. That is the only phone she has. And since it's still holding a charge enough that we could hear the ringing from outside the house, we can assume it has not been lying on the floor here for much more than a day, two on the outside."

"That means she's not here," the sergeant argued. "It doesn't mean she's been kidnapped."

"The phone was on the floor next to the table. It had been dropped there. And it was left there."

"So she dropped her phone on her way out the door," the sergeant said.

"Look at this house," Duffy countered. "It's not clean, but it's neat. There isn't one thing out of place. Everything, down to the last cereal spoon, has been put back in its designated spot. Everything except that cell phone, the one item

Ms. Bledsoe would probably have been most cognizant of the whole time. No, the phone on the floor is very telling, sergeant. There's no sign of a struggle, but that phone makes it kidnapping for me, and if that's the case, I'm afraid we have very little time left to find Ms. Bledsoe."

Chapter 9

"You were extremely helpful," Duffy Madison told me. "I would not have been able to adequately evaluate the crime scene if you hadn't been there. Thank you."

All this buttering up was taking place in the parking lot of the Bergen County office building, after another interminable trip, this time from Ocean Grove to Hackensack to pick up my car. Duffy had nattered on about the case in a monologue, almost nonstop, since we'd said our good-byes to the Ocean Grove police department and headed northwest to our—or my, at least—home county.

I'd been taking notes, as he'd . . . is there a word that could make it sound like he didn't actually order me to? *Instructed*, perhaps. Gentler, without actually being polite.

The three murders of crime writers were perplexing at the very least, he'd said. They weren't the same kind of writers. One, Missy Hardaway, lived in New Hampshire and wrote "cozies," the kind of mystery that features no "bad" language, no graphic violence, and, above all, no explicit sex. (You can kill anyone you want—except the cat—but you can't have your heroine *shtup* anybody or you're toast.) She had published two books in trade paperback with a small publisher headquartered in Baltimore.

The second dead writer, J. B. Randolph (I didn't think any of these were their real names), wrote tough thrillers. The initials instead of a first name probably indicated that her publisher wanted readers to think the books were written by a man, or at least not to think about the author's gender at all. Randolph had written seven books, all stand-alones. They'd managed some success, but she was hardly a household name.

The third was Marion Benedict, a lab assistant and an unpublished writer who had created two e-book short stories on her own and was at work on her first full-length novel (the first two had not been purchased by a publisher, and she'd been talking about self-publishing), a police procedural about a beautiful but shy forensic lab technician, when she was found murdered.

I did not get to ask Duffy how the women died because he literally never stopped talking during the ride, but he volunteered the information anyway somewhere around Exit 143B (Irvington/Hillside) on the Garden State Parkway. "Ms. Hardaway was found at her home in Nashua, New Hampshire, with trauma to her head; she'd been hit from behind with a manual typewriter she kept in her writing room but did not use," he said. I thought—but, again, didn't get the chance to say—that no writer uses a typewriter anymore, and certainly not a manual one, so it had probably been a decoration—or an inspiration. Some people get a charge out of the good old days of writing. Give me a good word processor and the ability to cut and paste, and I'm a happy woman.

"J. B. Randolph was electrocuted directly by current from her desktop computer," Duffy went on as I scribbled. "She lived in Manhattan, Kansas, and had no connection to either of the other victims or Ms. Bledsoe, according to the research I've done and have been given by the other three police departments. If the women weren't all crime writers, they would seem to have been chosen at random. Because they clearly *weren't* random crimes, the motive must somehow be tied to the idea of writing crime fiction."

I knew Sunny Maugham's reputation well enough to dismiss the idea of a jealous rival doing her in. She was generous to a fault with other writers, had been working with the same editor for decades without so much as a hint of friction, and was considered one of the truly nicest people in the business. If I hadn't been so busy taking dictation from Duffy, I might have had a moment to be truly worried about possibly being in very severe danger.

But on he went: "Marion Benedict was found in her home in Philadelphia. She rented an apartment over a pizzeria and wrote in her bedroom. Her death was perhaps the most gruesome of the three."

I considered asking him to let me off here, but we were still on the Parkway, and getting out to walk while other cars zipped by at eighty-five miles an hour could make me an even more gruesome statistic, so I took a breath and told myself simply to write the words I heard and not to think about their meaning.

"She was found literally choked to death with printouts of rejection letters stuffed into her throat," Duffy said. "She suffocated."

He was right; that was pretty bad.

"In Ms. Bledsoe's case," he continued, the words just coming out as if he had already written them down and was now reading off cards, "the abduction is unusually subtle. The other victims were reported missing but immediately found murdered at home. Ms. Bledsoe is missing from both her Upper Saddle River home and her beach house in Ocean Grove, indicating she was taken and kept longer. There is a reason the criminal has changed his pattern, but it is not yet apparent."

He had then recited various observations from each of the crime scenes, from Sunny's house, which had shown no sign of any serious altercation, to the newest data (as Duffy would call it, despite the fact that it was all from his own mind) from the house in Ocean Grove, with its incongruous card table and folding chairs—really not the kind of place a woman like Julia, whose books had achieved a very high level of success, would usually be expected to own. "It is odd that she chose that house for her writing retreat and that she had clearly been there recently but had not seemed to do much more than exist there. Even the backyard did not show signs of much activity, and that would have been the route to the beach, surely one of the draws for Ms. Bledsoe to make the drive down."

He had never speculated on the kidnapper's motive or any possible identity for the criminal. I knew he wouldn't; that

Holmesian brain would never admit any thought that hadn't been created from facts. Guessing was simply not something Duffy Madison would ever do.

And whoever this guy was, he clearly knew all about what Duffy Madison would and would not do.

Now in the Bergen County parking lot, I could put away the note pad and accept his compliment. "I am happy to be of help," I said, and to some degree I meant it. "I'll type these notes up and e-mail them to you tomorrow morning; how's that?"

"Oh, that's no good," he answered.

I had been reaching for the door handle; now I stopped and regarded him. "I beg your pardon?"

"Ms. Bledsoe has not yet been found. Every minute counts." His tone indicated that I was no longer the brightest third grader in the class.

"And my typing up thc notes is going to get her rescued faster?" I *knew* he was crazy. Now the deep psychosis was going to come out. I reached for the door latch again.

"Of course not," Duffy said. "Type up the notes at your leisure. But you can't leave now. We have work to do. I want you to lend the same expertise at Ms. Bledsoe's home in Upper Saddle River. It's possible there is something there that I missed, as well. And *that* might get her rescued faster."

"Upper Saddle River?" I moaned wearily. "That's got to be a half-hour drive."

"Thirty-three minutes," Duffy corrected. It occurred to me to mention that specificity might not be the most important thing at this moment. "Assuming there isn't much traffic."

"You can't be serious." Then I realized he was about to inform me that he was nothing *but* serious, and I cut him off at the pass. "If you wanted me to go with you to Sunny's house in Upper Saddle River, why did you bring me back here?"

Duffy looked uncomfortable. "I thought you might want to get your car or need to go home to freshen up," he said. "Ladies do that, don't they?" Maybe he really was four years old. Had I ever written a love interest for Duffy? Now that I thought about it, the answer was no. He'd probably never had anything but a professional conversation with a woman in his "life."

"Well, it's always welcome, but if we're going to—" I caught myself. "Hold on. I'm not going anywhere with you anymore. You're the consultant with the cops. Go consult. I'm a mystery writer. I have revisions that need to get done. Call me with any updates, and good night, Mr. . . ."

"Madison. Duf—"

"Whatever." This time I opened the car door and got out. And I was about to slam it, harder than I probably should, when a wave of guilt, probably sent across thousands of miles by my mother telepathically, hit me between the eyes. I turned back and looked at Duffy. "Look, there's nothing at Sunny's house that I could see if you didn't see it. If you really believe that I am responsible for your existence, then you have to believe it the whole way. That means I can't know anything you don't. So I'm sure you didn't miss a thing. Just keep on investigating. Duffy Madison hasn't ever failed to find the missing person." I closed the car door, respectfully and quietly. "Good night," I repeated.

He probably wouldn't have heard me, but he was in the process of lowering the passenger window. "I saw the table and the dust in Ocean Grove. You interpreted them. You're the writer. You have the same sensibility as the victim here. You can help."

The fatigue that had set in was too strong. I shook my head. "Not tonight, Duffy. I don't have anything left in me. You keep working the case tonight without me. I guarantee you'll make more progress that way, and I bet by the morning you will have found Sunny Maugham. Meanwhile, I'll get your notes together. If you still feel like you need me in the morning, go ahead and call, okay?"

He looked like a disappointed puppy, but he nodded once. "Fair enough. You've already gone above and beyond the call of duty. Thank you for your help, Ms. Goldman. I'll call you tomorrow morning either way, if that's all right."

I assured him it was, then turned and walked to my car as his tires crackled on the pavement. I didn't look back, got in, and drove home without checking in the rearview mirror to see if Duffy Madison was following me.

Once there, I got out my key and opened the door. Being inside my very own house was the most comforting feeling I could remember having in a long, long time.

The revisions—I hadn't been kidding about those—were waiting, but I decided first to put some water on to boil and make myself some pasta. Comfort food on a day when comfort was definitely a scarce commodity. Once the water was on the stove, I opened a bottle of red wine, let it breathe for close to ten seconds, and poured myself a glass. I don't have a fireplace, but it was July, so that was just as well, and I plopped myself down in front of the TV, put on a rerun of a sitcom I probably thought was stupid the first time it had aired, and luxuriated in the depths of ordinariness.

When the water boiled, I cooked some penne to the proper al dente, got out a jar of Alfredo sauce, and reveled in how badly I was treating my body. I probably would have eaten the whole box of pasta if those damn revisions hadn't been calling from the back of my mind. Deadline was less than a week away; there was no avoiding them.

I got the laptop out of the case I'd been lugging it around in all day, then decided I'd do this right and actually go to my office and the desktop computer I had there. That would feel more like a responsible professional doing work.

It actually did seem right to work in the office, which still wasn't straightened up, but I didn't care about that right then. I touched the *R* key on the computer, which I always do to wake it up, and sure enough, it blazed to life. Well, "blazed" might be a trifle optimistic. My computer is a few years old. It rumbled to life.

There were, it noted, two hundred and sixteen e-mails in my inbox, accumulated since I'd left this morning. I knew it would take me precious time to sort through them, but it's a compulsion. I can't work if someone is trying to get in touch with me. What if it's Steven Spielberg wanting to adapt a Duffy novel to the big screen?

Stop laughing. It could happen.

Alas, Steven had forsaken me once again. Most of the e-mails were either junk that the spam filter hadn't managed to, you know, filter or messages from one of the LISTSERVs I joined around the time *Olly Olly* was about to be published. The lists, for those interested in crime fiction, get an author in touch with people who might want to read her books, and they have been very helpful to me. I also love to get into discussions about my books and those of other writers in the field with the people on the lists. They're really very respectful and extremely interested in the subject matter—sometimes I feel bad that they read so many more of the books in my own genre than I do.

I checked the subject lines on most of the e-mails and deleted many off the bat. Even on the lists, there are books I haven't read or subjects on which I know I won't have a pertinent comment. With so many messages a day, one must manage one's time.

That left about twenty messages that actually had some relevance to my day. Some were from readers who wanted to make a comment on the latest book (latest to them—I was probably two installments ahead, but they didn't know that) or ask for a bookmark. I'm happy to send those when I can get a snail mail address. Some people ask for the bookmark, which I always autograph, and don't give me an address. And it's so hard to stick those suckers in through the slots in the Internet.

I answered two or three reader e-mails (and I never know what to say; I'm bad at accepting compliments, but I think it's bad policy to disagree with people who think my writing is wonderful) and moved on. There was one from Sol, not asking about the newly completed manuscript but hinting that he wanted to know when he'd see it. Sol can be subtle. I shot him back a message that I was doing revisions and would have it for him in a few days, ahead of my deadline.

Three e-mails to go now. One was from a media newsletter reminding me that my subscription would soon expire—in four months. That got deleted. Let them get back to me in three and a half months.

The next was from my mother, who reported that she had felt a lump in her breast, correctly diagnosed it as a benign cyst, had it removed and biopsied, and was now in perfect health. That's my mother. She'll have a health crisis, go through any amount of suspense having it resolved, and never think that maybe her daughter might be able to support her through her time of need. I would have called her immediately, but it was late now where I was and not where she was, which meant she'd be twice as energetic as me, and that never leads to a pleasant conversation. I wrote a sticky note to call her when I got up in the morning (Mom rises with the sun in Colorado) and secured it to the frame of my computer screen.

I almost deleted the last e-mail without reading it. The return address, itsamystery@anonymous.com, certainly didn't ring any bells. But the "mystery" part was definitely in my wheelhouse; it was possible this was another reader who'd just discovered the Duffy books, which is always nice, or someone in the mystery community with a request for something (an appearance, maybe, or a signed something or other for charity, things that are easy to do and make the author feel like a good person). It was worth checking. I opened the e-mail.

Immediately, I was sorry I'd done that. Sprawled across the screen, as if taken from random publications for a ransom note, were words in various fonts, colors, and sizes. The message read,

You THINK **you** *CAN* FIND
Sunny Maugham? **Just Try!**

And then at the bottom . . .

YOU **could** *BE* **next**.

Even as the word left my mouth, I felt stupid for shouting it: "Duffy!"

Chapter 10

Duffy, who had to be a good many miles away by now, did not appear at my door, which was distressing. I stared at the e-mail for a while longer, felt my stomach tighten, and picked up my phone.

I could have called Brian Coltrane. I could have called Paula. I could have called Marty in the Morris County Prosecutor's Office, although I'm not sure I have a number other than his office phone. I could have called my father, which definitely crossed my mind, but he was hours from here and would only have told me to call the police.

I didn't. I called Duffy Madison.

There is no way to explain that. I'd met the man who claimed to be my fictional creation only hours before. I was certain he had severe emotional problems or a mental illness that created his delusions. I didn't know his real name, his background, his intentions, or his reliability. I had no reason to trust him. But he had struck me as so much the character I'd been writing, who always comes to the rescue and always knows just what to do, that my first (and second, truth be known) impulse was to cry to him and make him help me.

It was a simple stroke of luck that Petrosky had given me Duffy's cell phone number, because I certainly wouldn't have asked for it, but he wanted me to talk to his consultant and work on the Sunny Maugham case. Now it appeared I would have no choice.

Besides, I was scared shitless.

Duffy answered the phone on the first ring. "Ms. Goldman," he said. "I'm glad you have changed your mind about coming to Ms. Bledsoe's home. I can pick you up in a half hour."

I'd rehearsed what I was going to say after I got finished hyperventilating, which had taken some minutes. "Duffy, I think the kidnapper knows that you contacted me. In fact, I'm sure of it."

In my mind, I could see his eyebrows drop into a concerned expression through the momentary pause on the line. "What makes you certain?" he asked.

I told Duffy about the e-mail and he did not waste any time. "I'm on my way out the door," he said. "Make sure yours are locked, and don't let anyone in until I'm there. Understood?"

I did, in fact, grasp the meaning of his words and told him so. I disconnected the call and sat looking at the threatening message my computer seemed eager to send me.

For half an hour.

How could Sunny's kidnapper (since there now seemed to be no doubt that was what had happened) have discovered that I was involved in the investigation? I wasn't that puzzled over his finding my e-mail address; it's listed on my website with a link (under "Contact" on the home page). Authors have to promote their work.

I mentally counted the people who would know I had spent the day with Duffy Madison as a consultant to the consultant, working to find Sunny Maugham. I started with Petrosky, who had suggested it initially, and moved on to the sergeant and a few uniformed officers in Ocean Grove. They knew I was there.

But Rita and Brian knew I was planning on finding out who this "Duffy" character was from the night before. Naturally, there was no reason to think either one of them had anything to do with whatever Sunny was going through; I wasn't sure Brian had even *heard* of Sunny Maugham. But they could have talked to other people, and those people could have mentioned it to someone who ended up being the wrong person. The world is a random place.

Marty Dugan knew I'd been asking about Duffy Madison. It would have been easy for him to find out what case Duffy was consulting on for Bergen County. I couldn't possibly see Marty as Sunny's kidnapper, but again, how could I know to whom he was telling his story about the crazy author in his spare time?

The kidnapper, of course, *could* have been watching the house at Ocean Grove. He *could* have been one of the uniform cops, although that seemed unlikely (the other three abductions took place outside New Jersey). He *could* have been in the Bergen County offices and seen me with Duffy.

In fact, this person could be anyone on the street, anyone at any book convention I'd ever met, any fan, any critic, anyone who had ever attended one of my book signings.

And then there was Duffy.

My Duffy, the one I've been writing for years, was beyond reproach. There was no chance, zero, none that he would ever under any circumstances consider something cruel or illegal. He was not violent. He was not angry by nature. He was not at all unhinged. True, he could be excitable in the name of good, and he was not always the most polite person you'd ever met (especially when dealing with those he considered unintelligent), but kidnappings and murders? Never.

But *this* Duffy? The one who had clearly appropriated the identity of a fictional character, wormed his way into the favor of the chief investigator for the Bergen County prosecutor, and then found an excuse to confront me with the tale of a fellow mystery author who by coincidence had been helpful to my career and now needed help in the most desperate fashion? The one who had wanted very badly to take me from a small house filled with police officers to another, more than two hours away, where it was a fair bet there would be no one but the two of us in an empty building? The one who had thought I needed a break to *freshen up*? That Duffy? He could be anyone, literally. He could have all sorts of mental issues besides the obvious ones. He could have aligned himself with a law enforcement agency to have better access to public records and crime files. For all I knew, he was not "consulting" with the prosecutor during the times the other three authors were taken and therefore could have been anywhere.

Why had I called this guy for help, again?

It was just then I had that thought that I heard Duffy's car pull into my driveway. Now having convinced myself that the man was a deranged kidnapper and murderer, I went to the door and let him in out of a ridiculous sense of propriety: how could I turn him away when I was the one who had called him in the first place?

"Let me see the e-mail," he said the second his foot hit the threshold of my entrance hall (okay, it was a tiny space with ceramic tile floors leading to the living room—you have to call it *something*).

"Nice to see you, too," I said, ushering him into the house and pointing him toward my office. He strode purposefully, just like in the books, through what he must now have been thinking of as "the crime scene" and kept going until he realized he had to wait for me because he didn't know which room was the office.

"This way," I said in what I hoped was a dry voice.

But if my tone had the desired message in it, Duffy hadn't noticed it. He walked through the office door and went straight for the desktop computer whose screen was still glowing brightly in the room. (I hadn't actually turned on the lights when I walked in because it wasn't dark yet and had neglected to turn them on afterward.) The offending message was still vividly displayed in all its gruesome glory.

"Aha," Duffy said, as if that actually meant something. He sat down in my work chair without an invitation or permission but did not touch the keyboard. He reached into his pocket and pulled out a pair of purple latex gloves, which he snapped onto his hands.

"Does my computer have some illness I should be concerned about?" Apparently getting a virus was more than a metaphor.

"It wasn't a virus that caused this," Duffy said. I had always thought I'd given him a sense of humor, but it's so subjective. "This came from Ms. Bledsoe's abductor, almost certainly."

That was not good news. He seemed to be jumping to conclusions after a quick glance. "How do you know?" I asked, and even as I said it, I knew I'd regret doing so.

"All the crime fiction authors in this pattern have gotten e-mails like this one," Duffy answered. "They were found on the hard drives of the three before and then Ms. Bledsoe. It is the perpetrator's calling card, his way of introducing himself before the game actually begins."

Yeah, I'd been right. I regretted asking.

"You're not making me feel better, Duffy," I said.

He didn't turn away from the screen but had not yet touched the mouse or the keyboard. "I'm not trying to alarm you, Ms. Goldman," he said. "I'm merely stating the facts of the case."

"The facts of the case are alarming me," I admitted.

"Facts are facts." The man was a virtual wellspring of reassurance.

"What does the message mean? How can this guy know I was involved in the investigation? I wasn't before I met you." Duffy would analyze the situation dispassionately, clearly, and intelligently. Why wasn't that making me feel any better?

"That is an excellent question," he said, eyes never leaving the screen. It was like he wanted that message—which I never wanted to lay eyes upon again—burned into his retinas so that he could analyze it endlessly for as long as he wanted until it told him something useful. "It is destructive to speculate without sufficient data."

"We have data. There are a finite number of people who had the information that this person now has. We can assume, then, that one of them told him, no?" When I'm writing Duffy, the hard part for me is finding a puzzle that will be difficult to solve, because he's written as such an observant and analytical character. Now, I was hoping this was the easiest case he'd ever have to solve.

"Not necessarily," he answered, tearing down any hope I might have been trying to build. "The perpetrator in this case might have been watching at any of the points we were visible to the public, which is virtually any time since we met that we were not alone in the conference room at work or in my car. He might have been following you before you came to see me this morning."

My god, was that *really* just this morning? This had been the longest day of my life, and I hadn't even gotten any revisions done.

"So where does that leave us?" I asked.

"With only a few facts." Duffy looked up because the doorbell rang.

I think I might have stopped breathing. Could the kidnapper be so confident that he'd ring my bell and walk in without any trepidation? Would it help that Duffy was here?

"I hope you don't mind," Duffy said. "I called the investigator after I spoke to you. Would you let him in?" He gestured toward the door as the bell rang again.

"The investigator?" Wasn't Duffy investigating?

"Of course. You know I'm just a consultant. You wrote that for me. Mr. Preston is the investigator assigned to Ms. Bledsoe's case."

Of course. If there was one thing you had to love about Duffy, it was the matter-of-fact way he condescended to you. Without anything else to do, I got up and went to the front door.

I looked through the peephole, which was entirely unhelpful. A man was standing there. He might have been the Mr. Preston Duffy was speaking about. He might have been the kidnapper. He might have been a Jehovah's Witness on the graveyard shift. I had no idea what any of those people might look like.

I took my chances and opened the door.

"Ben Preston, Bergen County Prosecutor's Office," said the man, who looked much better than the squashed version of himself I'd seen in the peephole. He held up identification in a folding case. For the first time in my life, I examined such a thing closely. It looked like it was real, and so did he. I opened the door wider.

"I'm Rachel Goldman." I held out my hand, and Preston (if that's who he *really* was) took it.

"Is Duffy Madison here?" he asked. "I hate to bother you at this hour, but I got a call from him and it seemed urgent."

"Oh, he's here," I assured Preston. "Follow me." If this man *was* the criminal, he was doing a great job of concealing it. I locked the door behind him, then decided I would walk very quickly to the office. If Duffy knew the guy, he was Preston. If not, I would be walking in front of a deranged killer and kidnapper.

Maybe that wasn't the best plan. "Duffy!" I shouted. "Mr. Preston is here!"

Duffy's voice came back sounding slightly irritated and a little puzzled. "Yes, I know. Lead him back here, please."

Big help, Duffy. We'd have to go through a narrow corridor. I'd have preferred to have Duffy meet his "colleague" out here.

Ben Preston looked at me a moment. He had nice blue eyes and dark hair. If he was planning on kidnapping me, I was probably being abducted above my pay grade. Then Preston seemed to pick up on my vibe. "Would you like me to walk ahead?" he asked.

There is no greater sign of idiocy than the impulse to give up one's life rather than risk seeming rude. "Oh no," I said. "There's no need."

"Yes, there is," he answered. "Which room is it?"

I pointed down the hallway. "Third on the left. You'll see."

Preston headed in that direction without hesitating. Because I couldn't think of anything else to do, I followed him. When he reached the fork in the hallway—one way toward my office, the other way toward Paula's—I said, "Left," and he followed the direction.

Inside the office, I saw Duffy Madison get up and walk toward Preston. "Thank you for coming, Ben," he said. "We've got another one."

Duffy showed Ben the e-mail message and sat back down in the swivel chair. He reached into his pocket again and produced another pair of latex gloves, which he offered to Preston. Preston waved his hands to decline.

"If there's been a crime committed, it wasn't committed here," he said to Duffy.

"True. I like to be thorough."

There was a long-suffering quality in Preston's voice when he answered, "I know."

I sat down on the sofa and considered very strongly the option of breathing into a paper bag. "Okay, fellas," I said. "Exactly how petrified should I be?"

Preston said, "Not very," at the very same time that Duffy said, "You should be very concerned."

I pointed at Preston. "I like your answer better."

He smiled, and it was a nice smile. "There's not much reason to be worried," he said. "This is just an e-mail. It's made to look scary, but it really doesn't say anything that can be considered criminal. And you don't fit the profile of the other women this person has targeted."

"I don't?"

"No," Preston answered. "They were all mystery writers."

There was a fairly long silence in the room. Its comfort level varied depending on which inhabitant one was considering. Mine was pretty low. "That's what I do," I informed Preston.

His jaw seemed to loosen a little; it swung around once or twice. "It is? I'm very sorry, Ms. Goldman. I'm not familiar with your work."

"Mr. Preston, this guy has killed three crime fiction writers; has kidnapped a fourth, whom I actually know and like; and now he's sending me messages that say I could be next. So whether or not you've read my books is hardly what I'm choosing as my top priority."

"Exactly my point," Duffy said. "It is a very serious area of concern."

I gave him a look that would have been withering if he were a normal human being. Maybe that was it—maybe this wasn't a person at all, just a collection of quirks and tics that had come to life when I'd hit my fourth printing on *Olly Olly Oxen Free*.

Preston decided to cover his awkward faux pas by concentrating on the computer screen. "Is there any way to trace the e-mail?" he asked Duffy.

"I've tried not to touch the keyboard, but if past experience is any indicator, I tend to doubt it," Duffy answered.

"Go ahead and try. The only fingerprints you'll smudge will be Ms. Goldman's, and we already know she uses that computer."

Duffy nodded. He set to work on the keyboard, and with his rapid typing, a number of windows opened on the screen in quick succession. I couldn't keep up, but among them were definitely at least one search engine whose name I'd never seen before, a home page for the prosecutor's office (which I assumed was Duffy logging into his account for access), and something that flashed by so quickly that all I could see was the words *Original Source.*

A few more minutes went by with nothing but the clack of the keys audible in the room. I'm not sure I heard my own breathing. I'm not sure I *was* breathing.

Finally, Duffy turned toward Preston and looked perturbed. "It's encrypted at least seven different times," he said. "Whoever this person is, he or she is good."

"I don't think 'good' is the word I would use," I muttered. Nobody seemed to hear me or the sound I appeared to make.

"Is it necessary to confiscate the hard drive, do you think?" Preston asked. "Think we'd get anything from that?"

Yeah, they were going to confiscate . . . huh?

"Whoa!" I shouted. The two men, startled, jumped just a bit and turned to look at me. "I write for a living, no matter what you might have heard, Mr. Preston. I keep everything I write on that computer. If you take that computer away, you take away my livelihood. You're not going to do that."

"You really should back up your data, Ms. Goldman," Duffy scolded.

"I *do* back up my data," I shot back. "But I work on that machine. What are you going to get from my hard drive that you can't get from the server that sent me the e-mail to begin with?"

A full minute of computer gobbledygook followed, of which I understood the words *computer* and *e-mail.* That was it. As you might imagine, I was largely unconvinced, although the flood of fluid Geek was impressive. And after it was all over, Duffy shook his head. At Preston.

"I don't think taking the hard drive is necessary," he said.

"Couldn't you have just said that before?" I asked.

"I will need your e-mail password and the name of your domain, Ms. Goldman," Duffy went on.

I gave him Paula's phone number and suggested he call her in the morning. "She keeps all those files," I told Duffy. "I have no idea. What's a domain?"

They started to talk again. "I retract the question," I said.

Preston looked at the message on the screen again. "Not much more we can do," he said.

I was actually glad, because my eyelids were in the second stage of droopdom, and I wasn't sure how much longer I could stay awake, scary e-mail or no scary e-mail. "Well, thanks for coming," I told him. I didn't tell Duffy anything.

That didn't stop him from piping up. "There is something we can do," he said, suddenly looking excited and rubbing his hands together. "I can't believe it took me this long to think of it. And it can be of great help in the Bledsoe case."

Preston's eyelids fell to half-staff. "What can you do?" he asked Duffy.

But the figment of my imagination shook his head. "It's not what *I* can do," he answered. "It's what *Ms. Goldman* can do."

Now, you have to trust me when I say that I had no desire to play straight man to a guy pretending to be my fictional hero. But he was playing the role with such intensity that I really didn't see an alternative to asking, "Me? What can I do?"

Duffy Madison, if that's who he was, smiled. "You can answer the e-mail," he said.

Chapter 11

"So let me get this straight." Brian Coltrane sat across the table from me looking concerned with a side of stupefied. "You followed this guy who said he was a character in your book all the way down the shore to Ocean Grove, came back to your house and found a threatening e-mail, and called *him* to come help you?"

"I'm not proud of it." Sandy, the waitress at the Plaza Diner, had just put down our lunches: a Greek salad for me and a pizza burger with fries for Brian. Sandy, working her way through Ramapo University, knew not to listen in on the conversation, and besides, she had other tables. "But he has this way of making you believe in him. You met the guy."

"Yeah, and I thought he was a nut. So did you, the night at BooksBooksBooks." Brian dug into the pizza burger, but with a knife and fork. He doesn't like to pick food up. He is what we call in New Jersey a "crazy person."

"I still do," I protested, spearing some vegetation on my fork. I should have told Sandy to leave out the black olives, but I thought she'd know that by now. I ate lunch at the Plaza at least twice a week, one of those times with Brian. "But he's the best I can do, and he checks out with the Bergen County prosecutor. At least in that area, he's Duffy Madison, and he's for real."

"And you're playing along with this crazy game of e-mail tag with a kidnapper who might have killed three women?" Brian could actually look worried while wiping marinara sauce off his chin. It's part of what women who aren't me find "cute" about him. He says. "How is that supposed to help? Both these investigators—the fake one and the real one—said they couldn't trace the source of the e-mail like they can with a phone call. What's the point of continuing the contact?"

I sipped my diet soda. I won't call it a Diet Coke, because what passes for such in a diner is made through a fountain machine and usually tastes considerably like straight syrup in warm water. But hey, they put a lemon in it, because when you order a sweet drink, what you want is a sour one. I love the Plaza, but they can't make a soda. And yet I order it every time. I'm an optimist.

"Duffy says that engaging the perpetrator in an online conversation might get him to say something that can help the cops find Sunny Maugham," I said. "The idea is to goad him into thinking I'm not paying him close enough attention so he'll say something incriminating or telling."

I thought Brian's eyes would pop out of his head, but then his sunglasses, which he insisted on wearing because we were near the window and "with contact lenses there's always glare," would have held them in. I'm guessing. "So the plan is to taunt this dangerous guy and get him mad at you?" he said. "This guy's gonna get you killed, Rache."

To be fair, I had thought—and said—variations on that very theme when Duffy had suggested I respond to the e-mail the night before. But Ben Preston had said the response would not be designed to seem insulting or challenging to the sender of my e-ransom note.

"What we want to do is open a very impersonal sort of dialogue, at least from your end," he'd said. "What do you normally do when a fan sends you an e-mail about your book?"

"A fan?" I echoed. "I'm not sure that's how I'd put it." I have a problem with the concept of having fans. It somehow seems pretentious to assume that if someone has read my book and enjoyed it, that person is now a fanatic about it. Fanatics, it has been my experience, are not people who are especially reasonable. "If readers get in touch, I always try to respond. I write an e-mail back thanking them for reading the book, saying how glad I am that they liked it, and usually mentioning books they might have missed or the next title to be published and when. It's a fun part of the job, but it's not one I've ever been incredibly comfortable with."

"Why not?" Duffy had asked.

"Because I'm not convinced that I'm good enough at what I do to have people feel so strongly that they will take the time out of their day to get in touch and say so to me."

"You think they're lying?" Duffy was having trouble grasping the concept.

"I think they're mistaken," I said.

Ben Preston took over the conversation, largely because somebody had to. "That's exactly what I want you to do with this guy," he said. "Send back an e-mail that sounds like a form letter, something that indicates you've received his message but haven't read it. You might want to send it through your assistant's e-mail account."

"No," Duffy interjected. "There is no sense in getting Ms. Goldman's assistant involved. Let's not give this man any e-mail address he doesn't already have."

Preston thought and nodded. "Good thinking." He turned back to me. "Anyway, respond with an impersonal e-mail. Let him think his attempt to terrify you has gone unnoticed. They hate that."

"But if I do something he hates, isn't he more likely to get mad at me and maybe come after me with a typewriter or a passel of rejection letters?" That one still seemed unbearably cruel to me. "Aren't I sort of inviting him to come and force me to pay him some attention?"

"I don't think it'll get that far," Preston answered. "In fact, I don't think it'll ever get past the e-mail stage. We'll be lucky if he responds at all. What we want is for the guy to see what you send back, feel like he needs to better articulate his point, and, in the course of doing so, give us a hint to his location or the place he's holding Julia Bledsoe."

Bringing up Sunny and calling her by her real name were low blows—the two investigators were reminding me that she was out there somewhere, probably terrified and in great danger, and I was bringing up petty concerns like not getting kidnapped myself. Dirty pool. But effective.

I ended up sending our mystery man a very formulaic e-mail, which read,

> Thank you for getting in touch! It always is a pleasure to hear from a loyal reader. With your permission, I'll add your e-mail address to my newsletter mailing list, so you can keep up with Duffy and his adventures! And again, thank you so much for taking time out to contact me. Sincerely, Rachel Goldman.

"That should be impersonal enough," I said to Preston. Duffy, reading over my shoulder and seeing his name, flinched a little.

"Yes, it should," Preston said. "Your character is named Duffy, too?" He looked a little perplexed.

"Yeah," I said. "Go figure." I hit the send button, but I'm pretty sure I wasn't actually breathing when I did it.

Now in the diner, Brian had the same look that Preston had sported. "I can't believe you did that," he said through mozzarella.

"At the time, it seemed like the right thing to do," I said. I took another sip of the swamp water. "Can I have some of your water?"

Brian handed it over. "You do this every time. Just order a different drink."

I pulled on the straw, hard. "I don't want to hurt their feelings and tell them their cola sucks," I said when I came up for air.

"They run a diner. They don't care what drink you order as long as you pay for it."

"Cynic."

He made a point of catching my eye and holding it. "Rachel, seriously, what are you going to do about this guy?"

"The kidnapper?" I knew what he meant. I was playing for time to think up an answer to the *real* question.

"The guy who thinks he's Duffy Madison."

"What do you care? You don't even read the Duffy books." It was true; Brian buys four copies of every book I write and doesn't read any of them; his taste runs to nonfiction. I personally can't understand why anyone would read anything that was actually true.

"Stop evading the question." Brian, alas, has known me a long time.

"What do you want me to do, Brian? You want me to refuse to help find Sunny Maugham because the guy who's doing his best to find her claims to be a character I made up?" Just for that, I took a French fry off his plate and ate it.

"How about trying to find out who he really is?" Brian challenged. "You're not doing a thing but buying his story. You research those books. You know how to dig in, how to act like a cop on an investigation. This is the weirdest thing that's ever happened to you—"

"What about Walter Messinger in tenth grade?" I said.

"Okay, the second-weirdest thing. But at least Walter wasn't dangerous."

"That's your perspective."

Brian glared at me. "Stop it. I'm worried about you."

I broke into a crooked smile, and I wasn't even trying to do that. "I know," I said, patting his hand. "The fact is, I'm a little worried about me, too."

"This guy is *crazy*," he said.

"Maybe so. And the one who's kidnapping these women is even crazier." I took a bite of salad. It wasn't as good as the French fry.

Brian looked very serious. "How do you know they're not the same person?" he asked.

I didn't eat much after that.

* * *

I got back to the house determined to find out something—anything—about the man who called himself Duffy Madison. I wasn't sure how to do it, but as Brian said, I have been doing research on crime novels for a few years now, and that meant thinking like a detective. You had to assume that anyone you met or saw could be capable of a crime and make no assumptions until you had facts. It meant being constantly vigilant and aware. It meant taking nothing for granted.

Which is why I was more than a little concerned to find my front door unlocked.

I knew I'd locked it—manually, with the key, from the outside—when I'd left this morning (after doing some actual revisions, about twenty pages) for lunch with Brian. And I knew that I never, ever leave the door unlocked. So I didn't check when I got home; I just put the key in the lock and turned it.

But there's a different action in the lock when there's a dead bolt moving inside. You can feel it. And this time, I didn't feel it.

Now, a TSTL character would walk into the house armed with a candlestick or a penknife, try to be quiet, fail, walk into a bedroom without looking behind the door, and get herself into some hideous situation because the author is too lazy to write someone with a brain.

Not me. My first impulse was to call the police. But there's a problem with calling the cops to tell them your door was unlocked: they're going to tell you that you *think* you locked it when you left but you really didn't. They'd come if you insisted on it, but you'd be in the odd position of feeling embarrassed if someone *wasn't* in your house intent on killing you.

So maybe the thing to do was call the pseudopolice: Duffy and/or Preston. They knew there was a possibility I was in danger, so they wouldn't consider me a hysterical woman for being worried.

I got the phone out of my pocket and was looking for Preston's business card in my purse when the front door of my house swung wide open in a quick, jerky motion. I gasped, dropped my purse, and had what I considered to be several small heart attacks that were probably just the Greek salad reminding me of something.

"I thought I heard your car in the driveway," said Paula. "Why are you standing out here?"

Of course. Friday. Paula was working this afternoon, and she had a key.

"Um, I was just texting," I said. "Anything going on I need to know about?"

"Adam called to say he'd sent out *Little Boy Lost* to three more production companies. It seems like the movie world heard someone was on it, and now he's optimistic he might be able to get it to auction."

What? A book of mine being bid on by more than one producer? "Adam's been into the mushrooms again," I said, more or less to myself.

"Sol called about the manuscript, and I said you were doing revisions," Paula continued. "Want to come inside?" She seemed confused by my inability to move, and frankly, it was a little bit worrisome to me as well. I followed her in.

"You also got a call from a Mr. Preston. He just said to call him back. Do I know him?" Paula asked as we walked from the front door toward my office.

"No," I told her. "We just met yesterday. He works for the Bergen County prosecutor."

She gave me an interested look. "Ooh," she said.

"Yeah, keep dreaming. Listen. I have stuff for you to do."

Paula, no matter how overworked she was, always looked eager when I gave her more responsibility. I often considered giving her a raise, but then I'd have to cut back on her hours so I could afford her. It was a conundrum. "Stuff?"

"Yeah." I sat down in my desk chair without swiveling toward the computer screen, which is my natural tendency. Paula did not take out a pad to jot down notes; she knew she'd remember what I said, and so did I. "You remember the guy the other day who called and said he was Duffy Madison?"

She grinned. “Of course. What a nut.”

“Uh-huh. I want you to do some digging. He works as a consultant for the Bergen prosecutor.”

Paula’s expression went from amused to serious. “Mr. Preston? He’s Duffy Madison?”

I shook my head. “As far as I know, Ben Preston is Ben Preston. But ‘Duffy’ has convinced them, after a series of vetting processes, that he’s for real. He has an SSN, a birth certificate, a driver’s license, Selective Service, everything. What we need to do is find out who he really is.”

“We?”

“Okay, you. Get the numbers on his ID if you can find them. Call Max Cogdill at the IRS. See if they have any records for him. Then see how far back those records go and if he can be traced to a time before he was using this name.”

“How do I find that out if all I have is ‘Duffy Madison’?” Paula asked. It was a fair question. I wished I had the answer.

So I improvised; that’s what writers like me do. I’m a pantser. “The birth certificate will note a place of birth. That’s something to start with. Call the town in question, the clerk or somebody, and see if you can find any records of the guy. If his name really was Duffy Madison, there will be school records, old classmates, people like that. If it wasn’t, the birth certificate is fake and we have him in a lie. That along with the prosecutor gig might be enough to get him to fess up. It’s something to start with, anyway.”

Paula nodded, looking determined. “Cool. Anything else?”

I glanced quickly at the computer screen as I hit the mouse button to start it up. “Uh . . . no. Have you been checking my e-mails?" I doubted Paula would have neglected to mention if a raving maniac had gotten back to me, but the possibility always existed until confirmed or denied. Duffy taught me that. Or I taught him. The line was blurring.

"No. Should I?" Paula showed not suspicion but perhaps curiosity.

"No, absolutely not. I'll handle that end. If there's anything important that you need, I'll forward it to you." I turned my back on her, politely, telling her I was getting to work now. I heard Paula get up and walk back toward her office.

The first order of business was to call Preston. Maybe they'd made an arrest and he was calling to thank me for my exemplary bravery and effort in helping to incarcerate a dangerous killer.

Hey, you dream what you dream, and I'll dream what I dream.

"I've been monitoring your e-mail," he said once I'd identified myself. It was a lovely greeting, I thought. Invasion of privacy as an icebreaker. "The guy hasn't responded to you yet."

"Great. It gives me something to look forward to. Why did you call me, then?"

"I wanted to know about your relationship with Duffy."

Well, that was a new one. "My what with who?" I asked. I thought it was a legitimate question.

"You and Duffy. How you know each other. The two of you were acting strange last night, uncomfortable in an odd sort of way, and I need to know if what's going on between the two of you is going to compromise my investigation." I didn't know Preston well, but I couldn't hear a smile in his voice, which meant that—contrary to all logic—he wasn't kidding.

"I don't have a relationship with Duffy," I said. "I met the man two days ago and only talked to him at length yesterday on the way back and forth to Ocean Grove. What are you getting at, Mr. Preston?"

"It's Ben, please." Like that was going to help him after what he'd just dumped in my lap. "And I'm not getting at anything. It's just that I'm a pretty decent judge of human behavior, and there was something going on between you and Duffy last night."

"There isn't anything that's going to interfere with your work, *Ben*," I said. Okay, so there was a little more emphasis on the name than I'd planned on. "You can rest assured of that."

"That's fine," he said. And then he didn't say anything else.

"I'm just wondering if anyone's bothered to call Sunny's editor and her agent," I said. "If she was planning on traveling, they might know—well, her agent would, anyway—and even if she wasn't, the attacks seem to be based on being an author. They'd have some insight, wouldn't they?"

"That's very nice advice," Ben said. "But we've already had people talk to them. Her agent is Mandy Westen and her editor is Carole Pembroke. We've gotten what we can from them to begin with." Was he being a wiseass? I could out-wiseass him any day of the week. I'm a writer.

"So you called to check in on me and Duffy?" I asked. "Isn't *that* a little odd all by itself?"

"I had to be clear on that point," Preston said. "Now I'm clear."

"Okay," I agreed, because frankly, what else was there to do? "So let me ask *you* something. How well do *you* know Duffy Madison?"

There was a pause. Preston's eyes were probably crinkling; I'd seen him do that the night before. I was, of course, impervious to such things. Except that I was imagining him doing it now. "Impervious" is a relative term. When you use it like I do, anyway.

"We're not dating, if that's what you're asking," Preston said.

"It wasn't, but thanks for clearing that up. I mean, do you trust him? Has he told you much about himself? What can you tell me about Duffy?"

I could hear Preston's county-issued chair squeak. He must have leaned forward. "I don't know that much about him personally. He's all business when we call him in on a case." Then he paused, but not long enough for me to jump in. "Why?"

"Are you aware that I write books with a character named Duffy Madison?" I asked. "A character who's a consultant on missing persons cases for the Morris County Prosecutor's Office?"

Preston had clearly never read one of my books, but it was possible he'd heard about them. The "coincidence" of my character and his consultant having the same name (and job) should certainly have been a topic of conversation among the investigators.

"You mean you just changed counties when you used him for a character?" Preston said. "I thought you just met Duffy a couple of days ago."

"I did. And no, I didn't change counties. I'd never heard of your Duffy Madison when I started writing the books four years ago."

I could pretty much hear the light bulb go off over Preston's head through the phone. "Right around the time Duffy started working with us," he said. I'm not sure he was even conscious of being on the phone anymore.

"That's right. Kind of a big coincidence, don't you think?"

I thought that confronting Preston with this information—leaving out the part about Duffy believing I had psychically given birth to him—might lead to some revelation that would prove conclusively the man who was working for him and the man I'd been imagining for five books now were different. In that mine was imaginary, and his was crazy.

"How is that possible?" Preston asked.

"That's an excellent question. How do you think it could be? Because I've been going at it around and around in my head since Tuesday, and I haven't come up with anything." I checked my e-mail again; still no new communiqués from the creep with a thing for mystery authors. That was good, right?

"I thought you said you met him two nights ago, on Wednesday," Preston said. Investigators. They never let *anything* go.

Well, this was a problem. I didn't want to out Duffy as the complete nut job I thought he was, just in case he wasn't. In that case, I'd be ruining his career. On the other hand, if he were a bloodthirsty madman, it was probably better his employers know that.

So I hedged my bet. "He called Tuesday night asking me about Julia Bledsoe, but I didn't know her by that name, so we barely talked," I said. It was within driving distance of the truth and could be seen as at least some cause for further discussion without suggesting openly that Duffy be fitted for a jacket with very, very long sleeves.

"Uh-huh," Preston said. So he wasn't a scintillating conversationalist. There are other things that can be important. Like those crinkling eyes. "That doesn't really answer the question, does it?"

"I said since Tuesday, and that was three nights ago," I explained. Again.

"The question about why he seems to be a version of your character, despite you never having heard of Duffy when you started writing." Oh yeah.

"I can't explain that," I said, and that was precisely the truth. I mean, I *could* explain it, but the only reasonable way to do so would be to suggest that Duffy was nuts, and not being a licensed psychoanalyst, it wasn't in my province to say that. "Can you?"

"No, and I don't like it." Next Preston would be telling me that mysteries give him a bellyache. Men can be driven by role models they get from bad movies.

"As an investigator, how would you research it?" I asked. I'd given Paula a list of tasks to perform, but maybe Preston could simplify the problem or use the resources at his disposal, which were undoubtedly better than the ones Paula or I had.

"I could ask Duffy," he said. *Brilliant, Holmes! How does the man do it?*

"I've already asked him," I said. That was probably a mistake. Duffy's explanation would not help anyone's case here, and Preston's inevitable question would be . . .

"And what did he say?" Can I predict them, or what?

"Well, he couldn't explain it, either," I said. Certainly, Duffy couldn't explain it *adequately*, and that was one way of interpreting the question.

"Odd. Normally he'd mention something like that to me." Normally? Something like that? How often did these situations come up?

"Well, maybe he's embarrassed. Maybe he thinks the other guys in the office will read the books and make fun of him." Now I was acting like Duffy's mom. Be nice to my boy and I'll bake you cookies.

"Duffy doesn't embarrass easily," Preston said. That was true, at least of the Duffy I wrote. One time I had him emerge from a sewer pipe wearing nothing but boxer shorts and a snorkel, and he hadn't even flinched.

"Maybe you shouldn't bring this up just yet," I suggested. "Observe him for a while and see if you can pick up on anything."

I couldn't hear Preston nod, but I was sure he did just that. "That seems reasonable. In the meantime, I think we should talk about how you conceived of this character. Are you free for dinner tonight?"

Well, that came out of left field! It was so unexpected that I said, "Yes, I am," without thinking once about it. That's not like me.

"Great," Preston answered. "I'll pick you up at your house around eight. Okay?"

I was off the phone before I realized what had happened. Did I have a date with Ben Preston? Or were we conferring about one of his colleagues?

It was best not to think about it, although deciding what to wear was definitely going to be a problem. I got up and walked into Paula's office.

The room was larger than mine and did not look out on my somewhat muddy backyard. It was decorated as Paula would have it—I'd insisted on that—which meant that everything was done in subdued colors, tastefully accented, and completely neat. I feared for Paula's mind.

She was staring at her laptop, which she kept open on her desk, when I walked in. She looked up with the same "Do you have something else for me to do?" face I'd seen before, when I actually *had* something else for her to do.

"I was talking to Ben Preston, the investigator on the case in Bergen County," I told her. "We were talking about this Duffy guy and whether he's legit."

"There's some question about that?" Paula asked.

I shrugged. "From Preston's end, anyway. Next thing I know, he asks me to continue discussing Duffy over dinner tonight."

Paula's eyes widened a little, and she let a tiny grin show on her face. "And?"

"And the question becomes, is this a date?"

She snorted a little. "Yeah! It's a date, Rachel! If he'd just wanted to compare notes, he could have kept doing that on the phone. You're going on a date. That's okay with you, isn't it?"

It was okay with me. It had been a while since I'd broken it off with the last guy I was seeing, whose name was Phillip. Not Phil, Phillip. I should have known right away. I am a serial monogamist but hadn't been monogamizing with anyone for about six months. Phillip had left a scar. Mostly one about how stupid I was to date him to begin with.

"Yeah, it's okay. But what—?"

"We'll talk about what you'll wear when you're getting ready to go. What time?" I told her. "Fine. Before then, we'll discuss possibilities. I'll get some organized. Don't worry at all about that." She rubbed her hands together like a comic book villain and turned her attention back to her computer screen.

"Have you found out anything about Duffy yet?" I asked.

"Too soon." She was engrossed.

I tiptoed back to my office to avoid disturbing her. There are days when it's hard to tell which one of us is the other's assistant.

Rather than ponder that, I decided to turn my attention to Sunny Maugham. There had to be something I could do; Duffy himself had said I had a unique insider's perspective on the case. Well, he'd said *something* like that.

I pulled up a file listing members of the Mystery Authors Association. The MAA is not a trade union; it's more like a social club for writers who like to get together and complain about their publishers, worry about electronic books, and try to figure out how to get their novels to the front table at Barnes & Noble.

Sunny and I had really only talked that one time. I couldn't be counted as a close friend of hers or even someone who knew her habits. I was a little bit in awe when we met at the hotel bar and thanked her profusely for her help. However, given the six-ton brick of guilt Duffy and Preston had dumped on my shoulders, I wanted to at least do what I could in her most dire hour.

They say that kidnapping cases grow cold after forty-eight hours. According to Duffy, Sunny had been missing four days at least. That wasn't good.

All I could think to do was call some of my acquaintances at the MAA and do the research. I started with Emily Estebrook, whose real name was Bess Adelstein.

"Bess," I said after the usual catching up, "have you heard about Sunny Maugham?"

"I did." Bess sounded worried. Bess, like most good authors, is a touch dramatic. "An awful thing."

"Have you heard from her lately?" I asked. I knew Bess and Sunny were at least better acquainted than Sunny and I were.

"Not for a month or so," she answered. "We weren't in close touch all the time; we usually called when one of us had a book that needed a blurb on the cover."

"How did she seem when you talked to her?" This wasn't going much of anywhere.

"Nothing special. She was working on a stand-alone. Something about a woman who solved crimes through playing the flute. I didn't get it, but Sunny could make anything work."

"You're talking about her in the past tense," I noted.

Bess's voice caught. "My god, I am," she said. "I'm an awful person."

"No, you're not."

She didn't react directly to that. "Hey, what's this interest in Sunny? You thinking of writing something about it?" Crime fiction writers have a code: *nothing* is off-limits.

"Not me," I said. "I'm sticking with Duffy Madison."

If Bess read my books, she'd know that Duffy investigates missing persons cases and would point out that it would be right up my alley, but the sad fact is, most of us don't read the others' books. That's out of a real concern about inadvertently "appropriating" ideas, a need to disengage from the genre when not actually writing something ourselves, and a deep and abiding envy that every writer feels for every more successful writer, even the ones we truly love. It's not personal; we just think our books should be on best sellers lists. It's okay if yours are too. So long as they're not higher than mine.

Bess clearly had no new information on Sunny, but she did suggest I call Mary Alice Monroe, whose real name is Connie Bailey. Before I could call Connie, Paula walked into my office with a puzzled look on her face.

"There's no such person as Duffy Madison," she said.

"Tell me something I don't know."

"No, you don't understand. This is the age of no privacy at all. The Internet has everything that ever happened to anybody ever. You want to know what Napoleon ate for lunch the day he got back from Elba? I can find that. But so far, I can't tell you anything about this guy who thinks he's Duffy."

If Paula couldn't find anything, there was nothing to find. That sent an unintentional chill up my spine. I gawked at her for a moment. "You're scaring me."

That just made Paula look more determined. "I said 'so far.' Just give me some more time." And she marched back to her office with a look I wouldn't want pointed at me. Whoever Duffy really was, he'd have to contend with Paula now. I almost felt sorry for him.

I gave Connie Bailey a call and got just about the same story as I had from Bess Adelstein, but she directed me to Margaret Teasdale (Susan Oswego), who had seen Sunny just two days before she had been reported missing.

"She was in a really good mood," Susan said. "She'd started seeing some new guy, and she thought it was going to be something for real."

Klieg lights went off in my head. Sirens sounded in my ears. For a mystery writer, this was the equivalent of saying that someone had been standing behind Sunny with a six-inch kitchen knife, a .38 revolver, a bottle with a skull and crossbones, and a large noose in his hands.

I tried not to sound breathless. "Did she mention the guy's name?" I asked.

Susan didn't respond right away; I got the impression she was thinking. "Bart, maybe? Bill? No. Brad. She said the guy's name was Brad."

"Did you tell this to the police?" I said.

"The police? I never got a call from the police," Susan answered. "Do you think it's important?" The woman writes about a sleuth who gets clues from a talking horse—and outsells the Duffy books by a very wide margin.

Susan went on about Brad, how she didn't know his last name but was pretty sure Sunny had met him at her gym, if I thought he had something to do with Sunny being missing now, and if she (Susan) had been wrong not to think it was an important piece of information.

Two Edgar Award nominations. I ask you.

The second I disconnected with Susan, I texted Duffy and asked where he was. Turned out he was driving through Mendham, not far from where I was, so we arranged to meet at Caffeinated. Even though I'd be seeing Ben Preston tonight on what Paula had now officially decreed a date, I thought this kind of information couldn't wait. And I did feel the tiniest bit guilty about going behind Duffy's back to Preston. I wasn't sorry I'd done it, but it did feel a trifle devious.

* * *

Duffy does not drink coffee in the books, and he was not drinking coffee now. He had a Diet Coke from the cooler Ruthie keeps next to the counter and ate nothing. I was going to get a chocolate chip muffin, but with Duffy eating nothing and a date later in the day, I decided to abstain, cursing both myself and Duffy mentally.

I told him what Susan had said, and when I mentioned the name "Brad," I hoped that he'd immediately scream, "Aha!" and hop into his car to go rescue Sunny. That's not what happened.

"This is the first time I'm hearing about Ms. Bledsoe having a suitor," Duffy said thoughtfully. *A suitor*. That's the way the guy talks, even when I'm not writing his dialogue for him. "This is very interesting."

"Interesting? I'd think it would be enormous."

"It's significant, certainly," Duffy said. "But it will take some research to find out who Brad might be."

"How many Brads can there be in Upper Saddle River?" I asked. I was getting a little disappointed that I hadn't solved the case all by myself with a few phone calls to the other writers.

"First, we don't know that his name really is Brad or Bradley," Duffy said, taking on a professorial tone. He sipped his drink and didn't even burp, which was not at all fair of him. "Second, just because Ms. Bledsoe lives in Upper Saddle River, there is no reason to think that the man is a resident of the same town. And third, even if there is such a man, it is by no means certain that he is the perpetrator of this crime."

"If he's not, how come you never heard about him before this?" I said. Challenge the man. If a guy isn't going to act the way you want him to act, what's the point of creating him? I started to rethink the chocolate chip muffin.

"Suppose he's a married man and doesn't want his wife to know about the relationship with Ms. Bledsoe," Duffy suggested. "It wouldn't do much for a man like that to present himself to investigators and make that relationship a matter of public record."

Well, if he was going to insist on being logical about it . . .

"Well, what else is going on in the investigation?" I asked. "Did Sunny's cell phone tell you anything helpful?"

"There are no calls to a man named Brad," Duffy said. Okay, so get off the "Brad" thing; I feel stupid enough already. "Beyond that, all we know for a fact is that the phone was used right up to a few hours before you and I entered that bungalow in Ocean Grove."

"So that means Sunny was alive at least as late as yesterday," I said.

Duffy let a little air out through his lips and looked uncomfortable. "Not necessarily," he answered. "Just because the phone was used, there is no evidence that Ms. Bledsoe was the one who was using it."

Way to bring down the room, Duffy.

"So where does that leave . . . you?" I'd almost said "us" and then reminded myself that I was a writer of fiction and not an actual investigator. I wasn't part of this process. I should, in fact, shut up and leave the real cops to handle it.

Except there had been a threatening e-mail on my screen that was not addressed to Duffy Madison or Ben Preston. I had, as they say, flesh in the game.

And I was not crazy for *that* expression as soon as it suggested itself to me.

"How terrified should I be about being next on this maniac's agenda?" I asked Duffy.

He made a show of taking a long drink from the soda bottle and responded after a moment's thought. "I don't think there's any immediate cause for alarm. Keep in mind that the previous . . . incidents happened months apart. This is a person who likes to plan his moves meticulously. And we are still holding out hope that Ms. Bledsoe will be found alive and well, which would mean you are not yet the top priority for our kidnapper."

Why wasn't that more reassuring? "Thanks a heap, Duffy. I'll sleep so much more soundly tonight," I said.

"You're quite welcome," he answered with no hint of irony. "Would it be possible for you to take a trip to Ms. Bledsoe's home with me? I'd still very much like to get your perspective on her writing office, especially. There might be something there that could help."

"I can't tonight," I told him. "The fact is, I have a date."

"Oh." I couldn't tell whether that was disappointment about my not being available to him when he had summoned me or he was displeased with the idea of me having a date with someone. I chose not to ponder that for long. "Perhaps tomorrow, then."

On a Saturday? Well, Sunny did need rescuing. "I'll be glad to go tomorrow," I told Duffy. Maybe *glad* was overstating it.

"All right, then," he said, so I thought the conversation was at an end. But Duffy apparently hadn't caught the sign he'd actually sent himself. We'd both driven here; a five-minute conversation didn't seem sufficient, somehow. "You haven't really reacted to what I told you, now that you've gotten to talk to me."

What was he talking about? "I don't understand," I said. "What do you mean, 'what you told me'?"

"About my being your fictional character," he said, his voice suddenly much lower in volume. "About you creating me."

"I don't see how that's possible," I said, because I've never had much experience dealing with seriously crazy people. I mean, my mother is a little off, but . . .

"And yet, here I am," Duffy answered.

I'm sure I stared at him. "Don't you think it's more likely," I said, voice in what I hoped was a soothing mode, "that you took on the personality in the books a few years ago?"

"I've never read your books," he insisted. "I didn't know they existed until early this week."

"Maybe you did and you've forgotten," I said. I'd decided that Duffy, in whatever former existence he'd had, must have suffered some awful trauma that had caused amnesia, and he'd picked up this persona as a way of coping. If I'd been around during their heyday, I might have had a nice career writing for soap operas.

"I don't think I'm the one in denial here," he said.

* * *

That pretty much ended the meeting. I bought a chocolate chip muffin to go. (I swore I'd eat it the next day and then devoured the whole thing in the car on the way home, a six-minute drive.) Once I got back there was no respite: Paula walked into the office, and her expression indicated not much more joy in Mudville than when we'd spoken last.

"What I have to tell you isn't going to make the situation a whole lot clearer," she said. Paula sat on the lumpy sofa. This whole room needed a makeover. Adam had better sell *Little Boy Lost* to television. TV is where the money is.

"You've been looking into Mr. Madison's past?" I asked.

Paula nodded. "And I have a little more. There is actually a picture of him in the Poughkeepsie, New York, high school yearbook from 1998. I printed out a copy."

She handed me the picture, which wasn't especially clear, but was definitely a younger a version of the man who'd been claiming he had come full blown from my brain. Under the picture, which I noticed included some blemishes the air-brush had not been able to hide (and somehow made him look more endearing) was the name "Duffy Madison," followed by the quote, "When you eliminate the impossible, whatever remains, however improbable, must be the truth." That's what he *would* choose.

"So he was using the name in 1998, but he doesn't remember it?" I thought aloud.

Paula took the picture back and answered, "It gets stranger."

"How is that possible?"

She fixed me with a look. "I tracked down three people also listed in his class. Said I was writing an article about a notable classmate of theirs and wanted to get their memories of him."

Paula was clearly playing up the drama. She could have been *in* a soap opera. "What did they say?" I asked.

"That they don't have any memories of him. Nobody remembers anything about a guy named Duffy Madison in that class."

Okay, that could be explained. "How many people graduated from that school in 1998?" I asked.

"I don't have an exact count, but it's probably less than two hundred," Paula said. "Of course, it's possible that these three people didn't know Duffy, but one of them said she was a member of the Classics Society. Said she thought at the time that it would help get her into an Ivy League college."

"So?"

"So look again." Paula handed the picture back. "Under his name."

"There's an oddly irritating quote from Sir Arthur Conan Doyle," I said.

"And under that?" The teacher was easing me through the difficult part of the lesson.

"Okay, fine. Duffy is listed as being in the Classics Society. So how many people were in that?"

"Six."

That wasn't good. "You'd think she'd remember him, wouldn't you?" I wheezed.

"I'll make some more phone calls, but that's what I've found out so far." Paula stood up. "This guy is a mystery wrapped in an enigma."

I let out a long breath. "That doesn't make me feel better."

"Sorry."

"It's not your fault. You're a gem. Don't ever think I don't know that."

Paula smiled as she turned back toward the door. I started to swivel toward my screen, then stopped and looked back at her.

"Hey." Paula stopped, ready in case I had something else to ask her. And I did. "Where'd that woman end up going to college?"

"She got an associate's degree at a local community college and now works as a hostess at an Outback Steakhouse."

So much for the Classics Society.

Chapter 12

"Have you heard from our friend yet?" Ben Preston sat across the table from me and looked concerned. The air was scented with garlic and tomato, and his serious tone seemed somehow incongruous.

"Which friend?" I asked.

"The one with the interesting 'handwriting' in e-mails," he noted with a wry expression.

"Nope, haven't heard from him," I answered.

"Good. I never much cared for that plan." Ben took a sip of wine and did not do that thing that the oenophiles think make them look superior where they swirl it around in the glass and then stick their noses in. That's just silly. Do I carefully examine the label of a Snickers, hold it up to my nostrils, inhale its deep fragrance, and then take a tiny taste before letting the cashier at the Rite Aid know if I'm willing to buy it? I do not.

"You disagreed with Duffy about that?" I asked. "I'm surprised. I thought you listened to every word he said."

"I listen, but I don't always agree. I'm the investigator; he's the consultant."

Ben had met me at the restaurant bearing one tiny tulip, an orange one he gave me before we walked inside. The waiter had already placed the little flower in a glass of water, making it look like a toddler swimming with water wings on his arms. So Paula had been right: this was indeed a date.

"I thought I understood how you guys operate," I said.

"There's always more to learn, and besides, you didn't call me when you were creating your first book." *Creating. Is that not adorable?*

I felt like taking notes for my next book, but the scoop-neck top and pants Paula had approved for me tonight didn't have ample pocket room for a reporter's notebook, and my purse was on the floor next to my chair. It would have been showy for me to reach over to get it. In any number of ways. "So why did you go along with the e-mail plan if you didn't think it was a good idea?"

Ben considered, then tilted his head a bit to indicate it was a compromise. "I didn't have a better idea," he admitted.

"Have you given some thought to what I told you this afternoon?" I asked him. "About Duffy being a little too much like the character in my novels?"

I tried to remember Paula's advice about the date: "Make sure he asks about you and doesn't just talk about himself. Make sure he doesn't call the waitress 'honey.'" (We had a male server. That would have been a real mood killer.) "And above all, see if he's a generous tipper. That's key."

Ben leaned forward, now being both interested and serious. "Yes, I have. And it's weird. It's weird that you chose a name for your character that just happens to be the same as the guy who has that specific job for us. It's weird that you started writing the books at the exact moment he appeared at our door looking for the job. And it's weird that he never mentioned any of that to us in the office."

That was lovely summing up, but it didn't really create much of what you'd call "progress." I looked Ben Preston over. He wasn't a classically handsome man in the "male model" sort of mode. He was more the guy-next-door type, heavy on the "guy." But his movements, his expressions, his words all seemed just a little rehearsed, like he was used to having women (and some men) admire his good looks as he walked by and he was trying not to disappoint them. It was the first date I'd been on in a while (damn you, Phillip!), and we were talking business, but that was mostly my doing. I hadn't yet had the opportunity to see how well Ben tipped the waiter. That didn't seem especially vital just at the moment. Except, I imagine, to the waiter.

I wasn't swooning for Ben, but I could be persuaded to under the right circumstances. For reasons I didn't understand, though, I seemed subconsciously intent on sabotaging any hint of romance: I kept talking shop. Ben's shop, which, after considerable revisions to fit my twisted imagination, would become my shop.

"So what do you think it means?" I asked him. If Duffy Madison was the reason Ben and I had met, he was also the reason we had something to talk about. And the perspective on Duffy from someone who worked with him would be invaluable in dealing with the flesh-and-blood model as well as the Duffy who lived in my tortured mind.

"Damned if I know," Ben said.

"Thanks. That's a huge help."

"I'm serious; I have no idea what to make of it. I've done all the checks on Duffy the department does with all new employees, and he came up clean every time. He's not living under an alias. The ID records he has are not forgeries, and even his fingerprints check out."

Wait. "Why would Duffy have been fingerprinted before he came to work for you?" I said. "What do you have to compare them to?"

"He taught an afterschool class in forensic criminology at a middle school in Hackensack," Ben said. "You teach in a middle school, you have to have fingerprints on file."

What? "When?"

"About seven years ago. Before you were writing him by a wide margin."

My head swam just a bit, and it wasn't because I had drained my wine glass in record time. "None of this makes any sense. If Duffy—"

Ben held up a hand. "Are we going to spend the whole night talking about Duffy Madison?" he asked. "Would you rather be out with him tonight?"

Hell no! "Of course not," I answered. I can be genteel when necessary. And the thought of being out on a date with Duffy had certainly sobered me up in a hurry. "Tell me how you got to be an investigator. Were you a police officer before?" That's the way most of the prosecutors' investigators start, although Ben was younger than most of them.

He nodded. "I was a cop in Metuchen, down in Middlesex County," he said. "But I had to quit due to a disability and took on the job here when it was offered. The physical demands weren't quite as stringent."

A disability? "Were you wounded in the line of duty?" I asked.

He sniffed a little in amusement. "I fell down the stairs carrying a box of Christmas decorations."

"Must have been quite a staircase."

"I just hit it the right way. Compressed two vertebrae and broke my left arm. Luckily, after I healed, physical therapy and a lot of time got me to the point where I don't really feel it that much anymore."

Our dinners came, and there was less talking because the pasta primavera (mine) and chicken marsala (Ben's) were intoxicating. I did take time to notice that Ben was delicate in his movements, favoring his right arm, and drank water, not wine, with the dinner.

When we came up for air, he asked me how I'd gotten the idea for Duffy Madison the fictional character. I guessed that let us out of the don't-talk-about-Duffy pact because now it wasn't his Duffy but my Duffy. So I left out the part about being in the shower for reasons I didn't fully understand and said that I'd wanted someone who had access to law enforcement but wasn't a fully qualified officer. "That was so I could cover over any mistakes I made in procedure by saying that Duffy wasn't really a cop."

"And why'd you put him in the prosecutor's office?" Ben asked, wiping a little marsala sauce from the corner of his mouth.

"Before I started looking into it, I didn't know the prosecutors' offices had their own investigators," I said a little sheepishly. "I thought local police departments handled every crime in their jurisdiction."

"Everybody thinks that. In New Jersey, we don't work that way."

"Obviously. So when I created Duffy—and I'm insisting that I did in fact create Duffy and hadn't ever heard of your version before I did—I started talking to some cops, who told me exactly that. They sent me to the prosecutor, and luckily, I found a source there who could tell me how things really worked. It didn't hurt that he loves mystery novels but hates it when they get procedure wrong."

"What's his name?" Ben asked. And there was something just a little bit off about his tone when he asked. Suddenly, I wasn't sure I wanted to put him onto Marty Dugan.

"His name's Martin Dugan," I said. Okay, so he had nice eyes and I caved. "Do you know him?"

Ben shook his head. "I don't know that many guys in Morris. We talk more often to the Passaic and Essex people. We share a larger border with them."

Eager to move the conversation, I said, "Duffy. What can we conclude about Duffy?"

Ben sighed. "Look. I just met you yesterday, and you seem like a very nice, reasonable woman. So much so that I asked you to come have dinner with me tonight in this really homey restaurant. And I'm glad we're here. You're charming, you're pretty, you're engaging, and you're funny. But here's the thing: I've known Duffy Madison for four years. He has helped me solved cases I thought were lost causes. He's never told me anything—*anything*—that turned out not to be true. So if you were me, who would *you* choose to think was the nut?"

He had a point, although not one I was especially well inclined to admit. "Wow," I said. "You really don't have any chance of getting lucky tonight."

Ben sat back a little and smiled. "Really? None at all?"

I hadn't intended to sleep with him anyway, so I answered, "Nope. You're completely on your own."

"I did say you were pretty." That was true. I was about to rethink my position. "And I meant it. But I've never known an author before, and that's really interesting. I want to know more." So, naturally, that's when his phone buzzed, and Ben looked at it, then straightened up as if something surprising had shown up on his screen. "It's Duffy," he said.

Duffy. The man was everywhere. In my head, in my life, on Ben's phone; you couldn't swing a dead cat and not hit Duffy Madison. If my books had made him this ubiquitous, I'd have paid off my mortgage by now.

Ben hit the button on his phone and put it to his ear. "Duffy," he said, and then listened for a long moment. His jaw tightened, and I thought I could hear his teeth grinding, something you really shouldn't get to hear from a man you've decided not to share a bed with. "Okay. I'll be there as soon as I can." A moment. "No. I'll do that. Okay. Right."

He put the phone into his pocket and turned his attention to me while signaling the waiter for our check. "I have to go," he said.

"Something from Duffy?" That couldn't be good. If I were plotting this adventure, at this point, Duffy would be getting really deep into trouble and things would take a dark turn. From Ben's face I could see that real life was essentially in the same story structure segment that I would be. I didn't like the feeling.

Ben nodded. "Yeah." He took the check from the waiter and handed him a credit card before he could walk away. The waiter, without a word, took the card and the check back to process. "I have to go see him right now."

I was the mystery writer and the witness, of sorts, in this escapade; I understood the drill. "Can you drop me off, or should I call a friend for a ride?" I asked.

"You should come with me. Duffy's intercepted an answer to your e-mail. Our mutual friend—the one with the interesting e-mail font decisions—just got back to you."

I picked up my purse and followed him to the door as soon as the check was signed. I have no idea how much Ben tipped.

Chapter 13

Duffy Madison did not react when Ben Preston and I arrived together, and he did not comment on my clothes, which were a little dressier than anything he'd seen me in before. I had no way of knowing whether he'd seen Ben dressed for an evening out in the past and chose not to think about it. But I could see the wheels in his brain turning when he saw us—even through his lack of a reaction. The guy was a champion at not reacting. If he thought I didn't see that, he just wasn't paying attention.

It was possible I was overreacting. But news of a fresh message from Sunny Maugham's abductor, in response to what I'd sent him, had me just a little on edge. The next time someone who has kidnapped four women and killed the first three gets back to *you* about an e-mail designed to infuriate him, you may judge me, and not a moment before.

"I'm not sure what to make of it," Duffy said, "but it certainly does leave us with some avenues of investigation."

The reply, from the same somehow-untraceable e-mail address as before (what do I know about technology?), read,

> **I** am <u>not</u> TYPICAL. **Do** <u>not</u> **treat me** LIKE **a** typical "*fan.*" **I hold** *your FATE IN* **my** hands. **Ask** *Sunny*. WHEN *you* **can**.

Well, that wasn't encouraging. Duffy, who had seen the message long before Ben and I got to his office, chewed on the end of a pen despite not being called upon to write anything down. It was a habit I'd given him. Right now, I found it annoying.

"We got a response," he said. "Much as we would have expected. He's not happy about being sent a form reply."

"Swell," I answered. "Now we've got him pissed at me. Nice work there, Duff." He grimaced. I knew he didn't like to be called "Duff." This adopt-a-fictional-character's-personality thing could be played both ways.

"I'll say it again: I don't think this contact was a good idea," Ben told Duffy before we could get into a "guess Duffy's habits" contest (which I had the eerie feeling I'd lose). "We've increased the danger to Rachel, and we haven't found out anything useful about the sender."

"Oh, but we have," Duffy replied. "We've found out that he doesn't like to be thought of as typical. That's very useful."

"It is?" That was me.

"Certainly, Ms. Goldman. A person who does not believe himself to be typical has often had that message delivered to him by his parents, peers, even therapists, perhaps. There could be psychologists who have spoken to him. The chances that he has been involved in the criminal justice system just rose considerably. There is a much higher likelihood of a paper trail with someone this volatile."

"You're not making my stomach feel any better," I told him.

Duffy had the nerve to look surprised. "My apologies," he said.

"Those are places to look," Ben said, rolling a chair by the computer screen on Duffy's desk. "But I'd hardly call them a breakthrough."

"I never used the word 'breakthrough,'" Duffy pointed out. He can be annoyingly accurate when you don't need it.

"You said it was very helpful." Ben, who had worked with Duffy for years, clearly knew how to push his buttons the right way to get results.

Sure enough, more came from the mind of the fictitious loony next to me. "Look at the message, Ben. Like the last time, this person has chosen a number of different fonts and type sizes for his message. Each choice is a clue to his brain."

"I get that he wants it to look like an old-style ransom note, but I don't get why," Ben said.

Nobody had gotten *me* a chair, so I rolled one in from the outside reception area, but I could hear Duffy through the open door. "Look. It's really very simple. Notice how each time he refers to himself, the type size increases and he uses a bold face. Yet each time he refers to 'you,' meaning Ms. Goldman, the size decreases, and the type is italic, lighter, and less forceful."

"Okay, so he's being insulting with the typeface," I said. Might as well throw in my two cents, given that it was my life the guy was threatening. At least, it sounded threatening. "What good is that knowledge?"

Duffy didn't turn around to look when I was talking; he kept his gaze fixed steadily on the screen. "He did the same thing when referring to Ms. Bledsoe as 'Sunny,'" he went on. "And he underlines the word 'not' both times he uses it. He wants to make sure the word is noticed and obeyed. This note is all about control. It's about the sender taking control and denying it to you and Ms. Bledsoe."

"You have a degree in psychology," I said, really to myself. I'd given him that, too.

"Yes, and this note tells me that the man who sent it is unquestionably trying very hard to dehumanize his victims, to make them seem less than significant in his mind," Duffy said.

"'Victims.'" That word hit me right between the eyes. "You think Sunny is dead. And you think that I'm next."

Ben swiveled in his chair and looked at me with concern. "That's not what Duffy is saying, Rachel," he said. "Right now, we know that Sunny is probably the victim of a kidnapping. She's been missing for four full days we know about. This guy seems to have knowledge of her and her situation. But Duffy using the word 'victim' is not any indication that anything worse than that has happened to her. Right, Duffy?"

Duffy continued to stare at the screen. "There is no evidence to support either theory right now. But the length of time Ms. Bledsoe has been missing is not a good sign."

Someone gasped. Pretty sure that was me.

"Duffy—" Ben began.

I held up a hand. "There's no point," I told him. "He sees things that way. You can't make him not see things that way."

Duffy was always right. That was something that needed to be understood. In the books, every theory he has is proven out by the end. Every one he shoots down turns out to be stupid or a bad guy lying. He doesn't cloud his thinking with what he wants to be true; he deals just with what he knows to be true. So when he says something, it always—*always*—turns out to be correct.

That meant Sunny Maugham was dead. And if Sunny was dead, there was a very good chance that the next "victim" was already chosen. And everybody in that room knew it.

That would be me, too.

Chapter 14

Ben Preston didn't let me wallow on my expected fate for more than a second. "Duffy," he said, clearly in an effort to move the conversation in another direction, "is there anything here that can give us an idea of the sender's location?"

"No." *My* Duffy was usually more help than that.

My head reeled. I was a dead woman walking. I had no future. I'd have to find someone to water my plants. I should have a letter of recommendation for Paula in my files. Perhaps moving to Ecuador was an option. I could write in Ecuador.

Note to self: call Brian, Sol, Rita, and Adam before leaving for Ecuador. Did I know any cities there? Was there a place to get ice cream when you finish a manuscript? Could I pack Paula in a really large suitcase with air holes?

"But there is some encouraging data from Ms. Bledsoe's cell phone," Duffy went on. "I think from that, we might be able to begin to zero in on her location."

"You buried your lead, Duffy," I said.

He looked up. "A newspaper term."

"Yeah. It means you saved the most important piece of information too long and told us the less vital stuff first. Bad reporting." I had started out wanting to be a newspaper reporter, after all.

"What came through on the cell phone?" Ben asked. He was good at keeping us on topic, I'd noticed.

"There were no calls made a few hours before we found the phone," Duffy reported. "So while the battery life would indicate that it hadn't been left there long, it had not been in use for some time."

"How does that help?" Ben asked.

"It doesn't. But a review of the calls that were made and received revealed something more interesting." Duffy punched a few keys, and ahead of the latest e-mail from my creepy pen pal came a printed list of the calls Sunny Maugham had made and received just before Duffy and I invaded her bungalow in Ocean Grove. "Look here."

He pointed at a list of incoming calls, all in a row, that came from the same number. "These calls were made within the two days before Ms. Bledsoe vanished," Duffy said. "You'll see there are eleven of them, and they are concentrated almost entirely into an eighteen-hour time span."

"Are they from a guy named Brad?" I asked, remembering what Susan Oswego had told me about the man Duffy had suggested was Sunny's "suitor." "Do you know where he is?"

Ben Preston didn't know about Brad, so it took a minute for Duffy and me to explain. But all the while, Duffy was shaking his head.

"We don't know if the man who called her is named Brad or even if it was a man," he said. "The phone was a prepaid mobile phone purchased at a convenience store the day it was used."

"So how does that help?" I asked.

"If we know where the convenience store is that sold the phone, we can narrow the focus of our investigation," Ben explained. "It takes the search down from all of Earth to a much more manageable area. Where was the phone sold, Duffy?"

"In Passaic, on Main Avenue," Duffy answered. "And the local police were kind enough to question the owner of the place, who said that he didn't remember the man who bought it but had security video that could provide some help."

This seemed like it was exciting Ben and Duffy, but it wasn't doing much for me. "Okay, great," I said. "So instead of having to look for this guy in Istanbul or Minsk, now we can limit the search to northern New Jersey. Swell. And we might have some grainy security video that could show someone who called Sunny but might or might not be the person who took her. So explain to me why I should be encouraged at all."

Duffy looked surprised, as if surely I had missed the simplicity in what he had told me before. "The security video will be anything but grainy," he said slowly, like he was explaining it to a five-year-old who had recently suffered an unfortunate blow to the head. "It's digital. We can isolate the buyer and get a clear picture. We will at least have a view of the person we can distribute to police departments and hope for a sighting very soon."

"Has that been done yet?" Ben asked, perhaps trying to reassert his authority. He was, after all, the real investigator on this case.

"Yes. I got in touch with the Passaic County office and used your name. I hope you don't mind," Duffy told Ben. Ben waved a hand to dismiss the notion; of course he didn't mind. "We should be getting a look from them any minute now."

"They're working late?" Ben's eyebrows arched.

Duffy smiled just a trifle naughtily. "You authorized the video technician's overtime," he said.

"I'll take it out of your fee."

"If we find Ms. Bledsoe unharmed, it will be well worth the expense," Duffy noted, not specifying whether he meant the department's expense or his own.

"Guys, I need a ride home," I told them. "Being scared out of your wits makes a girl tired. Can you call me a taxi or something?"

Ben stood up. "I'll drive you," he said. "This is our first date, after all." Oddly, he was looking at Duffy when he said that. Duffy, very deliberately, did not move a facial muscle. "You'll call me when you get that video image?"

"First thing," Duffy said. He turned toward me. "I will see you in the morning, Ms. Goldman."

"You will?" I wondered if this was some kind of test to see whether I was going to get lucky with Ben Preston tonight.

"Of course. You assured me you'd come along to Ms. Bledsoe's house for a look around."

Oh, yeah. "Can you give me Sunny's home address for my GPS?" I asked.

"I will pick you up at your home. About ten, given the lateness of the hour right now. Is that convenient for you?"

Sure it was convenient, if I never intended to get any work done again for the rest of my life. "Shouldn't be a problem," I told Duffy.

"Good." He started to turn away when a "whoosh" sound came from his computer. "Hang on. I think we're getting that image from Passaic County."

I froze, and I don't know why. I'm not sure what I was afraid to see on his screen. Ben turned to look, and Duffy sat riveted in his chair, fascinated but also in a strange way giddy. He clicked on the file coming in.

"Is the guy at the bodega sure that this is the man who bought the phone?" Ben asked as the image started to download.

"He's only sold one such phone in the past week," Duffy answered. "This has to be it."

"We'd better get a break soon," Ben said, "or Special Agent Rafferty will come and show us stupid cops how it's done."

"Special Agent Rafferty?" I asked.

"There's an FBI agent who's been paying attention to these abductions because they're taking place in a number of states," Duffy explained. "She's been e-mailing Ben and me, threatening to take over the investigation if we don't solve it soon."

"She's a pain in the ass," Ben noted for color.

Soon enough—or too soon, depending on one's perspective—the picture came up, clear and sharp, on Duffy's screen. It showed a figure, in a blue sweatshirt (in this heat?) and baseball cap—Red Sox—pulled down tight over his forehead. He was hunched over the counter at the small store, which was crowded with shelves groaning with products for sale. His elbows were on the counter, where the clerk, who must have been in his early twenties, was placing the phone down for inspection.

"Well, the search is over," I said to Duffy. "We can close in on every guy on the eastern seaboard."

"It's not a great image," Ben agreed. "Do we have the whole video? Maybe there's a section where he's not bent over like that."

Duffy looked deflated. "This is not the picture we were hoping for," he admitted. "But the tech at Passaic said this was the best image he could take out of the video."

"Any chance the tech is our guy?" I asked.

They stared at me as if I'd suggested that we should be looking in Carpathian graveyards because I suspected Dracula was involved. "The other three crimes took place in other states," Duffy said quietly, using his best placate-the-mental-patient tone. "It is almost impossible for the Passaic employee to have been in all three places."

"It was a thought," I mumbled.

Duffy turned his attention back to the screen. "Maybe I can refine the image more efficiently," he said. "We might be able to get more facial detail that way, but it's never going to be a clear portrait."

"It's obvious he knew there were security cameras," Ben said, running his fingers through his hair. "What does that tell us?"

"That he's not an idiot," I said. "You can see the cameras in those stores; that's the idea. They want you to see that you're being filmed so you won't shoplift to begin with."

"But he planned for it. Had he been there before?" Ben looked at Duffy, who shrugged.

"Casing a bodega because he planned to buy a mobile phone there?" Duffy answered. "A little extreme, I'd say. My guess is he simply assumed there would be cameras and prepared for them."

"Yeah," Ben began, and then looking at Duffy's screen, froze.

"What?" I asked. I turned toward the screen.

The picture from the security camera was being dismantled, bit by bit (byte by byte?), slowly, until it became yet another message in early hostage-taker:

Seen enough?

"That's not good," Ben said.

Chapter 15

There just wasn't any point in continuing that evening. Ben drove me back to where I'd left my car—you meet in a public place on a first date, even with a law enforcement official with dark hair and blue eyes—and I went home, with plenty of thoughts in my head and none of them pleasant.

I breathed a sigh of relief when my front door was actually locked, and I managed to make it all the way into my office without scaring the living crap out of myself. One must be grateful for small favors.

There was a sticky note on my computer screen from Paula, who had still been there when I'd left for my wildly romantic evening of suspects and threatening e-mails. It read, "More info on 'Duffy.' See you AM." Paula goes to sleep early and generally does not have madmen chasing her unless she wants them to, which she rarely does.

So I revised exactly two pages of my manuscript and was immediately ready for bed. I took off my makeup, washed up, and went to bed. I believed that it had been a full day.

My first order of business the next morning was indeed to call Paula for the latest on my character wannabe. Duffy said he'd be coming at ten; I got up at eight thirty because . . . well, because Paula was at my door at eight thirty. She'd probably been up since five; going to bed early means getting up early, like Ben Franklin said.

"I assume you're here to tell me more," I began.

"Are you okay?" Paula asked. "You look gravelly."

She wasn't used to dealing with me before a more sociable hour. And I remembered that I hadn't told her about the nut who was cyberstalking me now. So I told her, and once she recovered, I said, "So this is what I sound like when I spent much of the night thinking about a crazy person who likes to send me e-mails," I said. "Especially when I have another crazy person trying to protect me from him. What can you tell me to alleviate my fears?"

"Not much."

"That's not helpful."

"Well, maybe this is: I can't tell you anything that's going to make you more fearful, either."

"It's a start," I said. "What'd you find out?" If I kept asking, there was a distinct possibility she might actually tell me.

"Nobody ever seems to have heard of Duffy Madison before four years ago," Paula reported. "People from his high school—teachers who must have had him in class at some point—don't have any memories of him. I can't find a record of who his parents were or even whether they're still alive. This is a man who truly sprang from your imagination onto the streets of Hackensack."

"You didn't come here this early just so you could say that," I suggested. "You're holding back for effect, aren't you?"

"Maybe a little," she said guiltily. "There are two interesting leads. One is his college yearbook; he went to Oberlin in Ohio. And in his yearbook, he's listed as having been a director for a section of Model UN."

Try as I might, I couldn't really make a significant connection there. "Model UN?"

"Model United Nations." Like that helped.

"I didn't think it was Model Unwanted Nitwits. How does that help us find out something about this guy?" When I was talking to Paula, I stopped thinking of him as "Duffy" and went back to "unnamed maniac."

"Think about it," she urged. "He was helping high school kids get through a mock session of the United Nations. He was in charge of some of them. It's not something that can be done alone in a room from far away. *Somebody had to see him.*"

"You appear to be taking this really personally," I pointed out.

"I have the scent of blood," she said.

"You said there were two things. What's the other one?"

Paula was grinning when she said, "There's some indication that he might have gone to the senior prom."

This was getting a little scary. "Remind me never to get on your bad side," I told Paula.

"It's not pretty."

I thanked Paula, and seeing that I was a work in need of much progress, she left. I was showered and dressed by the time Duffy showed up in the driveway. I had decided to be outside waiting for him. He'd been in the house before, but I wasn't comfortable with him coming back just now. Not until Paula found out who his prom date had been.

"Do you really think this trip is necessary?" I asked him as I buckled in.

"We still have no strong leads to the location where Ms. Bledsoe might have been taken," he said. "We have to follow every possible idea until something suggests itself."

I studied him as he drove. He was intense without being tense. He was all concentration without seeming like he was obsessed. He was all business without being emotionless. He was a perfect model for the character I write regularly. Observing him would be a terrific tool for future books. It's not always easy to come up with new things for Duffy. And yet, here was Duffy in front of me, flesh and blood. I could ask him anything.

What I finally decided on was, "How can you remember nothing before four years ago?"

"Do you remember before you were born?" he asked.

"Of course not."

"It's like that."

"How can you explain your existence? It's not like every character every author ever wrote is now walking around living a slightly different life that author imagined for him."

"How do you know? Maybe we're all characters that were imagined by an immense author and everything we do is fiction." Duffy never moved his gaze from the road, never referred to notes, had no GPS on.

"Very metaphysical . . ."

"Duffy. Duffy Madison. Nice to meet you." So he did have a sense of humor. My Duffy always had.

"Surely you can understand how weird this is for me," I said.

"Imagine how I feel. Last Friday, I had no idea you existed. I thought, like you do, that I must have undergone some hideous trauma that my mind insisted on blocking out. I spent a year with a therapist trying to uncover that lost memory. But it wasn't there. Now I know why."

This was going to be a long ride, and the distance wasn't even very far. "How can you make that leap?" I asked. "There are a million other explanations ahead of the idea that you just came into being because I typed some words on an iMac."

"Like what?"

"Like maybe that wasn't a great therapist. Like maybe it wasn't some emotional experience you were trying to block out. Maybe you got hit really hard on the head."

"Where's the scar?"

"Under your hair; what do I know?"

There was silence for a while. "If you were writing this scene, what would happen now?" Duffy asked.

"You and me in the car? I don't write science fiction."

He was agitated enough to steal a half-second glance at me before he stared once again into the distance. "You write stories in which a character with my name—" He stopped himself. "—in which *I* investigate cases of abduction. Ms. Bledsoe has been missing more than four days. We have no substantial leads. What should I do now?"

I closed my eyes. It was typical of Duffy, in either incarnation, to foist the responsibility onto me. "You're asking me how to find Sunny?"

He nodded without turning. "What we know is that she was home five nights ago. We know that because her sister saw her there that night. We know she was in her Ocean Grove bungalow within the last three days, because her phone was found there and it was still holding a charge. We know she had received a series of threatening e-mails and had failed to report them to any authorities."

"And we know that she was seeing a guy named Brad that she was really excited about," I added.

Duffy shook his head. "We don't know that. We know that another author, someone who knows Ms. Bledsoe, said that was the case. Until we can substantiate the suggestion, we don't actually know that to be the fact."

"Fine. Any progress on finding this Brad guy?" I had opened my eyes a while back; had I forgotten to mention that? Duffy was calm, but small, dark circles under his eyes and dryness in his lips indicated it had been a while since he'd slept well. He always did get emotionally involved in his investigations.

"We don't have much to go on," he answered. "Ms. Bledsoe's sister has never heard of the man, and neither has her ex-husband."

"Sunny is divorced?"

"Yes. I've told you that before."

"But before I knew Julia Bledsoe was Sunny Maugham."

Duffy did not address that directly. "She was married to a man named Zachary Wharton for seven years. They've been divorced for four. I'm surprised you didn't know that." Duffy's tone was not accusatory; it was more in the area of perplexed. "I thought the two of you were friends."

"Well, we were professional friends. Not even. Acquaintances, really. You know how it is: There are friends, and there are *friends*."

There was no irony in Duffy's voice. "I wouldn't know," he said. I resolved to write some friends for him as soon as possible. I might be able to shoehorn in at least one when I got back to my revisions.

"I'm guessing Zachary is not a suspect in the abduction," I said.

"It would be odd if he'd kidnapped and murdered three other women just to warm up for this one," Duffy agreed. "But we haven't eliminated any suspects yet, since we have so little to go on. Still, I have met Mr. Wharton, and he is considerably taller than the man in the convenience store video."

"You met him? What's he like?" Duffy reads things by observing people; he can tell you more about yourself than your spouse. There are times that can be incredibly valuable.

"He's a forty-seven-year-old venture capitalist who spent six months in prison for insider trading fifteen years ago. He is meticulous in his manner of dress, scrupulous about his conversation, and emotionally distant, probably as the result of a difficult upbringing. He says he has not seen Ms. Bledsoe in almost a year, has no reason to be upset with her, no longer pays her alimony because her income is higher than his, and has no idea who might have a grudge against her."

That actually didn't tell me much. It's so much easier when you can decide what the clues will be ahead of time.

"Do you believe him?" I asked.

"I have no reason not to," Duffy answered. "Yet."

We pulled up to a large, single-level home at the end of a cul-de-sac. It was gloriously tasteful, a relief in this neighborhood of alternating McMansions and older homes of ostentatious overindulgence. From the look of the house, I'd say it was built in the 1970s, and that made its grace and beauty even more remarkable. Most things built in the seventies look like the architect was on drugs. Because he probably was.

It had a lovely circular drive with impeccable landscaping. A fountain, which appeared to be naturally fed, trickled quietly on the left. A scent of chlorine in the air suggested there was a swimming pool. On a day like today, that was a major plus.

Who knew Sunny Maugham had been doing *this* well?

"It's not a bad little place," I told Duffy, "when one is trying to be thrifty."

He got out of the car as I did and took it in without irony. That would teach me to write a guy without irony. "It's valued at two-point-four million dollars," he said.

"I was joking, Duffy. Roll with it."

He didn't answer. He walked to the front door—natural wood and polished to a mirror shine—pulling a key from his jacket pocket. Yes. It was ninety-six degrees out, and Duffy

Madison was wearing a sports jacket. I was going sleeveless and wishing someone had invented personal air conditioning.

Duffy opened the lock and then the door. We walked inside.

There was something distinctly weird about being inside Sunny Maugham's house without her knowledge. This was different than the bungalow in Ocean Grove, where Sunny had probably just gone to break the routine and have a swim in the Atlantic. This was her home. This was her private space. And she didn't know I was there. I didn't care for the vibe.

It was not, as I had half expected in a place this size, imposing and museum-like. Like Sunny, the place was unpretentious. The room did have nicely polished hardwood floors, but its decorations were simple and unassuming. There was a small stuffed puppet of Oscar the Grouch on one of the sideboards.

"What are we looking for?" I asked Duffy.

"I'm looking for anything that might be different from the last time I was here," Duffy answered. "I expect to find nothing of the sort. *You* are looking for anything that wouldn't be immediately noticeable to a law enforcement officer but looks wrong to a writer of crime novels."

"I'm not going to find anything like that in the front room or the kitchen," I noted.

"No, you won't. The office is toward the back, on the right. I'll show you."

Duffy led me across the room and into a dining room that made me want to eat there every Sunday night. Homey, warm (well, hot today, but emotionally warm), and inviting, without the egotism that money often inspires. But we weren't there long. I followed Duffy through the dining room and into the back room of the house, where Sunny wrote her books.

It was the exact office I wanted to have when I grew up. It wasn't perfectly neat; that would have put me off and irritated anyone else who walked in. A writer with a completely organized mind? Why not become an accountant and leave room for more of us crazy people?

The computer on the desk (which had papers stacked semi-neatly on either side) was high-end but a few years old. The desk had actual writing surface, something mine completely lacked. And there was box of fine-tipped roller pens next to the stress ball, the reading glasses, and the voice recorder.

Sunny's workstation faced a wall. Behind and to the right were glass doors to the back deck, which was large, cedar, and friendly looking. I was starting to regret not being closer to Sunny.

File cabinets sat on either side of the room. Wooden ones that looked like actual furniture and not some Office Max steel-with-wood-veneer special. The printer sat on one of them, light still on, waiting for the next installment in one of Sunny's three (!) best-selling series.

"What do you see?" Duffy asked quietly, as if we were in a library.

"It's organized, but not obsessively," I said. "She can work without worrying about glare from the deck reflecting in her computer screen, but she can turn her chair toward the glass doors and look out on the backyard anytime she wants. The printer is close by, but not so close that she can't pick up documents without getting out of her chair. She can write on the desk, again by turning the chair. But the keyboard is ergonomically placed and has a wrist rest on it to avoid carpal tunnel."

"Good," Duffy said. "Keep going."

"Keep going? What do you expect me to see, a hologram of what happened when she was taken? That's it." I looked around the room again, fighting the growing feeling that it would be really good if I could work there instead of Sunny, because that was cruel and petty. There are times I'm not crazy about being in the same head as myself.

"You see more; you just don't know it yet." Duffy was doing his best to speak with a soft, moderated tone, trying not to break the mood. He stood to one side, positioning himself away from me and in as innocuous a spot as he could find, under one of Sunny's Agatha Awards (given out for best traditional mystery) on a shelf with some books from other authors.

One of them was mine. *Olly Olly Oxen Free.* I immediately felt even worse about any thoughts I'd had about Sunny that weren't warm and positive. I wondered if I should go over and autograph it for her and caught myself in that burst of ego, meaning now I was completely ashamed of myself.

I walked to the exact center of the room and bore down to the task. I was going to find Sunny Maugham, and I'd do it before anybody else because I was determined and I had special talents. Duffy, or whoever he was, had said so himself.

What was there? This looked like a very standard office, albeit a very nice one. It was, as I had noted, the very kind of space in which I wished I could work. That meant it was the kind of space in which many writers like me would have liked to create. So maybe I needed to experience it myself to see how it would drive on the real highway.

Without asking Duffy, I walked to the desk and sat down on the swivel chair. Real leather. I have some ethical objections, but I had to admit that it felt really good. There was a strong possibility that I might take a nap at Sunny's desk before I left the room.

I swiveled toward the desk. The computer, which the police had no doubt examined within an inch of its life, was still turned on but in "sleep" mode. So I hit the *S* key (in honor of Sunny) and it came to life. The screen began to glow.

There was no way I'd be able to interpret Sunny's files. Also, I had no desire to see anything she hadn't decided was ready for public consumption yet. That would be prying. I would shudder to think of anyone reading my work before I declared it ready. Her desktop was not terribly idiosyncratic; things were labeled "2nd Draft—Riches" and "First-Pass Pages—Cradle," no doubt two upcoming manuscripts in various stages of editing.

I want it stated for the record that I did not open Sunny's hard drive or look at any personal files. I was here to try to find clues to her location, a reason someone would want to abduct her. But I did take a quick peek at one file: "1st Draft—Standalone," just to get a glimpse of one page. I would not read for content, I decided, but for format and style of work.

I didn't learn anything except that Sunny couldn't spell or punctuate. Her gift was for storytelling. I closed it quickly, feeling like a Peeping Tom.

"There's an e-mail she saved as a Word file," I said to Duffy. "It's from her agent, I think. I'm going to print it out." The activity would give me an idea of how her office worked. Duffy had probably already seen the e-mail.

When I hit "print," however, I was rewarded with a message that the printer was out of paper. And there wasn't any in her desk drawers.

I stood up again. Okay, so this home office wasn't set up at all like mine, where everything could be seen mostly because it was never put away. I noticed a door cut into one wall, dark and unobtrusive. I walked toward it.

Duffy noted where I was going and said, "That's a supply closet."

"Exactly what I'm looking for," I told him, and reached for the doorknob.

Of all the things I've done in my life, I most wish I hadn't reached for that doorknob and opened that door.

It was a standard supply closet, small, with shelves on both sides and directly in front of me. A light went on overhead as the door opened; it must have had a motion detector that sensed when the door was open, an ergonomic touch I found very intelligent.

Slumped on the floor of the closet was Sunny Maugham. Her eyes were open, but she wasn't seeing anything.

She had a fountain pen sticking out of her neck.

Chapter 16

I'd never screamed in horror before. It doesn't help.

Duffy was at my side in an instant, gently pulling me by the upper arms away from the closet and directing my eyes away from the hideous sight inside. "Okay," he said quietly. "Hang on. I'll take care of it."

"Take *care* of it? That's Sunny Maugham!" As if there had been any question at all about that point.

"I know," he said. "Let me call my office so we can do something about this."

I would have pointed out that it was clear there was nothing anyone could do to help Sunny, but hyperventilating makes it so difficult to speak coherently. I sat down in Sunny's chair—feeling guilty about that, of all things—and put my head down, forcing myself to breathe more slowly than I wanted to.

In the background, which meant that he was probably directly next to me but my mind was in another state entirely, I heard Duffy talking on his cell phone to someone or another, and the words "deceased," "homicide," and "immediately" were the only ones that got through to my foggy brain.

Keeping my head down was helping. It wasn't helping with the fact that Sunny Maugham, possibly the best-loved author on the mystery circuit, was lying dead less than ten feet from where I sat, clearly the victim of a terrible crime. I'd been asked repeatedly over the past two days to come to her house for a look around and had avoided it until this moment. Could I have prevented this by showing up sooner?

I don't remember much of the next fifteen minutes, except for Duffy, after he got off the phone, kneeling down on the floor next to where I sat, my head still hanging down, and trying to soothe me.

"People are on their way," he said. "They'll help you. They'll get you out of this room, out of this house. Do you feel like you could walk outside now? We can wait outside."

I just shook my head hard.

"Okay," Duffy crooned. "You can stay there. That's fine. We're going to do everything we can."

I felt cold and clammy. I felt the way I imagined Sunny felt. Let's just say that I wasn't handling it especially well, and that's why I think Duffy's next words were inspired less by his tremendous empathy—as I write him, he doesn't score strongly in that area—and more out of a grim concern that if I couldn't actually be removed and didn't stop behaving like I was, there was a strong possibility I might throw up all over his crime scene.

"I told the executive producer at Monarch Entertainment about your book, *Little Boy Lost*," he said out of nowhere.

Oddly, that had exactly the effect Duffy had no doubt desired. I focused, lifted my head, breathed normally, and looked at him. "How did you even *know* anyone in the movie business?" I asked.

"Clearly, from one of the cases you did not make up," Duffy explained. "I know Mr. Ventnor after having worked on a case that involved his company's New York office. He recognized my name. I thought perhaps I could help."

"That was very nice of you." Being in shock makes you sound like an idiot.

"It was nothing at all," Duffy said. "I hope it helped."

Before I could answer, there were people in the room. Other people. Some of them were in uniform. Some of them were not. One who was in uniform, though not a police officer's, seemed to pay special attention to me and helped me get up and walk out of the room. When I instinctively turned to look into the closet, she made sure she blocked my view and said, "You don't need to see that."

I wished I never had seen that, so she definitely had a point.

The outside air, hot as it was, felt good. It smelled of whatever trees those were outside Sunny's front door, and it felt real, not like the artificial environment air conditioning had created inside that awful room. I'd never want to work in a room like that one.

The woman in the EMT uniform sat next to me on a bench outside Sunny's house, talking while she took my blood pressure and pulse readings. I think she might have taken my temperature at one point, too. I'm pretty sure she did so with an oral thermometer.

My mind wasn't clearing, so when Ben Preston arrived at my side, I was surprised and confused. Ben took my hands and asked me what had happened. In retrospect, he must have gone inside before I'd been aware of him, talked to Duffy, and decided Ben was the best one to debrief me.

It wasn't as difficult as I'd anticipated to tell him what had happened. For one thing, Duffy had been in the room when I'd discovered Sunny's . . . body . . . and could corroborate anything I said or even add details I had undoubtedly missed.

There was also the fact that I really didn't know anything other than what I'd seen in the closet, and that was more than enough.

But when he asked me, gently, about how Sunny had looked, I had to think hard. You'd guess that such a sight would be seared into my retinas for life, but the mind has a way of removing the things that are especially horrible just to keep us going through the day. Unfortunately, that is not an especially useful brain function when a crime is being investigated. For Ben's purposes, it would be better if I could remember every detail.

"It was a black fountain pen," I remember telling him. "It must have had one of those metal nibs on it, you know?" My mind began to let me remember what I'd seen, which was really somewhat cruel of it. Never had the term *blissful ignorance* been more apropos. Stupid mind, letting me remember.

"I know," Ben said with concern in his voice. "What else did you see in the closet?"

I stared at him. "Wasn't that enough?" I asked.

"I mean, what other details did you notice? Maybe you saw something I didn't. You write about murders. What clues did you see?" He was trying to get me to focus; I understood the technique. That doesn't mean it didn't still piss me off.

"I don't know."

"Think." Ben was getting less attractive by the second.

"I *am* thinking."

"I know," he said calmly. "But if you were writing that scene, what would you expect to see?"

"What I saw. I'd never write that scene. I don't write anything that bloody." Duffy Madison, in my novels, solves missing persons cases. There isn't always even a murder.

"*Was* it bloody?" Ben asked.

That got me, and I considered. "Come to think of it, no."

"You're the mystery writer. What does that tell you?"

My head was starting to clear a little. Ben was good at what he did. "She wasn't killed in the closet; she was brought there from somewhere else, in the house or outside, and posed there for us—for *me*—to find."

"Very good. And that tells us something very useful about the guy behind all this. We didn't necessarily know that in the other three cases. If he changed his method for this, that would be surprising. If he didn't, well, that helps us with the other three."

I shook my head; it was still too much. "But Sunny's dead," I moaned, the words coming out of me with difficulty. "I didn't come here yesterday because I was out with you, and

I didn't come here the night before because I thought Duffy was creepy, and now Sunny's dead."

Ben put an arm around my shoulder. "I know, and I wish it weren't true," he said. Cops usually go with, "I'm sorry for your loss," but he was showing a little more sympathy (and versatility) than that. "But don't for a minute think it would have made any difference if you'd shown up yesterday or the day before. There's no chance she was dead that long. You would have found an empty house."

That shouldn't have made me feel any better; Sunny was just as dead. But for some reason, Ben saying what he said had lifted the patina of guilt I'd been covered with since I opened the closet door. Okay, since I stopped screaming after opening the closet door.

"Thanks," I croaked. His arm stayed around my shoulder and squeezed it a little.

"No charge," he said. "Now, I have to get back inside. You okay out here?"

I nodded. It was a lie, but it was what he needed me to do, and I did it. I was not okay and wasn't going to be for some time, but I was strong enough that I didn't need to keep Ben Preston from his work. He got up and walked inside.

It was the twenty-first century and I was looking at more than seven seconds of downtime, so I checked my voice mail. I could have checked my e-mail, but a new message from my gruesome pen pal was the last thing I needed to see at that moment.

There was a voice message from my agent. "Get in touch," Adam Resnick said with a note of urgency in his voice. "It's about *Little Boy Lost*."

Well, there's psychological trauma and despair, but then there's an encouraging call from your agent. I pressed Adam's speed-dial button and waited.

"Resnick, Resnick, and Johnson."

"Who are you kidding? You're the only one in the office," I chided.

"Yeah," Adam said. "But it looks so good on the stationery. Are you ready for some news?"

I could have told him about Sunny. I *should* have told him about Sunny. The publishing world is nothing if not an enormous circle of gossip. But I wanted to hear about my book, the one I'd been slaving over, the one that could get me out of my current rut and get me—dare I say it?—money. "Hell yes, I'm ready for news," I answered. "What's up? Did the producer call with an offer?"

"Better."

Better? What's better than a movie producer wanting to buy my book? "The producer called twice?" I suggested.

The smirk was audible. "Better," he repeated.

"Okay, you've passed cute and are headed directly toward obnoxious," I told Adam. "What the hell is going on?"

"I got a call from another production company. They want to read *Little Boy Lost* with an eye toward making a Duffy Madison TV series."

All right, so maybe that *was* better than a producer calling. "Really?"

"No, I'm making it up. The one thing they teach you in agent school is always call up your clients with fake good news because they love that."

He said that someone at Beverly Hills Productions (which apparently was based in Santa Monica), a guy named Glenn Waterman, called his office unsolicited, saying that he'd "heard good things" about something called the Duffy Madison mysteries, which he'd never heard of. (Thanks for the ego boost, Adam—you could have left that last part out!)

He said there had been no market in Hollywood for mysteries lately, then someone had made a TV movie for a "women's channel" and gotten ratings through the roof. Waterman wanted to jump on what he'd decided would be a bandwagon and had remembered he'd heard something about *Little Boy Lost*, so he ordered his assistant to read it and write "coverage," which is the Hollywood version of a book report. She (the assistants are always women) read *Little Boy Lost* and made a recommendation.

Waterman bought it himself as an e-book, then immediately didn't read it and called Adam. Then he had signed disclaimers saying he wouldn't steal my work—which seemed damned nice of him—and gotten to the point that he and Adam were talking about an "option," which Adam explained is when a producer "rents" your book in the hope of selling it to a studio or network. Waterman had not read the book; he wanted to meet the author first because "that's where the power is." Hollywood people are crazy.

"That's amazing," I said when he was done with his tale. "Do you think there's really a chance?" Having a movie made of your book greatly improves sales on your current and previous books and can make you, if not a household name, the author of a household name. But a TV series was the gravy train. They have to pay you every time they make a new episode and every time they show it. The money, for sure, was not bad. I might be able to afford an office like the one Sunny had.

Oh yeah. Sunny.

"There's always a chance, baby," Adam said. "And since Waterman called on his own, without me breathing down his neck about it, I'd say the chance is pretty good."

I thanked him profusely, even though the renewed thoughts of Sunny were making me less ecstatic than I would have been under other circumstances.

I stood up and didn't feel light-headed; that was an improvement. "How long before I should start annoying you about this?" I asked Adam.

"I'd give it a couple of weeks, easy. People in Hollywood don't like reading. It requires too much imagination."

We hung up, and I walked over toward the inevitable ambulance. Someone would have to cart Sunny's body away after the detectives and everyone else was finished with the crime scene. I wondered if they had contacted Sunny's sister yet, the one who had first called with some concerns.

I never write the scene where the victim's family is notified. I don't do sorrow well. I'm much better at anger and repressed tension. Maybe I just don't want to face the open, over-the-top emotion that goes with irreplaceable loss. I never make Duffy inform the family, either. For one thing, he's not an official employee of the law enforcement agency, and for another, I hate to burden him with that kind of pain. It would really damage him to be the bearer of horrific news.

So why was I walking toward the ambulance? Shouldn't I be headed in the opposite direction?

All but one EMT were inside, taking the necessary readings and recording all the data they found for the investigation and, perhaps, a trial if the killer was found and brought to a courtroom. None of which seemed terribly likely at the moment. I was starting to conclude that this man was somehow superhuman, able to outwit any investigator (Duffy *never* doesn't find the victim in time!), incapable of being tracked or discovered. He would do whatever he wanted to do and get away with it.

Believe me, I was not forgetting that the next thing he would want would be to do to me what he did to Sunny, only in another creative "author" way.

A woman hit with a manual typewriter, one electrocuted with her word processor, one suffocated with rejection letters, and now Sunny, stabbed in the neck with a fountain pen. What was he planning to do to me? Bury me under dozens of volumes of Encyclopedia Britannica? Could you even find those anymore?

I reached for my phone again. Distraction. That's what I needed. I'd call Brian.

"Ms. Goldman?" Shit. Someone was going to make me deal with reality. I turned to see a woman in a conservative gray suit carrying a voice recorder. "Are you Rachel Goldman?"

I admitted to being myself because I wasn't really thinking sharply enough to come up with an alternate identity. She reached for my hand, and I gave it to her. "I'm Special Agent Rafferty, FBI."

Ben and Duffy had mentioned the FBI agent monitoring their case, and they'd rolled their eyes at the thought of her. But the imposing figure in front of me didn't really seem like the "meddling little lady" cops might disdain. "Wow," I said. "You must be really impressive." I wasn't really firing on all cylinders.

Special Agent Rafferty shook my hand and looked closely at me, as if trying to see the roots of my mental illness in my eyes. "How so?" she asked.

"I don't know any female officers or FBI agents, and I've done a decent amount of research on criminal justice," I explained. "I'm glad to meet you." Maybe I could patch up the faux pas with a little sisterhood.

She took a moment. "Research," she said. Then she stared at me. "You're *that* Rachel Goldman? The author?"

Now, you have to understand, that *never* happens. For one thing, mine is hardly the most distinctive or unusual name an author could have (and I never even used a pseudonym). And among people who have met me outside BooksBooks-Books and other such venues, I am not exactly a household name. Someone who recognized my work was a rare treat.

"Yes, I am," I said. "You've heard of my books?"

"Heard of them? I *love* them!" Special Agent Rafferty looked like she'd just met the president of the United States, or Justin Bieber, depending on your personal preference. "I never miss anything you write!"

I almost asked for her voice recorder to immortalize this moment and have it to play back in my dotage. "I'm so glad you enjoy the novels," I said modestly.

Rafferty blinked. "Novels?" she said. "I didn't know you wrote novels."

What did she think I wrote—papal decrees? "Sure. I write the Duffy Madison mystery series." Remember? How you loved them ten seconds ago?

Now she looked *really* confused. "But I just spoke to Duffy inside. He's real. Did you name a character after him?" She scratched at something imaginary on the right side of her head.

"No. I've been writing mystery novels for four years. What did you think I had written?" It's one thing to be dissed; it's another thing to be dissed when the person doesn't even know they're doing the dissing.

"You're Rachel Goldman. You write books on the philosophy of the criminal justice system. I've read every one."

"I don't. I write mystery novels. I swear." Then it hit me. "You mean *Roberta* Goldman." I'd heard that name before, of course.

"Oh, that's right!" No apology, nothing. She didn't even have the decency to look mortified. Between this and finding the dead body of a professional acquaintance, it had hardly been worth getting up this morning.

"How can I help you, Agent?" If she wasn't going to shower me with praise, we might as well get on with this.

"Special agent," she corrected, probably out of habit. "Well, you can tell me about what you found inside." Voice recorder out, red light lit.

"You saw it," I noted.

"Yes, I did. But I want you to tell me about it." For a gushing fan of . . . somebody . . . Special Agent Rafferty was not terribly pleasant, I thought.

"Duffy and I went inside so I could have a look around the house," I said.

"Why?"

"Why?"

"Yes. Why were you brought in to look over the scene? You're not a criminal justice employee or a forensics expert. Why you?" This woman was about as not Lieutenant Isabel Antonio as she could be without changing species.

"Duffy felt it would be helpful to get another writer into the house to see if there was anything unusual that someone outside the field might not notice," I told her.

Rafferty scowled. Really. A full-on scowl. I've used the word to describe disgruntled expressions before, but I'd been doing the term a disservice. This was a real scowl. Rafferty looked like she wanted to spit. Possibly at me.

"So that's what *Duffy* thought, huh?" Her inflection was all I needed to infer a few things, mostly that Rafferty didn't like Duffy Madison.

"I was just trying to help," I said. I sounded even more like a five-year-old than you're already thinking.

"And what did you see?" Rafferty continued. "Was there any useful observation in there from you? Did your writer's sensibility help the investigation?"

"I found the body," I said, a little more starch in my voice. "That didn't help Sunny Maugham much, but it was more than anyone else had managed to do." *You go, girl! Get a little of your own back!*

"Yes, let's talk about that," Rafferty said. I didn't like the almost happy tone. "What made you get up and open the closet door?"

"I was looking for paper." That seemed simple enough.

"Why? You were just *observing*. What did you need paper for?" There was something ominous in this interview, but it was sneaking up on me. I knew it was there, but I wasn't sure I could get out of its way.

"I wanted to print something out, to get a sense of what it felt like to work in Sunny's office." That was, in fact, why I was looking for the paper. It's important to tell the truth to someone who could arrest you. My mother taught me that after her first pot bust. (She got off with a fine.)

"Why? What would printing out a file do to help?"

"It was to get a feel for the office," I said again. "It was supposed to give me a better idea of what Sunny's system was, so that I could tell if anything was amiss."

"And something was." No expression on her face. We could have been discussing fabric softener sheets.

"I didn't find that out until I opened the closet door." Okay, so maybe there was a little attitude in my voice at that point. We were discussing the death of a woman I'd known, who might even have thought of me as . . . no, we weren't really friends. But it was upsetting.

"How did you know it was a closet?" Rafferty asked.

What did that mean? "I don't understand." That's what I say when I don't know what something means. Snappy, huh?

"I mean, how did you know that was a closet?"

I still wasn't getting it. "Well, the fact that there were all these supplies in it sort of gave the purpose away." Mom never said anything about being snarky to the officer, but I was still betting it wasn't the best strategy. She'd baited me, giving me the same straight line twice.

"The door. The closet door." I must have been staring blankly. "You'd never been in the room before, correct?"

Yes, madam district attorney. "That's right."

"So if you'd never been in the room before, how did you know that door led to a utility closet?"

It was a good question. How *had* I known? "It seemed logical. She wasn't storing paper or anything she'd need nearby in the desk. There was a door just to the left of the desk; I figured it was a closet." Because that was exactly where I'd put the supplies if I could afford to have an office like that, and everything else in the room was exactly the way I would want it, so it followed. I felt it was probably best not to mention my office envy to the detective.

"There are six filing cabinets in the room. You didn't go to any of those. You walked directly to the closet." A mouse walked up to me and asked if I knew what it felt like to be lured into a trap, but I ignored it.

"I figured the filing cabinets had files in them. The door looked like a closet." Whoa. My eyes narrowed involuntarily. "Why are you asking?"

"I'm just trying to understand."

Wait. There was something else. "Besides, Duffy told me it was a closet." Okay, so I was already on the way to the door when Duffy mentioned it was the supply area, and I had assumed that, but it should have bought me at least a little credibility.

Instead, there was the sneer again. "Duffy," she said.

"What is it with you and Duffy?" I asked.

She, naturally, ignored the question. "How well did you know Ms. Bledsoe?"

This was not progressing along the path I'd anticipated when it seemed Rafferty was a big fan of my books. "Not all that well. We spoke for a while at a mystery book conference once."

"What did you talk about?" She had put the voice recorder in a breast pocket, where it could still record, and pulled a reporter's notebook out of her back pocket. She started writing in the notebook.

I folded my arms. "Do I need to call an attorney, *Special Agent*?" I asked. Because it sure was starting to sound like I might.

Not a blink. "Why would you need an attorney?" Blandest tone you ever heard. The last time someone asked you to pass the salt, they had more passion in their voice.

"I'm wondering that myself, but you're making it sound very much like I'm on the verge of being arrested. If I am, I'd like to stop answering questions and call my attorney." I stopped short of the cliché, "I know my rights."

"I wasn't planning on arresting you," Rafferty said. "Unless you'd like to make a confession."

"Depends," I said. "If you're arresting people for watching trashy reality shows, I'm ready to be handcuffed."

Rafferty's face was as impassive as a Halloween mask of a police detective, only less expressive. "Far as I know, that's still legal," she said.

"Then I think I might exercise my right to remain silent. Other than to say that your interpersonal skills might use some polish."

Her eyelids stood at half-staff. "I'll take it under advisement." I turned to walk away, but she added, "I thought you wanted to help find the person who killed your friend."

I'll admit it, I stopped walking. "You know, impersonating my Aunt Harriet really isn't going to help you much."

Rafferty just stood and stared. She looked like she was thinking about the last time she was really bored.

"What is it you want to know?" I whined.

"What did you and Ms. Bledsoe talk about when you met at the book convention?" she said. Lord knows, *I* wouldn't have remembered what had gotten this little chat fest going, but she did.

"We talked about book promotion," I said. "Sunny was very helpful in giving me some pointers on how to get my book noticed."

"Then how come I thought you were Roberta Goldman?" Rafferty asked. Perhaps on her planet, that would have constituted a joke.

"You don't venture out of the how-to-further-my-career section at the bookstore," I said. "If you wandered into the fiction aisles, maybe you'd come across my work. Is there anything else?"

"Yeah. Did you kill Julia Bledsoe?"

"No. Damn, that was easy. I assume I can go now." Once again, I started to walk away.

"Just one thing." Arrgh. I turned again and considered her. She didn't wait for me to ask what the one thing might be. Her eyes didn't soften, and her voice didn't show any signs of compassion. "Do you think you need protection?"

That came out of nowhere. "Why?"

"Because I hear you've been getting e-mails from the guy who did this," Rafferty said. "Personally, I doubt it, but if you're scared, we can assign you some extra protection."

I hadn't been thinking about that at that moment, so thank goodness Rafferty had brought it back to my frontal lobes for consideration. But I was still smarting from the grilling she'd just given me and wasn't going to admit to the amazon that I was afraid. "If you know I'm getting threatening e-mails, and you know it's from whoever did this to Sunny, what made you think I was the killer?" I asked.

"I didn't. But you have to eliminate as many possibilities as you can. Now the question is whether you want us to assign some extra police drive-bys to your house and maybe put a monitor inside to watch out for you. Do you want that?"

"No," I said without a long thought. "I have Duffy and Ben Preston watching out for me. I think I'll be all right."

Rafferty gave me a long look, like she was deciding if she wanted to say something. I almost turned away a third time, then figured I wouldn't give her the satisfaction. Sure enough, she spoke again.

"You'll be safe with Ben Preston," she said. "Be careful about Duffy Madison."

You know when something goes screwy in movies and they play that sound where the phonograph needle skips across the record? I heard that in my head. "Why?" I asked. "What is it about Duffy?"

"He's . . . run into problems with two other missing persons cases," she answered. "I'm just saying you should be careful."

Now *she* started to turn away. "Hold it," I said, and she stopped. "What do you mean, 'run into problems'? What's happened with other cases Duffy's worked?"

"I don't work for the prosecutor's office," Rafferty answered. "I wasn't there, but I heard about it."

"Heard about what?" I got out through my gnashed teeth.

"Twice he's had people he was looking for turn up dead. The guy's bad luck. Just stay away, is all I'm saying."

Chapter 17

"Duffy's had some bad luck once in a while, but for the most part he's been a real boon to the department," Ben Preston told me. We were getting out of Ben's car at my house, where he'd taken me after the inevitable hordes of people had vacated Sunny's place and he had enough time to drive me home. "Nobody bats a thousand."

"I'm not saying who, but I was warned to stay away from him," I said. "That's why I asked. I'm told that if I am in fact next on the list for this guy, Duffy Madison is exactly the man I want to avoid." Okay, so Rafferty hadn't said those words exactly, but the message had been clear.

"Don't tell me, let me guess," Ben said as I unlocked the door and we walked inside. "Eunice Rafferty was doing her voodoo scare thing again. She has some bug up her ass about Duffy, and I have no idea why."

We went into the kitchen, where I started a pot of coffee. I'd just turned the air conditioning back on, so it was going to be iced coffee, but there was no sense getting the ice out until there was something to pour over it. "There were two cases—and we don't get tons of missing persons cases just in Bergen County—that Duffy worked on, and they didn't turn out the way we wanted them to. It wasn't Duffy's fault, and he wasn't the black cat walking in anyone's path."

"The first three abductions took place in three states that weren't New Jersey," I pointed out. "Don't you have to look for someone who could have been in all those places at the time of the crime? Doesn't that sort of narrow things down?"

I have a counter between the kitchen and the dining room. I never actually dine in the dining room, so there were a number of boxes in there from when I had moved in that had never been completely unpacked. Kind of makes me wonder if I needed that stuff in the first place. Ben sat down on a barstool I had set up next to the counter.

He rubbed his chin as he thought. "Of course that would help identify a suspect," he said. "But we don't even have a pool of people to choose from yet. This guy has been really discreet, except when he's killing people."

"Well, what about motive?" I filled the coffeemaker with enough water and started it going, then I walked out to his side of the pass-through and stood looking at him while the coffee brewed. "No two of these women seem to have anything in common other than writing crime fiction. Why does someone want to kill women crime fiction authors?"

I realized then how tired Ben looked. There were creases under his eyes, which were not entirely white in their whites, and his smile was crooked, favoring the left side. "Has it ever occurred to you that this guy might just be crazy?" he asked.

I shook my head, probably too dismissively. "That's the easiest dodge in the mystery writing business," I told him. "You don't give your killer a motivation; you just say he's crazy. Even crazy people have motivations, whether they make sense or not. In the criminal's mind, what he's doing is perfectly logical and necessary. Just saying 'he's crazy' means that you don't know why he's doing this."

Ben looked at me blankly for a few moments. "I don't know why he's doing this," he said.

"Doesn't it make you feel better to tell the truth?" I asked.

"Not really, no."

I should have been more shaken up than I was; I should have been sad and terrified and angry and did I mention terrified? Sunny Maugham, everybody's favorite in the mystery world, was dead, and I had discovered her body. It was possible that, by pissing off the abductor, I had played a role in her death. And then there was the small matter of the very broad hints being dropped that I was next on the agenda. Yes, I definitely should have been a quivering mass of frightened gelatin lying in the fetal position on my bedroom floor.

But I wasn't. Maybe it just hadn't sunk in yet. Maybe I was in major denial. But maybe, just maybe, the training in concocting plots, figuring motives, designing clues, and most of all creating Duffy Madison was kicking into gear now, and I was taking a defensive stance, attempting as best I could to take control of the situation and protect myself from the oncoming threat.

Yeah, it was probably that it hadn't sunk in yet.

What I actually was, almost as much as tired, was pissed off. I started feeling like the heroine of one of Sunny's cozies, an amateur who would immediately start investigating the crime and way outpace the professionals because she was spunky or knew how to embroider or something. I wanted to find the guy who killed Sunny and beat him up. Except that I was petrified that I was next and wanted to be as far away from him as possible. I was not discounting Jupiter as a place to hide.

The coffee began to drip into the empty pot, which Paula had been kind enough to actually wash out, so I walked back around into the kitchen and got two glasses and a tray of ice out. As I prepared the glasses with ice and got soy milk out of the fridge, Ben stood and walked around, offering to help.

"You want to help? Figure out who this maniac is and catch him," I said. "That's your job. Mine is making up fake ones and then getting somebody to catch those."

"And so you made up Duffy Madison," Ben reminded me. He looked concerned, as if the whole Duffy-as-fictional-character thing had lost its amusement.

"I did. And once we figure out who your pal using the name I made up really is, we can determine exactly how crazy *he* is." I poured the coffee over the ice, much of which promptly melted, and got more ice to add to the drinks. "You want sugar or anything?"

"You got chocolate syrup?" Ben Preston asked. I nodded. "That's great in iced coffee." He opened the fridge, found it on the door, and extracted it.

I looked at him. "You cops really are just little kids with guns, aren't you?"

"I'm not a cop; I'm an investigator for the prosecutor of the county of Bergen." He squeezed some syrup into his iced coffee and stirred it with a spoon I handed him.

"That's pretty much a cop. And you used to be a cop."

"We were talking about Duffy," he reminded me.

"I don't have anything new to say about Duffy." The fact that my assistant was trying to track down Duffy's prom date seemed, well, perhaps an unflattering detail that was best left out of this conversation.

Ben took a long swig of his iced . . . mocha. It must have hit the spot, because he gave a contented sigh. "Well, I do. I think you're wrong about him. I don't think he's crazy."

"You don't? How do you explain—"

"I can't. I can't tell you why he has the same name as the character you made up. Maybe you'd heard his name and forgotten it; it's possible. Maybe you saw it on the Internet in doing some research and thought it sounded like a fictional character; that's possible, too. But I can tell you that Duffy Madison is the best missing persons investigator I've ever met, and you can't do that job as well as he does if you are mentally incapacitated." To punctuate his point, he drained the rest of his drink. "Is there any more coffee?"

But I was annoyed enough, and frayed enough, not to succumb to the charms of a fairly good-looking man drinking a sweet caffeinated beverage in my kitchen. "I believe that Duffy is a good investigator," I said defensively. "I made him that way. I created every piece of that personality; I know how he thinks, what he wants, everywhere he's ever been. It's the only way you can do what I do at all well." And just to show him I meant business too, I took a long sip of my iced coffee. He was right; chocolate syrup definitely would have taken some of the bitterness out. But I wasn't going to give Ben the satisfaction.

"You're changing your tune," Ben said. He seemed mystified by that.

"You're right."

"What does that mean?"

"Exactly what you think it does," I said.

"Jesus Christ, you really think that guy is some fictional character you made up, don't you?" Ben leaned back on the counter and seemed to be trying to take me in all at once, which at this distance couldn't be done without a special lens.

"It's the only explanation that makes any sense," I said.

* * *

Ben left a little while later, still shaking his head. I finally did call Brian, told him about my day, and, after all those hours, cried for a while. Scotch helped a little, but not that much. For one thing, I can't drink more than one glass. For another, even after I felt myself relax, Sunny was still dead.

I vegged out for a while, just sitting there in my living room with *The Return of the Pink Panther* playing on my TV. Even the unrelenting silliness on the screen wasn't helping. I wasn't mourning Sunny, exactly; I didn't know her well enough to feel comfortable doing that. I was feeling her loss from the world of mystery writing, which was depressing enough, but I was also just feeling drained and uninspired. It actually occurred to me to do some revisions then, but that seemed somehow disrespectful, and besides, they were revisions and I didn't want to do them.

So, as I often do when I'm out of sorts and have no logical reason to do so, I called my father.

I told him about Sunny. I told him about how I'd been asked to consult on her abduction, how I'd accidentally discovered her body, how that was making me feel somehow responsible, and how I didn't want to be responsible. I said that I wished today had never happened, but now I couldn't make it unhappen, and I'd be stuck with it for the rest of my life—and what was that going to do to me?

The one thing I didn't tell him about was Duffy. He'd have me declared incompetent and take over my affairs in court, right after having me committed to the most compassionate lunatic asylum in New York State.

My father, who has a logical and caring mind, listened without comment for a long time. When I was done ranting and just started sniffling again—which was exactly what I'd promised myself I wouldn't do—he spoke up.

"You know perfectly well that what happened isn't your fault, Rache."

"It feels like it is. I mean, if I'd just tried harder . . ."

"Your friend would be just as dead."

I stood up and started walking around the house, just because. Well, maybe because I could be sure then that I was indeed alone in the place. I hadn't checked my e-mail pretty much all day. Duffy would see if there was something from the guy who killed Sunny. I didn't want to know.

"Maybe that's the thing," I told Dad. "Sunny wasn't really my friend. I mean, she was a lovely person and I liked her, but we didn't really know each other that well. If it comes out on a LISTSERV or some of the other mystery underground, it'll look like I was just trying to climb onto her coattails, like I'm the worst kind of morbid namedropper. How do I make it not look like that?"

"Nobody's going to think you were doing that," Dad said patiently. "If anyone did, it would be someone who has no idea what kind of person you are."

There wasn't anyone in the dining room. I turned on the lights to be sure. There wasn't anyone in the kitchen, either. But I put some more lights on just to prove it to myself.

Then I made the biggest mistake I'd made in a day full of hideous events and certain errors. I told my father about the threats from the killer.

He did not take a breath or wait one second. "I'm on my way," he said.

Before he could merely hang up and hop into his car (which was undoubtedly his plan), I leapt in with, "No, Dad. Please. There's no need. I have some very good security people on me. The police are taking it seriously and helping me, I swear."

"So how will it hurt to add your father to the mix? I'm on my way."

"No," I said more forcefully. "The last thing I need right now is to be worrying about you at the same time I'm worrying about me."

"So here's the solution: don't worry about me. Nobody's threatening *my* life over the Internet. I'm on my way, Rachel."

"No, you're not." Improvise. Writers improvise all the time; it's what we do whenever we don't know what's coming next. "I promise I'll call you if things get worse, but I really can't be distracted with you here, Dad. I shouldn't have said anything."

There wasn't anyone in the office, or in Paula's office, either. You can bet lights went on in both. I shuddered a little when I passed the door to the basement stairs. I sure as hell wasn't going down there. That's what a TSTL character would do. Or was *not* going downstairs what made me Too Stupid to Live? Either way, there was no chance I was checking my basement.

"Of course you should say something," Dad answered. "I'll make a deal with you. Call me twice every day to let me know you're all right. First time I'm ready to go to lunch or to bed and I haven't heard from you, I'm getting in the car. No questions asked. Fair?"

It occurred to me that he could call *me* twice a day, but that would surely be worse than the way he proposed; my father has the worst sense of timing on the planet. It was one of the reasons I hadn't had sex in more than a year. He had a knack of calling whenever things were getting interesting, and yet I knew his interruption had to be completely unintentional. Dad never worked for the NSA.

"Fair enough," I answered, since it was the best deal I was going to get. Calling Dad twice a day wouldn't be that bad when it was for one purpose. I could just get him on the phone, say, "I'm fine," and he'd let me go almost immediately.

"I think it's best we don't tell your mother," he said, and then thought over what he'd said. "That's not a divorce thing, Rache."

I had saved my bedroom for last. This was a twofold decision: I thought it would make sense to end there so I could just go to sleep and try to forget the day, and also, if there were someone in my bedroom, I especially didn't want to know.

There wasn't. That was not especially unusual, but tonight I was glad of it.

"I get that it's not a divorce thing," I told my father, "and telling Mom is the last thing I'd want to do. She'd probably blame it on either the government or the lack of fiber in my diet, and I don't need to hear theories about either of those."

"A wise choice," Dad said.

I kept him on the phone, talking about pretty much nothing at all, for as long as I could, just to have a comforting voice there whenever I stopped talking. But after a while, I was tired, Dad was out of things to say, and Sunny was still dead. We said good night.

Within three seconds of my disconnecting the call, my phone rang. I had flung myself on my bed, lights still on in the room, makeup still on my face, clothes still on my body, just to rest my head against the air-conditioned pillow and try to get a moment's rest for my mind. I checked the incoming number.

Duffy.

I gave serious consideration to letting him go to voice mail, but a quick look at the phone indicated that he'd already left seven messages. That told me he had news, and it undoubtedly was not the kind that would trigger another run to the Cold Cow for a celebration.

Maybe, I decided, I didn't have to be a cozy heroine. Maybe I could just help Duffy from afar, on the phone preferably, and give him the clues that would lead to the killer's arrest. I made a mental note to cancel the flight to Jupiter. Help Duffy. That would do the trick.

"What's going on, Duffy?" I said when I hit the talk button (call it what you like; you hit it and then you talk).

"I have been calling you for ninety minutes," he began. "I've left seven messages on your voice mail. Haven't you checked your e-mail?"

Oh no, not one of those, please. Not tonight. "Don't tell me I've gotten another threatening message," I said. "I couldn't take that right now."

"I'm not telling you that. I'm telling you that I sent you four e-mails and you have not answered them."

"It's all about you, isn't it, Duffy?"

"Hey, I didn't ask to be created." That's the sense of humor this guy had. If I was going to buy in on this ridiculous theory, I'd start giving him more compassion in later books. Sol would tell me it was inconsistent, and I'd reply that the character has to grow.

This would, naturally, strip Fictional Duffy of everything that readers liked about him and would no doubt result in the cancellation of the series and the bulk of my income.

But then this version of Duffy wouldn't say annoying things to me. There are trade-offs in every business.

And now I could never kill him off. I already felt horrible about Sunny, and I couldn't even come up with a rationale for believing her death was my fault.

"What was it you wanted to tell me?" I asked. That pillow wasn't getting any more air-conditioned. I wanted to be sleeping soon.

"We might have a break, something that could help track down the murderer of Ms. Bledsoe. May I come to see you?"

"What, at this hour?" I could barely keep my eyes open.

Duffy's voice sounded incredulous. "It's eight thirty," he said.

It was? I looked at the clock next to my bed, and sure enough. The light through the windows was not entirely devoid of sunset just yet. How could I have so lost my bearings that I'd thought it was at least four hours later?

"Sure, drop in," I said. "We're always open."

Chapter 18

While Duffy was driving to my house, I decided to call Brian Coltrane and ask him to stop by, too. I decided this based on two principles: (1) I wanted Brian in the house just in case Duffy was the author abductor coming to take me away and kill me, and (2) I wanted to be sure that Duffy wasn't a figment of my imagination. Even though he'd interacted with others, including Brian, it was still possible I'd dreamed up everything that had gone wrong since he'd called my landline that first day. Writers are open to every possibility, and that can be a real pain in the ass.

There was a third motive for inviting Brian over, but it's one I don't really like to admit to myself: he was willing to stop at Adamstown Pizza on the way and bring me dinner.

He got to my door, edible Frisbee in hand, before Duffy, who was presumably coming from farther away, perhaps as far as the Andromeda Galaxy. "Cathy's starting to worry about us," Brian said as we settled our carbohydrate-rich dinner in my kitchen. "I wish you'd let her come over too."

"Next time for sure," I said, aware that Cathy had never actually set foot in my house. I like her well enough, but when a real friend gets romantically involved, there is a strain on the friendship. Brian had been hurt a number of times before, so I tend to see every woman he meets as a potential late-night decompression session after the inevitable breakup. Cathy had lasted ten months so far, a new record, but I wasn't letting her off the hook that easy.

Besides, there was no way I was letting her meet the lunatic who was on his way here even as we spoke.

"All right, but I'm holding you to next time," Brian said. "Now get me up to date on the Duffy impersonator."

I told him what I knew based on the research Paula had done so far. Brian already knew about the horrific day, about Sunny Maugham and the not-so-veiled threats sent in my direction. I had left out the Duffy stuff because in the shadow of everything else that had happened, it didn't seem especially important.

"So there's physical evidence that this guy existed before four years ago," Brian said, chewing on a piece of crust. I had gotten some Trader José beer from the fridge (don't knock it until you try it) so he washed down what he was eating with that. "But nobody she can find from that time remembers ever seeing him or even knowing he existed, is that about the size of it?"

"That's what it looks like," I said. "And I don't know what to do with it."

"Confront him," Brian suggested. "Tell him what you've found out and defy him to explain it."

"I've done that. He looks me in the face and tells me that there is no explanation other than he sprung to life the minute I configured pixels just the right way on my word processor. And since I don't actually have evidence that he suffered some mental trauma or was hit on the head by a heavy object, I don't have anything to refute what he says."

That, naturally, is when the doorbell rang. Even in my kitchen, with (literally) every light in the house turned on, with Brian in the room and a couple of slices of pizza still left in the box, I jumped a little at the sound.

Let's just agree that my nerves were a touch on the brittle side that night.

"That's him," I told Brian. "I'm dealing with him as if he really is Duffy Madison. I'd like you to follow my lead, but watch him closely. We can compare notes later, okay?"

That was a stupid plan, so I didn't give Brian time to protest and headed directly to the front door. And you'd better believe I looked through that peephole to make sure (1) that Duffy was the man outside the door and (2) that there was only one man outside the door. Both those things appeared to be true, so I opened up and let him in.

"There's been a breakthrough," he said even before I could lock the door behind him. "It's not a huge breakthrough, but it definitely is more than we had before. I think we can start triangulating a position."

"It's nice to see you too, Duffy. I'm a little shaky, but I'll get by. Thanks for asking." I started walking back toward the kitchen.

"I didn't ask," Duffy noted. Honestly, he was pointing out that he hadn't asked me about my state of mind, wondering why I would suggest that he had. Luckily, I speak fluent Duffy Madison, having invented the language all by myself. "I was telling you about—" He stopped short when we reached the kitchen door and he saw Brian standing there.

"Duffy, this is Brian Coltrane," I said before my creation could make some uncomfortable comment. "Brian's a very good friend, and I asked him over. He brought pizza; would you like some?"

Brian held out his hand. "Mr. Madison," he said.

Duffy looked at the hand as if wondering whether it was loaded. He took it, gingerly, perhaps trying to keep it from going off. "We met at the bookstore," he reminded Brian. "You told me to leave."

Brian nodded in agreement. "Yes, I did," he said. No note of apology.

"Okay, guys, no need to mark our territory. I just had the floor washed," I said. "Duffy, do you want some pizza?"

"No, thank you," he answered, sitting down on a barstool on the outside of the pass-through. You could see his eyes recording everything he saw, storing each detail for future reference and analysis. No doubt when the killer came and did me in with a sheaf of copy paper, Duffy would be able to pick out the one misplaced fork in the utensil drawer that would crack the case.

I'd still be dead, but Duffy would have his man. Right at the moment, it was small comfort.

"You said there'd been a breakthrough," I reminded him.

"Yes. I believe our quarry has finally made his first mistake." There are few things—no, there's *nothing*—Duffy Madison likes better than showing off how smart he is. "At my request, the crime scene team did a spectral analysis of the utility closet in which you found Ms. Bledsoe's body. There was some DNA evidence that did not match the small amount of blood found from Ms. Bledsoe. Specifically, some fingernail residue that did not belong to Ms. Bledsoe."

"Great. The DNA test tells us who the killer is, right?" Brian said. "So who is it?"

I couldn't get there fast enough because Duffy was busy showing off. "We won't know even if it's possible to identify the originator of the residue for some weeks, Mr. Coltrane," he said. "This is not crime fiction. The lab is overworked and the tests take time." He looked over at me. "But the key is that in finding the residue, the technicians also discovered something the killer left behind that might be useful in determining his place of origin."

Again, I speak Duffy, so I could follow. Brian, who doesn't read my books, needed the Rosetta Stone version. "You think you can figure out where this guy is from?" Brian nodded now; he got it. "What did they find?"

"A candy wrapper," Duffy answered.

I waited, but nothing else came. "A candy wrapper?" Sometimes it's best to provide a little prodding.

"Indeed." Duffy could have said *yes*, but why do that when you can sound more like a pompous know-it-all? Sometimes I wasn't crazy about this guy, and then I remember everything he does comes from my brain. Because even if he was just emulating the character I write, he was doing a really masterful job. It's disconcerting. "A cellophane wrapper from a hard candy, probably a caramel flavor. It was not a national brand, available only in the store where it was created. The wrapper bore the legend of K. Moore's Confections, a local candy shop in Syracuse, New York."

Maybe it was the impact of the day's events. Maybe it was the relative lack of sleep, or the disorientation, or the impending death threat, but I wasn't firing on all cylinders just at that moment. "What's the big deal about a candy wrapper from Syracuse?" I asked Duffy.

To be fair, I knew that I was inviting a lecture. Asking Duffy *anything* is inviting a lecture. But Brian, who had shown no interest in his beer or more pizza since Duffy arrived, was practically immobile now. He'd been listening to every word and was processing. Brian is a good thinker—I actually based some of Duffy's methods on him, although he doesn't know it—but he requires time to process the data coming in and uses logic to reach a conclusion.

"Where did the other crimes take place?" he asked before Duffy could begin his PowerPoint presentation that would undoubtedly accompany his answer to my question about the candy wrapper.

Duffy pointed at him like a proud teacher whose student had just mastered the times tables. "You've got it," he said. "The three other authors were taken from their homes in Philadelphia; Manhattan, Kansas; and Nashua, New Hampshire."

Brian, trying to set a record for clichéd gestures, snapped his fingers. It was a wonder a light bulb didn't appear right over his head. "And Sunny Maugham lived in Upper Saddle River, here in Jersey," he said.

"Precisely."

"It's not that the geography lesson isn't fascinating," I broke in, "but I don't really see what that has to do with the amazing tale of the caramel hard candy and why it helps us with the guy who killed Sunny."

"Think, Rachel." Brian was playing a very Duffy game, forcing me to reach the conclusion myself instead of simply telling me what it all meant like he was supposed to. Maybe I'd based more of Duffy on him than I'd initially realized. "We know all the places this guy committed his crimes, and not one of them is Syracuse."

"Yeah, and none of them is Paris," I noted. "Wouldn't it be more fun if he left a clue from there?"

"So far, the perpetrator has left us with no clues to his identity or his location," Duffy said, undoubtedly perturbed at having to concede the role of professor to someone else for even a few seconds. "But now he has indicated that in addition to his recent trips to Kansas, Pennsylvania, New Hampshire, and here in New Jersey, he has been to Syracuse, New York. And since no crime fiction writers from Syracuse have been reported missing, we know that he did no 'business' in that area. That leaves open the possibility that we're seeking a man from Syracuse."

Maybe he was waiting for the applause he must have heard in his head after that display of brilliance, but it was not forthcoming. Not from me, anyway.

Brian stared at Duffy with something like awe in his eyes. "It's brilliant," he said. "You can pinpoint his location through a candy wrapper."

"No, I can't," Duffy said, shaking his head negatively. "I wish it were that easy. But the fact is, there are too few facts and too many possible scenarios to make that true. The killer could have been passing through Syracuse while traveling from New Hampshire to Philadelphia. He might have ordered the candy through K. Moore's website. Someone might have sent it to him as a gift. It might not even be his candy wrapper. And those are just the most obvious possibilities. There are hundreds more."

For a guy who wanted to be brilliant, he was coming across as simply annoying. "So we're back where we started," I said and sat down heavily on one of the barstools. Brian, looking dejected, eyed one of the remaining slices of pizza but did not grab for it. Brian is more disciplined than I am. But I did take a swig of my now-tepid beer. The English are crazy. Warm beer.

"Oh, I wouldn't go that far," Duffy said.

"Make up your mind," I muttered. Alcohol, trauma, and fatigue: a classic combination.

"This is a breakthrough," he reiterated. "I told you it was not a huge breakthrough, but it is a beginning. There is no reason to think that this won't lead us to something very valuable indeed. I think there's a very good chance that even if we do not find the killer himself through the revelation of the candy wrapper, we will find someone who can lead us in the proper direction. I think the road to this killer goes through Syracuse, New York."

Suddenly, fatigue was winning over alcohol and trauma in my weary head. I needed to go to bed, and I mean soon. "That's nice for you," I told Duffy. "Now let's make sure that I lock the front door thoroughly after you leave. I wouldn't want to screw up your investigation by being the next victim."

"I was not planning on leaving just yet," Duffy said.

"Yes, you were."

"No, I don't think so," he went on. "Plans need to be made." I'm sure Duffy was a fantastic student in school, but I guarantee you he failed Hint Taking.

"I'm tired, Duffy. If I don't sleep soon, I won't be held responsible for my actions."

He stopped and looked at me. He seemed to be processing what I'd said, like a computer that had been fed contradictory data. "Of course," he breathed out finally. "It has been a long day."

Brian came with me as I ushered Duffy toward the front door. "I think I'll take off too, Rache," he said. "Cathy's going to think we're a thing." He put a hand on my shoulder and squeezed, then slipped out the door and left Duffy standing there even as I was trying to politely shove him out of my house.

If I could rewind back to five days before, I'd have cancelled the signing at BooksBooksBooks, disconnected my phone, and booked a vacation in Tahiti complete with my laptop to do revisions. I'd never have met Duffy Madison in the flesh, would be blissfully unaware of the rash of mystery author killings, and would have nothing but fond memories of Sunny Maugham, whom I would miss but not have to think of with a pen sticking out of her neck for the rest of my life.

Yes, things had been better back in the good old days, like this past Monday.

"Thank you for coming, Duffy." I opened the door a touch wider. But not too much. You never know who's lurking in the bushes.

"It wasn't a favor," he said, Mr. Spock persona solidly intact. "I was here to deliver news of the investigation."

"Yeah, I got that. Well, good night, now." An inch or two wider. No more. If a killer wasn't out there, mosquitoes definitely were. And they sucked blood.

Duffy did, thankfully, turn and walk out the door. Just as I was closing it, he looked back at me. "What time shall I come by tomorrow?" he asked.

The world kept getting darker and lighter. I must have been blinking. "Tomorrow?"

"Certainly. We have work to do." Duffy seemed to be trying to see me through fog, although there was none. The fog was in one of our minds, but don't ask me which one.

"What do you mean, 'we'?" I said. "*You* have work to do. You have to go find out who kidnapped and killed Sunny Maugham and those other three women. *I* have to revise the next book with you in it and worry every time my e-mail program makes a noise that indicates I've gotten a message. We have our assigned tasks. You go do yours. You don't need me for that."

Duffy Madison regarded me with what I'm sure he thought of as a kind and professorial demeanor but actually came across as unctuous and condescending. "You have the knowledge I've needed on this case. I've told you that from the start."

"Yeah, and how's it working out so far?"

He winced just a little. Duffy hates failing, especially when he doesn't get to the kidnap victim in time. I'm guessing, because this was the first time in my experience that had ever happened in my world.

"We have not done well," he admitted. "But that is not a function of your expertise. It's my failure to act quickly enough and the perpetrator's superior ability in concealing his identity and location. If we're going to find and stop this madman, it will be because you can anticipate your own acts and we can anticipate ways in which he might therefore try to strike."

There was something about the word "strike" that sent a shiver up my spine, and in this weather, any shiver was a significant achievement. "I don't know that I can help anymore," I said. "What is it you expect me to do with you tomorrow?"

"We need to research the modus operandi of this perpetrator. That can be done through the prosecutor's office and the police. But if we assume that you are his next target—and I'm afraid that is an assumption we must make at this point—I will need a complete understanding of your every movement, your thoughts, your intentions. With that knowledge, it might be possible to stay a step ahead this time. You present a unique opportunity. Before this, we had never known who the killer was targeting before she was abducted."

"Do you ever hear yourself talk?"

Duffy seemed puzzled. "All the time," he said.

"You don't try very hard to make the person you're talking to feel better," I pointed out.

"I deal in facts, and they help me to do what I do," he countered. "With facts, I can help keep you safe."

I closed my eyes in weariness and frustration. "Fine. What is it you want to do tomorrow?"

"Follow you through the day. Observe. Take notes. I want to be sure of everything you do and every person with whom you come into contact. There is not one aspect of your routine that should be hidden from me. Do you understand?"

"I'm really afraid that I do."

He went on as if I had not spoken. This was not unusual with Duffy. "Also, we'll be putting together a portrait of the man who has committed these crimes. I need to know where in Syracuse to start, and we'll begin with the candy company. But we also need to figure out how old he is, when he went to school, and the people who might have known him. It is impossibly difficult to put together a profile of a man who has no name and doesn't seem to have a past."

I looked at him. There was no irony in his voice. "Tell me about it," I said.

At least he had the good grace to smile.

Chapter 19

Duffy Madison arrived at my house the next morning at seven AM. It was a Saturday. He didn't even bring coffee. That's all I'm going to say about that.

"If I had brought you something, it would have interfered with your routine, and that is what I'm here to observe," he said, defending himself. "You should go through your day interacting with me as little as possible." I looked at him, sifting through the thousands of possible retorts to that suggestion. "I mean, pretend I'm not here."

"With a great deal of pleasure," I said.

He studied me with an intensity that was at once flattering and disconcerting. "I am here to observe your routine," he said, apparently under the impression that I hadn't understood that the six other times he'd said it. "What do you usually do at this time of day?"

I went into the kitchen to start coffee. If Duffy wasn't going to provide, I'd have to do so myself. Never rely on a man when you can rely on yourself, my father always told me.

I made a mental note to call Dad the minute Duffy left so I could complain to him about Duffy.

"It's the weekend, Duffy," I said, stifling a yawn. "At this time of the day, I'm generally sound asleep. But I had to get up because some lunatic was ringing my doorbell at seven on a Saturday."

Again the puzzled look. "That was me," Duffy said.

"Bingo." There was one coffee filter left. I wrote that down on a pad I keep next to the fridge that becomes a shopping list eventually. This was the fourth page I'd started, because I always seem to need a piece of scratch paper in a hurry and I never bother to protect the sheet with my list on it. Which was probably how I got this low on coffee filters to begin with. "So now you can observe me getting coffee and reading the newspaper."

He did nothing else for the next forty-five minutes. I drank coffee and read the newspaper. Duffy sat by and said nothing so unobtrusively that I almost had a heart attack twice when I looked up and saw him there, having forgotten he was currently occupying my house.

The *New York Times* sends some of its Sunday sections on Saturday, which technically makes them Saturday sections, but I'll take what I can get. One thing they always include in the Saturday bag is the Sunday magazine, and that's fabulous because it means I get an extra day to figure out the Sunday crossword puzzle. I took the magazine out of the blue plastic bag (you'd think the *Times* would be more into biodegradable materials) and walked from the kitchen to my office. Once there, I opened the lid on my printer/copier/fax machine and carefully folded the magazine back to reveal the puzzle. I pushed a few buttons on the copier, and it began making me facsimile crossword puzzles. I checked to make sure the copy that came out was properly folded to have both edges of the puzzle and the clues visible; you have to be careful with the Sunday puzzle.

I was taking the second copy out of the tray when I heard that voice behind me again. "Why are you making two copies?"

Third heart attack of the day; I spun. "Jesus, Duffy, don't do that!" I almost crushed the paper I had in my hand and pushed the button for a new copy.

"Do what?" He seemed genuinely confused.

"Don't sneak up on me like that. You scared me half to death."

Duffy's eyes were slits. "You knew I was here," he said, the truth so obvious it was practically painful to him. "Why do you make more than one copy of the crossword puzzle? Why don't you just write the answers in the magazine?"

"I always make two copies of the Sunday puzzle," I said, sitting down in my desk chair and choosing my pen very carefully. There's no writing surface on my desk, so I keep a clipboard nearby for this very purpose, and I clipped the first copy onto it for easy solving. Or at least easy writing of the letters. Solving was not the clipboard's responsibility. "That way if I make too many mistakes, I have another copy so I can start writing again."

"Why not just write in pencil on the original page?" he asked. It was like having an inquisitive six-year-old in the house; they want to know *everything*.

"Because I like pen better than pencil, and if I make too many mistakes on the magazine page, not only will I not be able to solve the puzzle, I won't be able to read the article on the other side of the page. Can I ask how your knowing this is going to track down our pal in Syracuse?"

"I don't know yet," Duffy answered. Well, that settled it, right?

"I'm going to do the puzzle now. Feel free to go back to not talking." Without awaiting a response, I started in on the Sunday. There's always a gimmick (real solvers call it a "theme") on Sundays, and this one was no exception. But I hadn't yet been able to figure out what the longer clues—the ones associated with the gimmick—had in common yet. I grazed over the clues looking for real gimmes and found a few I filled in quickly. It gives one a sense of confidence.

Once the easiest clues were out of the way (which, since the solver was me, didn't take long), I started in on what I could glean from the letters I'd already solved. Finding the proper crosses is what saves the bacon of many a solver every day. One clue asked for an "AL MVP in '76." I knew enough to figure that was a baseball clue, but I know nothing about baseball. So I swiveled in my chair and turned to every writer's favorite source of quick information. I Googled "MVP 1976" and was rewarded with two names. Unfortunately, the two names (Thurman Munson and Joe Morgan) both corresponded with the crosses I had, the *M* and the *N*. I looked at Duffy.

"You know anything about baseball?" I asked.

"A little," he responded. "Why do you ask?"

"I need to know if Thurman Munson or Joe Morgan was in the American League." I turned back to Google and quickly got the answer: Munson.

"That was for the crossword?" Duffy asked suddenly.

I swiveled to face him. "Yeah."

His eyes showed shock. "That's *cheating*," he gasped.

I turned back toward the puzzle. "Go back to being an observer," I said.

* * *

This went on through my completion—yes, with some help—of the puzzle. Now, I don't know where you come down on this, but I believe that the puzzle is supposed to be an avenue for information as well as entertainment. If I discover new facts through a tough clue that requires some online assistance, I believe that is in the puzzle constructor's mission, not outside of it.

That's my story, and I'm sticking to it.

Then Duffy followed me through my morning routine, which unbeknownst to him, did not usually include a forty-minute shower during which he was instructed to stay as far from that part of the house as possible and to take me at my word that I was indeed becoming cleaner. I also cut out my exercise regimen, which mostly consists of me doing some *Wii Fit* yoga and then power walking around the house, because there was no way I was doing any of that stuff in front of Duffy. So I didn't tell him about it.

He *did* watch while I revised some of the latest Duffy novel, which was disconcerting in itself. There had been enough times I'd felt the character standing over my shoulder, but now it was a literal reality, and that was more than I could take.

"Isn't there some investigating you should be doing?" I asked.

"I am observing you."

"Yeah I get that, Artoo, but the fact is that you're a distraction and you're making it hard for me to do my work." I stood and started throwing a stress ball I had on my desk into the air and catching it. It doesn't relieve any stress, but it does give me something to think about that isn't tied to the motivations of killers and the clues that might be dropped in to distract the reader's suspicions. Writing a mystery is intricate enough without an existential reminder that your character is a living being right in the room.

Duffy looked uncomfortable. "What am I doing that obstructs your working day?" he asked. "I need to see it as it would be if I weren't here."

"The only way that works is if you're not here. Don't you get it—I'm writing Duffy Madison with Duffy Madison on my couch! That's just too bizarre, even for me!" The stress ball hit one of the spinning arms on the ceiling fan, sending it shooting across the room and toward a pile of books I wasn't reading.

Duffy watched that and appeared to be debating whether to call in a psychological evaluation expert, a criminal profiler, or a SWAT team. "I can't help being myself," he said quietly. "How can I observe your routine if I'm not here?"

I thought of suggesting that he rent the house across the street and buy a telescope or some surveillance equipment, but I was afraid he'd take me seriously. "I don't know how you can," I said gently. "I really don't think this is going to work. I can't behave like myself with you here."

"Why not?" Maybe he really *was* just four years old. He asked questions like some of my friends' kids.

"Because I can't decide if you're really my fictional creation or if you just think you are. It's like I'm trying to figure out which one of us is the crazy person." There. It was out. I didn't feel any better, but at least it wasn't hanging over me.

"Neither of us is crazy," Duffy said. He stood up to pace as he talked. I'd written that for him. "It isn't unreasonable for you to be skeptical of me; to you, my existence doesn't make sense. And while my position on my origin is certainly unorthodox, from my point of view, having eliminated all impossible options, my conclusion is the only logical one. We have two different perspectives and therefore different ideas of what can be possible."

That really didn't help much, but it made me feel better. I must have smiled at him, because he stopped pacing and his posture relaxed. "So what you're saying is that we don't have to agree on this; we should just both continue to act on our own view of the situation."

He smiled now. "That's it," he said.

"Do you want to be some help to me?" I asked. The thought had just popped into my head, and suddenly it made all the sense in the world.

"Of course, if I can observe you while I do so."

I was already back at my desk. "Do you have a laptop with you?" I asked.

"No, but I have a tablet." He produced one from a messenger bag he'd stashed on the sofa.

"Good. I'm going to e-mail a file to you. I want you to read it and point out any inaccuracies you might find."

I could hear some curiosity in his voice, but I didn't turn to face him. "What file is that?" he asked.

"The next Duffy Madison book. Would you read it and tell me if you find any areas that aren't consistent with your character?"

Having sent the file, I swiveled to look at him. Duffy was all intent, already working on the tablet screen.

"I will be happy to," he said.

* * *

We proceeded that way for the next three hours. I kept revising based on my own notes and thoughts—some of my original ideas had been placeholders because I simply couldn't think of anything better at the time—and Duffy would occasionally draw my attention to a speech he felt didn't sound like him, but never an action he thought he wouldn't take.

"You really have captured me quite accurately for the most part," he said at one point.

"That's because I made you up," I reminded him.

He smiled a little. "That's what you say."

"Did you see anything that doesn't work?" I asked. Hearing from the character himself is not something a lot of (sane) novelists get to do; there was value here.

"There is one thing," he began. And suddenly I was hit with conflicting emotions: *Uh-oh. He found me out for the fraud I am*, followed quickly by, *Who the heck is this guy to tell me I don't know how to write him?*

Neither was expressed because Duffy's cell phone rang (he was using the theme from *Mission: Impossible* as a ringtone, which I thought was a little unsettling), and he pulled it out to look. "It's Ben Preston," he said.

Duffy clicked the button on the phone. "Yes, Ben. Actually, I'm with her right now. No, at hers. Because I was observing her daily routine to—yes. All right. We'll be there." He disconnected the call and looked at me. "We need to leave now," he said.

I didn't like the sound of that. "Is the killer in the vicinity?" I asked. I have no idea why I thought they could know that and still not pick the guy up.

"No. The FBI."

Chapter 20

Special Agent Eunice Rafferty could have been Clarice Starling's older sister, I'd decided since the last time I'd seen her. No doubt having found her calling while watching Jodie Foster track down Buffalo Bill, Rafferty was dressed impeccably and was actually trying to either hide or affect a backwoods accent. In either case, she was not being entirely successful.

She was a tall, strong woman (which I'm told is not Ms. Foster's build, but I don't really know), constructed to be a cop, based on the impression she gave that if the Empire State Building needed to be moved two feet to the left, she could be counted on to do the lifting. It was a marvel she had taken time out from the gym to come solve this crime.

"This is a serial killer working in multiple states," she was saying in the conference room at the Bergen County Prosecutor's Office, the same one in which Duffy and I had met. Her voice was husky, not masculine but close enough. "It's clearly the work of one man but in, so far, four states. I've watched you boys long enough. Multiple states makes it my jurisdiction."

"No one is arguing that the bureau shouldn't be involved in the investigation," Ben Preston answered. Ben, in a T-shirt with a Yankees logo on it and a pair of khaki shorts, had obviously been doing something other than work when Rafferty called to inform him that she wanted in on the investigation of Sunny Maugham's death. "We welcome the help on the case we're working. What I'm saying is—"

"We're not offering *help*," Rafferty cut him off. "I'm telling you that from this moment forward, this investigation is under the bureau's control. We may ask you to assist, but we are not ceding responsibility to you or any other law enforcement agency, including the New Jersey State Police." I hoped there were no troopers nearby to hear her say that. They don't take kindly to . . . anything.

"Fine," Ben said with an edge. "We relinquish control to you. But I'd like to remind you that the killer has already threatened Ms. Goldman here in two separate e-mails and might very well be planning to make her his next project. We intend to take all the steps necessary to prevent that from happening." That's not really what you want to hear from a guy you're thinking of dating, but these circumstances were far from the norm.

"Acknowledged and taken under advisement," Rafferty said. No, really.

"Hold on," I said. "Can I ask a question?"

"That is a question," I heard Duffy mumble behind me.

Luckily, Rafferty hadn't heard Duffy, or she might have shot him or something. "Go ahead."

"Will Ben and Duffy continue with me?" I asked. "I've gotten to know these two gentlemen, and I know they've been very quietly keeping an eye on me. Should I expect that to continue?" I thought that was a pretty respectful way to ask about my own interest—staying alive—in the midst of this attempted power grab among law enforcement agencies. It wasn't that I was completely attached to Duffy and Ben—maybe one more than the other—but I did want some assurance that *somebody* would be looking to see if a madman carrying a deadly thesaurus or an equally witty weapon was climbing in my bedroom window.

"We don't believe that you will be a target, Ms. Goldman," Rafferty said. "In fact, I'm not sure why you're here."

Wait. What? "So you're not going to offer protection?" Ben asked, sounding aghast.

"We don't see the need," Rafferty said. "The killer has never struck in the same state twice, and certainly not consecutively."

"But there have been those two e-mails," Ben protested. "The guy practically announced that Rachel would be his next victim."

"Boasting," Rafferty said, dismissing the notion. "A terror tactic to make himself sound more potent than he really is. We've had a profiler working on this guy. His MO is to move somewhere else next. We'll gather as much data as we can on the murder of Julia Bledsoe, and then we can better assess where this killer will most likely strike next."

"I really feel like I need the protection," I said. My voice sounded a lot smaller and weaker than I'd intended. It was sort of in the Minnie Mouse area when I'd been trying for Wonder Woman.

"I'm sure Mr. Preston and Mr. Madison can recommend some local firms that will be able to provide you with security," Rafferty said. "Now, at the risk of sounding impolite, Ms. Goldman, I'd prefer you leave the room so that we can discuss the strategy we're going to implement to catch this criminal."

I looked at her, and the anger boiled up. "At the risk of sounding impolite? That *is* impolite! How else could it sound?"

"I'm sorry you feel that way. Now, please." She gestured toward the door. "Just one thing," she added, and I stopped in my tracks. Was she reconsidering?

"Yes?"

"I believe I owe you an apology," Rafferty said.

I thought she owed me about four, but one was a start. "For what?" I asked.

"For not knowing your name. I read your book, *Olly Olly Oxen Free*. You're really good."

Maybe she wasn't so bad after all. "Well, thank you," I said. "Can I stay now?"

"No. But your character. I mean, you called him Duffy Madison."

"Yeah, about that—"

"Did you base it on him?" Again, a nod toward whatever Duffy was.

"No. He based himself on what I wrote."

Rafferty walked over to me, her clipboard in hand, briskly and surely. She thrust the clipboard toward me. "May I have an autograph?"

I probably even signed it; I don't actually remember.

Exiled to Ben's office, I felt more like I had during Take Your Daughter to Work Day when Dad used to shepherd me around his office collecting smiles and then park me in a safe place so he could actually get something done. He'd provide me with crayons and coloring books, and that was about it. I'm not sure it's what Gloria Steinem had in mind.

This time, I had a few more things at my disposal. The first thing I did was check voice mail, and there was a message from Adam Resnick. An author's agent always jumps to the head of the priority list, but when there's a possible movie deal in the works, he gets above the head of the priority list.

"It sounds like it's happening," he said, delight practically oozing through the cell tower and through the earpiece of my phone. "Glenn Waterman wants to meet with you. He's flying in from LA tomorrow for meetings in the city Monday and he asked about your availability."

Assuming I wasn't busy being abducted, I would have a decent amount of time on my hands. "I have revisions, and I'm a little behind," I said, "but I'll make time whenever I have to. What do you think is going to happen?"

"I think I'm going to call him back and tell him we're available," Adam gushed. "Any times to definitely avoid?"

I considered. Given the impending danger of kidnapping and murder, it seemed best to stay home when the sun was down. "Just not at night," I said. "I'll be in the rest of the time. Call me and let me know when I have to be in the city."

We commiserated about our ridiculous excitement level for a while, I told Adam I'd be sending him a revised manuscript soon, and we hung up. I felt it best to leave out the part where I was letting the character in my novel read and offer tips before I'd send the book out. The first rule of negotiating a movie contract: never let your agent think you need to be sent to somewhere you can't do harm to yourself or others.

I was about to call Dad when Duffy walked into the office. I looked for Ben behind him, but Duffy was alone. "I can drive you home now," he said. "If you'd like to leave."

Feeling like Daddy had once again come to take me away from this boring day, I gathered up my stuff (basically my phone and my bag) and followed Duffy out of the room.

"Where's Ben?" I asked. "Doesn't he want his office back?"

"He's still being briefed by the FBI agent," Duffy said with a tiny hint of contempt in his voice. "I have been deemed unnecessary."

We had reached the elevator before I understood what that meant. "You mean they're not including you in the investigation?" I asked.

Duffy seemed very interested in the floor. "That's correct. I am no longer consulting on this case."

* * *

He seemed so downtrodden about his demotion, or expulsion, or whatever that I tried to think of ways to distract him as he drove me home. "You started to say something you thought I needed to change."

Duffy's eyes stayed fixed on the road, and for a moment, he didn't seem to hear me. "Change?"

"In the manuscript. You said there was one thing that didn't work. It would be a great help to me if you could remember what that was so I can fix it." Okay, so I was buttering him up a little. The next time someone you created feels down and you try to raise his spirits, let's see what *you* do.

"Ah. Yes. It was the ending."

I waited. Nothing. "The ending?"

"Yes. Where I, that is, *he* finds the young woman being buried alive based on the pattern of the mower in the field."

"Yes, I've read the ending; I know what happens. What's wrong with it?" Hey, there are all sorts of ways to make a person feel better. I was experimenting with one that preserved my integrity as a writer, and maybe a little bit of my ego.

"It doesn't make sense, but that's not the problem." He was speeding a little, and that was uncharacteristic for this version of Duffy; he was on edge.

"Yes, it's a problem. What do you mean, it doesn't make sense?"

"The kidnapper buried his victim in an open field, where a groundskeeper mows regularly? And the only mark two days after digging a grave is that the grass is mowed differently? Otherwise it's perfect? None of that is consistent with landscaping practice."

Dammit! He was right. So I naturally invited another blow to my now-fragile writer's sensibility. "What was the character thing? What did the character do that you wouldn't do?"

"He got involved in digging the woman out himself. I would know that there was a possibility I could do more harm than good, that I might cause pressure on the wooden box in which she was being held and actually crush her under my weight and that of the uniformed officers."

"So how would you have gotten her out?" Now he had me talking like he was real.

"Well, I wouldn't have let it get to that moment to begin with. You have Duffy overlook the fact that the kidnapper is the young woman's professor at college because he is a friend of the detective 'Duffy' works with. I wouldn't let emotion get in the way."

I looked at him; he was without expression but gripping the wheel tighter than I'd seen him before. "You've told me what you wouldn't do. What *would* you do in that situation?"

There was a pause while he thought. "Assuming there was a way that the disturbance in the turf could be made relatively invisible, which is unlikely, I would try to determine where I would bury a coffin if I didn't want it to be found. I would consider the area where I could dig without being seen and the area with the lowest number of rocks and roots, so away from trees if possible. And once I determined where the most likely spot would be, I would dig opposite that site."

"Opposite?" Now I was the straight man.

"A criminal that clever would never use the most likely spot," Duffy said, as if it were obvious.

"So the way to catch the guy is to think of what he should do and then do the opposite of that?" How could that be right? The man was blowing my entire third act out of the water and appeared to be speaking in some alternate version of English in order to do it.

Duffy's smile was sad, like he'd realized that the pupil he was teaching wasn't all that bright. "Not exactly," he said. "But you're the creative one, aren't you? You'll figure it out."

Thanks a heap, Duffy.

Best to get off the subject and see about keeping myself alive. That really was the priority, I decided. "Duffy, what can I do to best protect myself?"

His eyelids fluttered a tiny bit; I was watching. It's something I've given him to indicate anxiety without being obvious about it. That didn't make me feel better, either. "If Special Agent Rafferty is correct, you are in no special danger," he said in as unconvincing a voice as I'd heard him use. "You should simply make sure your doors are locked at all times and be wary of any strangers who approach you."

"Like you approached me?" I asked.

No trace of irony, again. "Under the present circumstances, yes, if we were meeting for the first time, you would be well advised to be careful about me. Stay in public areas with anyone you meet and never follow another person into a dark area like an alley or a hallway without anyone else present."

"You don't think Agent Rafferty is right, do you?" I asked.

"*Special* Agent Rafferty," he corrected.

This time *my* eyelids fluttered, because that was an irritating response. You give characters some of your own traits because in the heat of a moment you're creating, you have no one else upon whom to model a reaction. "Fine. *Special* Agent Rafferty. You think she's going in the wrong direction, and I really am next on the killer's list. You think that, don't you?"

"Yes," Duffy Madison said. "I do."

That took me a moment to digest. Not that I hadn't been operating under the assumption that I was in a lot of trouble for a few days now. Indeed, I hadn't bought the load of sanctimonious crap Rafferty had been selling in the meeting, either. And I hadn't gained a whole lot of confidence in her when she'd fired Duffy from the case. But hearing Duffy say it was a punch to the gut. I took in some air and let it out slowly.

"What . . ." My voice was raspy; I cleared my throat. I made a mental note to use that for a character struck with bad news. "What should I do?" I asked.

"Perhaps you should ask the special agent." He'd been stung by his dismissal.

"I don't trust the special agent," I said. "I trust you."

A tiny smile, so small as to be almost imperceptible, flickered across Duffy's lips. "You should do all the things I just said you should do, and you should probably hire some private security."

"I don't have that kind of money," I told him.

"An author with a successful book series?" Duffy sounded honestly surprised.

"Makes just about enough to not have to take a day job to pay the rent," I said. I don't know why people think midlist authors like me are paid like steroid-infused outfielders.

"Even on a short-term basis, you can't afford a bodyguard?" he asked.

"Would one guy make that much difference?" I countered. "I don't have any experience in this kind of thing, except when I can manipulate the situation to be exactly what I need."

Duffy thought, never turning his head. But he did stretch his neck a bit. "In all candor, one bodyguard against the criminal we seek would probably not be very helpful, but he would be better than nothing."

"What about you?" I suggested. "You seem to be between gigs at the moment."

"Perhaps I am more valuable to you doing what I know how to do," he said. "I'm not especially useful in physical situations; I do better with mental exercises than push-ups."

That had a little more information in it than a casual listener might have caught. "You don't plan to stop investigating, do you?" I asked.

Duffy looked very determined. "No," he said.

Chapter 21

Adam Resnick, so excited he was working weekends, had called me Sunday afternoon with the news that Glenn Waterman had arrived from Los Angeles and taken up residence at a trendy downtown hotel in Manhattan. His office would call me to confirm a time and place for our Monday meeting, Adam had said, and then I should call him because Adam would not be at the meeting. Normally the call would go through the agent, but Adam said Waterman's assistant (nobody has a secretary anymore) insisted I be contacted directly. I balanced being professionally excited with being personally terrified. Excited won, but it was a photo finish.

Ben Preston had shown up at my door two hours after Duffy had left. Before he left, Duffy had personally checked every room himself (including the basement because Duffy was not as big a coward as me) and declared the place kidnapper free. Ben said the meeting with Rafferty had gone on another hour and a half, and in all that time, Rafferty had said a grand total of nothing that he considered useful, except for reiterating at least seven more times that she was in charge and he wasn't. Perhaps "useful" was the wrong word.

I'd offered to order in food—the last thing I wanted to do was cook—but Ben said he wanted to do some more work, looking into the convenience store video with a tech expert who might be able to clarify the image better. At the door, I think he was debating whether to try to kiss me, then decided it was better to appear professional to reassure me and left.

Wrong choice, Ben.

Brian Coltrane had called to tell me he wouldn't be calling for a couple of days because Cathy was annoyed with him for spending too much time with me. I felt that mentioning the increased probability of my being murdered would be considered passive-aggressive and told him I'd be here when he called again. Then I wondered if I would.

Finally, Paula had called, a real rarity for a Sunday, to tell me she believed she was close to discovering whether Duffy had used another name before four years ago.

"Where are you getting that from?" I asked.

"No fair telling," she answered, which made me wonder why she'd called to begin with.

Duffy Madison, bless him, did not call. He was the only one who either realized that I needed some alone time or was so absorbed in his own thoughts that inquiring about my status just never occurred to him. I was betting on the latter.

So after all the phone calls were done and the e-mails (nope, not one with any serious threats attached, except a message that encouraged me to "enhance" my "manhood") were read, I was ready to do some serious revisions. But first, perhaps a break from the tension. *You've Got Mail* on the Blu-ray player. That sounded about right: a *fun* movie about e-mail.

I brewed myself an iced coffee with a splash of chocolate syrup (Ben Preston had ruined me—he'd be responsible for the weight I gained now), positioned myself optimally on the sofa, slipped the disc into the proper electronic device, and armed myself with a remote control that had more buttons than the navigation console on the *QEII*.

I was just about to hit the play button when the doorbell rang.

After scraping myself off the ceiling, I threw on a pair of shorts and a fairly respectable top (had I forgotten to mention being in pajamas until the early afternoon?) and crept with great trepidation toward my front door. I had a strong aversion to looking through the peephole; I had somehow now convinced myself that just seeing the person I dreaded could mean my immediate demise. Nobody said I was rational; I'm a writer.

Pulling a move from the TSTL playbook, I attached the chain on the front door and took a deep breath before opening it enough to see who was waiting to do me in on my front step.

"What are you doing opening the door without checking first?" my father demanded. "I could have been a homicidal maniac."

That was what I supposed to do after I got home last night: call Dad.

I let him in, noting with some horror the size of the rolling suitcase he'd brought with him. "You don't really need to stay, Dad," I attempted. "You can see I'm all right."

"Yeah, but then you won't call again, and I'll be forced to drive down here again. Nope, I'm staying." He rolled the Chrysler Building into my living room and looked around. "You've redecorated."

"Did it ever occur to you that *you* could have called *me*?" I asked. "I would have told you I was okay and spared you the drive. And the packing. That must have been a lot of packing."

"I threw a few things in a bag. Is my room all set for me?"

Groaning inwardly, I set Dad up in my guest room and forgot about visiting with Tom Hanks and Meg Ryan. Dad did a perimeter search of his own, the third in a day, and found the same lack of intruders that Duffy and I had both discovered.

We sat on the sofa in the living room, and Dad, looking more concerned than when I'd come back from my prom at eight the next morning, asked me for an update, which I gave him. "So who are the suspects so far?" he asked.

"There aren't any I know about," I told him. "But the FBI generally doesn't call me with every new development."

"Well, you can't wait for the feds," he said, shaking his head at the very idea. "Who would you look at for this crime? You write crime novels."

"I write *fiction*, Dad. The criminals all do what I want them to so they can get caught."

But the look on his face would broach no such dodge. "Okay," I said. "If I were thinking about it—"

"I can't imagine how you'd be thinking about anything else."

I let that go. "The attacks have all been about writing," I went on. "One woman was hit with a typewriter, one electrocuted with her laptop, one suffocated with rejection letters, and Sunny was stabbed with a fountain pen."

"So where does that take you?" Dad was leading me in a direction that he had no doubt already traveled.

"It's business, not pleasure. There isn't going to be an angry ex-husband anywhere because these four women were unrelated. There isn't going to be a monetary motive because not all of them were successful, and even Sunny wasn't in Stephen King territory. It's something about crime writing specifically."

Dad looked like a proud teacher. In fact, he looked like Duffy when I had made a similar breakthrough. It was really starting to annoy me. "Okay, that seems right. So who would be mad enough at four crime novelists to kidnap and kill all of them?"

I closed my eyes to think and to get the idea of Dad and Duffy melding into one person out of my head. "It could be a lot of people. An aspiring author who thinks the writers were blocking his way to fame and fortune. A rival author who thinks they stole some ideas. They didn't have the same editors, publishers, or agents. One of them didn't have an agent at all. So that's a dead end. A book critic who really hates crime novels. A man who's tired of women writing stories about people like him getting caught after making stupid mistakes. It could be anybody."

"Well, it's a good thing I packed for more than one night," my father said when I was done.

That didn't sound good. "Why?"

"Because it sounds like we have a lot of people to talk to."

* * *

Paula volunteered (after I asked her) to come in on a Sunday. It was sweet of her. She reminded me, too, that working on the weekend was double time. That was less sweet but deserved.

She began by finding out who had represented each of the authors who had been taken and killed, and for the ones who had publishing contracts, who had acquired and edited their work. That would have taken me three hours but took Paula seven minutes. It would have been quicker, but she had never met my father before and spent two minutes getting acquainted.

Missy Hardaway, the author of the cozy mysteries, had represented herself in negotiations with Ballmer Press, the Baltimore-based publishing company, which was a three-person operation whose owner, Harrison Belechik, was also the editor, Paula told me.

J. B. Randolph had been published by Criterion, one of the medium-sized houses in New York City. Her editor was Madlyn Beckwirth, the publisher's specialist in crime fiction, and her agent was Lance Galbraith, one of nine agents working out of an office in SoHo, Artistic Reps Ltd.

Marion Benedict, who had lived in Farmingdale but was never published, had no agent nor an editor, which made that line of investigation seem stupid on reflection. On further reflection, however, came the idea that we really didn't have anything else to try. That fueled our thoughts, or mine, anyway. I can't tell you what Dad or Paula was thinking.

Sunny Maugham, I already knew, was represented by Mandy Westen, and her editor was Carole Pembroke at Arlington House. The police and the feds already had that information, but I wasn't going to let that stop me. I was pretty sure it was still legal to call an agent on the phone.

Paula had also furnished me with contact information for the agents and editors, which wouldn't be useful until the next day. Finding someone in the publishing business on a Sunday is roughly as likely as being hit by lightning while picking up your Powerball winnings. At your wedding.

"What else can we do?" Dad asked when all the data had been printed out in triplicate and distributed to each of us (Paula is nothing if not efficient). "If we can't call people today, what's left?"

"We need to Google all the writers who were targeted and see if there were people leaving nasty comments about them," I suggested. Okay, so I've Googled myself once or twice; it's not a crime. Some late nights you feel like seeing how your books are being received. Some late nights it's better not to look. The Internet is vicious; it's like high school, only everybody in the world is in your graduating class.

"I can handle that," Paula said, as I knew she would. "If there's a recurring pattern in the way they're heckled, I'll find it. That might lead us somewhere. I'll check reviews, too."

I sat at my desk, which makes me feel like Captain Kirk on the bridge of the *Enterprise*. You can swivel around and pretend you're in charge of things. Paula was my Lieutenant

Uhura, communicating via computer with the rest of the universe. Dad was my Bones, always questioning the morality of what was going on and never not on my side. And my Spock . . .

There was no choice; I had to call Duffy.

He answered on the first ring. "Is everything all right?" That was, coming from Duffy, touching. Other people would have tried "hello," but given his personality, I would have expected a dissertation on the use of the cellular phone to convey information in various digital forms and . . . I fell asleep in the middle of my own sentence.

"I'm fine," I told him. "Nothing's happened. But my father, Paula, and I are trying to strategize, and I thought it would be helpful if you could drop by and contribute. Are you in the middle of something?"

"I am attempting to triangulate the killer's location through travel patterns, Internet connections, and behavioral analysis," he said. A lot of people, I'm told, watch baseball games on Sunday afternoons in the summer.

"So not much, then," I suggested.

His voice had a low chuckle buried in it. "I suppose not. Would you like me to drop by?"

"I thought I said that. Do you like sub sandwiches?"

He hesitated. In the books, Duffy is a vegetarian, but without reading them, this Duffy couldn't know that. "Certainly," he said. *Gotcha!*

"Good. Can you stop at No SUBstitutes on Mayhall Avenue on your way?" Duffy couldn't find a way to say no, so I got Paula's and Dad's orders, gave him mine, and thanked him for the help. Duffy sounded a little sheepish but agreed to get to my house as soon as possible.

"He's getting subs?" Paula asked with a knowing tone.

"Yup. He doesn't know Duffy is a vegetarian." I grinned at her.

"Is he a vegan?" Dad asked.

"No."

"They make cheese subs," Dad contributed. That hardly seemed called for.

While we were waiting for Duffy, Dad agreed to go out for some soda and macaroni salad, because you can't have subs without macaroni salad. Duffy in the books wouldn't drink beer or wine, and I couldn't be a hundred percent sure this one didn't know that, so the diet soda, which he does drink obsessively in my novels, was for him.

Paula began to attack her laptop keyboard in her office, and that left me alone with my thoughts for the first time today. Which, although it was what I had wanted earlier, turned out to be not that good a thing.

It was fun to play detective with Duffy and my entourage. I loved rallying Paula, and having Dad around was always a kick—for a while. I knew that within three days, I'd want him back in his barn doing whatever it was he does in his barn. And Duffy, while certifiably insane, was at least interesting to observe in order to get ideas for my next book.

But sitting here by myself, the possibility—if not probability—that there wouldn't be a next book, mostly because I'd be dead, was sinking in. This guy had killed four other crime fiction writers for no clear reason. And he had made it clear that I was the very author he'd choose to dispose of next. So far, nobody had come close to finding him, not even the always stalwart and resourceful Duffy Madison, who only one female FBI agent seemed to think was even a little fallible. I'd have to ask him about that the next time I saw him.

Or would I? Did I want to know of Duffy's failures, if he was committing himself to keeping me breathing? Was it better to be blissful (if this was bliss, I'd hate to see despair) in my ignorance? The only reason I could think of to assume Duffy himself wasn't the mad killer was that he'd had plenty of opportunity to abduct or murder me in the times we'd spent alone and so far had not availed himself.

That wasn't very much. Who the hell had I just asked to buy me a sub sandwich?

I got up and walked to Paula's doorway, if for no better reason than to not be left alone with my thoughts. She looked up at me and took off the glasses she uses for the computer screen. "What's up?" she asked. The reporter's notebook she uses to take down my more profound thoughts was close to her right hand, I noted. Paula is the most efficient woman on the planet.

"You said you might have a breakthrough on Duffy," I reminded her. "I need to know what it is."

She grinned a cat-post-canary grin and shook her head. "I told you," she said. "Not until I'm sure."

But I wasn't playing that game now; I needed reassurance that I wasn't actually inviting a homicidal maniac into my house just because his route went past No SUBstitutes. "I can't wait that long; I need something to hang onto. Please. Who is this guy, best guess?"

Paula studied my face, and her smile faded. "I'm sorry," she said. "This is really getting to you, isn't it?"

I decided, consciously, to look away. "Having my life threatened puts a general crimp in my week," I said. It came out way more woe-is-me and way less snarky than I had intended. The sniffle right afterward probably didn't help. "What can you tell me about Duffy?"

Paula nodded, mostly to herself, I think. "There's a guy from Poughkeepsie, New York, named Damien Mosley," she said. "Average kid, nobody ever really noticed him. Went to the high school, got mostly Bs and didn't really make much of a splash. Father was an IBM executive, a minor one, in the data storage department. Mother was a homemaker, joined the PTA, that was about it. They kept to themselves and they never did anything to get people talking about them."

So far, I didn't see a reason to get excited. "So the guy has the same initials as Duffy Madison. So what?" I didn't exactly doubt Paula, but I honestly couldn't follow her reasoning.

"So Damien went to Oberlin College. Just like Duffy. And after that, beyond a driver's license and some credit scores, which are just about perfect, there isn't much in the public record about him. Until . . ."

I waited what seemed like an eternity but was probably just three seconds. "You're being coy. I'm having a nervous breakdown and you're being coy, Paula! Tell me what's going on!" I leaned hard on the edge of her desk. "I need to know if this guy is a serial killer or a real-life incarnation of my imaginary friend!"

Paula punched a few keys on her keyboard and frowned. "Well, I can't tell you that definitively," she said. "Like I told you, I need more time. But there's something very strange about Damien Mosley."

She was going to make me say it. "What?"

"He vanished just about four years ago. Right around the time—"

I closed my eyes. "Right around the time I started writing books and Duffy Madison made his first appearance at the Bergen County Prosecutor's Office."

Chapter 22

Dad got back before Duffy could fill our sandwich order and make his appearance, so Paula and I brought him up to speed on her research about the guy who had presented himself as my character. Dad listened with full attention and did not ask questions as the story was being told to him. He is a careful thinker, which was why his business career was successful, and he prides himself in taking a sober, reasoned approach to every problem that comes his way. He steepled his fingers and held them up to his lips as he listened, blinking very rarely, looking more serene with each passing second.

"The guy's a nut," he finally pronounced.

I waited, but there was no more from my father. "That's it?" I asked. "He's a nut? That's the best you can do?"

Dad had the nerve to look surprised. "What did you want me to say, Rachel? A guy shows up on your door and claims to be the character you've been writing for four years, come to life magically through your word processor? He takes a job doing what your character does and presents himself as the character in the flesh? His life closely parallels one of another guy, with his initials, who went missing at exactly the same time that you started writing your books, and you want me to say yes, he's your hero, the guy who's going to get you through this? The man's a nut. I don't know what he did or what made him decide he was someone else, but it couldn't be good."

That was the sum total of everything I didn't want to hear, and I didn't have an immediate response. I turned toward Paula. "Damien just vanishes and Duffy appears?" I asked. "Did his family file a missing person report? Why wasn't anyone looking for him?"

"His father died two years before, and Damien had been living in his own apartment in New Rochelle, New York, at the time he vanished. He wasn't married, didn't seem to have any friends, wasn't seeing anyone. Damien worked as a bartender, sometimes in two places at a time so he could get enough hours to pay his rent. His mother didn't report him missing because she had gotten used to not hearing from him." Paula was scrolling down the file of notes she'd taken.

"But somebody must have noticed. The bars he was working in knew when he didn't show up for a shift. The landlord figured out he wasn't paying his rent. Maybe his power company noticed he was leaving the lights off a lot." I was trying to poke holes in Paula's logic, but I was poking with a butter knife and what I needed was something on the order of an awl.

Paula shrugged. "The landlord filed an eviction notice after the rent checks stopped coming. That's when they contacted Damien's mom, who didn't know anything. After another two months, when it was clear he wasn't coming back, the landlord got to go into the place, send some possessions back to Mrs. Mosley, and sell the rest. By then, there was no trail to follow."

"So maybe he is the guy we know as Duffy, and maybe he's not," I said.

"This is why I didn't tell you sooner," Paula said. "I'm waiting to get a telephone number for the mother and to check with the state police on whether they've ever had a record of anyone using the driver's license, a credit card, or anything. I don't know what we're talking about yet."

Dad shook his head in disbelief and looked at me. "You didn't hear a word I said, did you?" he asked. "I'm telling you this guy you've been trusting is deranged and might be dangerous. You're just ignoring what I said."

"Yes, I am," I admitted. "I don't want to believe that, and I don't have a real hard piece of evidence to prove otherwise. This is how I work, Dad. You have to let me get through the process."

"Is this how you write books? By diving in and seeing what happens?"

"Actually, yeah."

Cue the doorbell: Duffy was here. I got up to answer the door and my father, usually a very calm and understanding man, grabbed my forearm. "Don't let him in," he said with great force in his voice.

"I have to. He has my lunch." Dad let go, and I let Duffy in, wondering if being sassy to my father was worth the admission of a possible lunatic to my home. It had felt like a good impulse at the time.

Duffy, unaware that his sanity was even more in question than usual, greeted me with a charming, "I believe Ms. Bledsoe was murdered in a basement or an attic."

"Did you get napkins?" I asked.

"Of course. Fibers in the closet in which the body was found indicate a good deal of dust at the scene of the murder, and the metal-tipped pen that had punctured her carotid artery bore traces of dichlorobenzene." We were already walking toward the dining room, where there was a table large enough for four people. I heard Dad and Paula heading in that direction as well.

"Oh, dichlorobenzene," I parroted back. "That seals it."

Duffy gave me a slightly irritated look. "It is the common ingredient in most modern mothballs," he sniffed.

"How could I have forgotten that?" I wondered aloud.

Introductions were made, with Dad eyeing Duffy the way one would glare at . . . a possible murder suspect. We set out the food on the dining room table. Paula had gotten glasses and utensils from the kitchen, and everyone except my father grabbed a sandwich with gusto. Well, Duffy's version of gusto, which was to actually reach across me to get his sub rather than wait to have it handed to him. He unwrapped it slowly, which normally wouldn't bother me, but it was the very height of suspense now. I saw Paula watching like a hawk as he revealed his chosen lunch.

A cheese sub.

We exchanged a look that couldn't decide if it was relieved or annoyed. But I know we were both wondering the same thing: Did he pick up that detail in one of the books, or is that an actual incarnation of Duffy Madison sitting across the table? Should I call him "Damien" and see what happens? Wasn't Damien the evil devil kid in some seventies horror movie? (I'm pretty sure I was the only one thinking about that last question.)

Dad, picking absently at his sandwich as if he was afraid it might bite back, did not look at our fictional guest but idly asked, "So Duffy, how do you intend to find the man who you think is now focusing on my daughter?"

Duffy, of course, didn't skip a beat. "The key is to provide security for Rachel while continuing to research the criminal's methods and possible psychology. I don't believe in profilers, but I do think that a person's communication can be very telling, and the e-mails he sent to your daughter are extremely valuable."

He then went into a detailed description and analysis of syntax, grammar patterns, and font choices, and I blanked out somewhere around the complete lack of alliteration in the threatening notes. Duffy was trying to show off how thorough he was, but he wasn't getting anywhere with Dad.

Once he took his first extended breath, my father leapt upon his opportunity. "How do we know you're not the killer?" he asked.

I almost dropped my sandwich. "Dad!"

"It's a reasonable question," Duffy responded. Not a bead of sweat, not a blink. Nothing. "You have the evidence that, in the three days I have known your daughter, I have done absolutely nothing the least bit threatening and have been endeavoring to keep her safe. We have been alone at least three times, once in her home, and no harm has come to her. And you have my sincerest declaration that anything at all harmful would have to get through me first before Rachel could be hurt." He took another bite, and some mustard squirted onto the corner of his mouth. Duffy dabbed at it with an inadequate paper napkin from the sub restaurant.

"So you're asking me to take your word for it," Dad responded. He took a forkful of macaroni salad and chewed it suspiciously, if such a thing is possible.

"I'm suggesting you exercise logic and *then* take my word for it," Duffy answered, his lip now mustard free.

Before my father could snarl at him some more, Duffy's cell phone buzzed, and he registered a slight look of surprise when he checked the incoming caller. He stood and tapped the phone. "Special Agent Rafferty," he said with a hint of superiority in his voice. So she'd come crawling back for his help, had she? Well, he'd be happy to pitch in now that she was acknowledging his skills and dedication, but only because he wanted to help save lives.

It was a lot to infer from a 5 percent change in his tone, but I'm an author, and we observe, then exaggerate. Saves millions in lawsuits.

Duffy listened for a few seconds. "Indeed. How soon?" He looked at me perplexed. "Tomorrow? Well, certainly, if you feel it could make that large a difference." He walked out of the room, and his conversation with the FBI agent—sorry; *special* agent—became unintelligible.

"Sounds like something's happening in the case," Paula attempted as a way of breaking the silence.

"Good," Dad grumped. "This needs to end soon."

"What is it with you?" I asked. "You're usually so non-judgmental, and now you're practically jumping down Duffy's throat every time he makes a sound."

He gave me a very stern fatherly look and said, "I take offense when someone threatens my daughter's life. No matter how much he resembles a guy you made up."

"Well one thing Duffy's right about, we have no evidence at all that he's anything other than what he appears to be, at least professionally. He is trying to help, and you're jumping to the conclusion that he is the serial killer."

Duffy walked back in, pocketing his cell phone. "I'm afraid I'm off," he said.

"No kidding," Dad mumbled, but Duffy didn't appear to hear it. Hey, some jokes are inherited father to daughter.

"What's going on?" I asked.

"Special Agent Rafferty believes there's a strong possibility the next abduction has taken place. There's a crime writer in Connecticut named Rosemary Cleland who apparently is not in touch with friends or relatives."

I knew Rosemary from some meetings I'd attended of a nascent writer's union in Manhattan. Her writing name was Lisbeth Pastel, and she wrote what I'd consider to be something more akin to romance novels that occasionally had crimes in them. And the union hadn't gone anywhere, either. I told all that to Duffy.

He shrugged. "She's a writer, and she's missing. The special agent wants me in Stamford as soon as possible. Apparently, I'm not quite the charlatan she'd assumed."

I suddenly felt a cold feeling in the pit of my stomach. "What if she's wrong?" I asked. "What if Rosemary isn't the next victim? I'll be here without anyone to help." I realized what that sounded like and added, "No one official." I looked at Paula, who waved a hand to tell me not to worry, and Dad, whose expression was not as severe as before. He caught Duffy's eye.

"You sure you can't stay?" my father asked. "I'm concerned about Rachel." There is no greater hypocrite than the frightened parent.

"Ben Preston will be here." Duffy turned toward me. "Call him if you need him. Ben texted me and said he wasn't going to Connecticut but would continue working the case from here." And then, saying this time that he had to rush out, Duffy left, leaving the three of us with the better part of four sub sandwiches and a lot of trepidation.

I'd had enough, I decided, of sitting around and waiting for something to happen. The hell with the publishing industry and its odd rules about not working on weekends (except writers, who work all the time). There were unprofessional ways of getting answers, and I was just pushed far enough to use them.

"Fire up your laptop, Paula," I said. "We're making some calls to people who are probably enjoying their weekend."

Chapter 23

It took some doing. Most of the websites for publishing companies, editors, agents, and even publicists directed the visitor to make contact either through e-mail or by calling the office switchboard, which would inevitably lead to a voice mail cul-de-sac on the weekend. So my initial attempts to start calling people who had known the murdered authors were a little slow.

But Paula being the amiable model of efficiency was the key to the matter. She got out the actual paper phone books I'd forgotten I had for Manhattan and started looking up the home numbers of those who might still have a landline. Matching names to authors and then eliminating those who probably weren't agents ("Dr. Lance K. Galbraith, Gastroenterology") was a tedious business, but in the end and with the help of universal 411 to find some out-of-towners, we had a working list of six people from the four victims, which was a pretty good ratio. I live in fear that Paula will someday find a real job.

We split up the list three ways only because Dad would not be denied. Paula and Dad used their cell phones while I reserved the right to stick to my corded landline, the only phone that never drops a call and has sound fidelity I can actually count on being clear enough to take accurate notes.

I drew Sunny Maugham's editor Carole Pembroke at Arlington House and the brother of Marion Benedict, the unpublished author from Farmingdale, because he was the only person who might have some idea of her work habits. I think Dad and Paula wanted to keep their own lists exclusive to professional contacts because personal ones would tend to be more emotional and therefore the conversations might be more unpleasant. In other words, they were taking the easier ones for themselves.

I called Bob Benedict first, not because I was anxious about grilling someone who had recently lost a close relative to an unthinkable crime, but because he was more likely to be answering his phone on the weekend. And my luck, he answered almost immediately. I had to explain who I was, and since I really didn't want to lie, that took some doing.

"I'm the author of some crime novels, and I heard about the awful loss of your sister," I began. "I'm so sorry to hear about it."

"Why are you calling?" Bob had the tone of someone whose dinner was being interrupted by a caller asking whether he was satisfied with his current cell phone service provider.

Again, not lying was the priority, but not sounding like a nut was pretty high on the list as well. "I read about your sister in the newspaper, and as a fellow writer, I felt the loss.

I was so shaken by the news that I felt I had to call and find out about her." I hadn't actually mentioned that *A Confederacy of Dunces* was published only because the author's suicide sent his mother to publishers on a mission. So what I *did* say wasn't all that loony. But then, my standards for crazy had been considerably shaken in the past week.

There was a considerable gap in the conversation, and I got the strong impression that Bob was staring at the receiver and wondering who this dizzy, impolite woman calling him while he was still in mourning might be. "Why are you *calling*?" he repeated.

It was clear my first answer had been insufficient. "Look," I said, cards on the table, "I never knew your sister. I don't know if she was a terrific writer or a lousy one. But I know that this killer is someone who is targeting female crime authors, and I have reason to believe I'm next on his list. So anything you can tell me about Marion would be a real help to me."

I held my breath for a moment while Bob considered. "Okay," he said, but his voice had a tone that indicated he was weary of the whole thing and wished his sister would just stop being murdered so lunatics like me would stop calling him on a Sunday asking how they could avoid being next. "What do you want to know?"

"How far had your sister gotten with her work?" I asked. If she had been in contact with an editor or agent coinciding with the ones Dad and Paula were calling or calling about, it was possible there was a connection and therefore a suspect would emerge. If not, I had a grand total of nothing.

"She wrote some mystery books," Bob said, as if Marion had been trying to jump to Mars from a standing position. "I read the first one, and it wasn't all that great. She couldn't spell, for one thing. I'm no expert, and I was finding typos all over the place."

Typos? Those can be fixed. "But was the story good?" I asked. "The characters?"

"What am I, a book critic? It was one of those things where somebody who doesn't really do that for a living runs around asking people about a murder and they just tell her anything she wants to know. Not my thing, but some people really love them, I guess."

I had to be more specific in my questioning. "Had she gotten any encouragement from people in the publishing business? Did she hear from editors, agents, that kind of thing?"

"I really don't know. Marion lived in Philly over a pizzeria. I live in Delaware. We didn't talk more than once a month, maybe. We weren't that close. She told me once, all proud, that she'd sent out her manuscript to a bunch of agents, but she never said if she heard back from any, which made me think she didn't. After a while, she didn't mention the books anymore. I was surprised the cops found a new one she was working on in a file on her hard drive."

"So she never mentioned a name, a publisher, an editor, nobody?"

There was a sigh from the phone. "I just said she never mentioned the books anymore. Then some guy comes along and makes her choke on rejection slips I didn't even know she had. So maybe I'm not the one to ask. Look, lady, the Orioles are in the sixth inning and it's Sunday, all right? Nice talking to you." He hung up, and I almost didn't blame him or the sleeveless undershirt I pictured him wearing.

No author ever gets to be published without a quantity of persistence, and after all I was the one whose life was probably in danger, so with that motivation in mind, I dialed the home number for Carole Pembroke, Sunny's editor, who as it turned out lived in Morristown, on the train line. I asked if I could come over and discuss Sunny, and she said she understood my grief (which I was embarrassed about because this call was more about fear) and would be happy to see me. She gave me directions, which I didn't write down because I have GPS.

Dad wasn't happy about me going alone but didn't want to sit in the car in the midnineties heat while I talked to Carole, so he allowed for it. It didn't take long to find her apartment, actually a loft in a converted school building; very trendy.

Carole said she was surprised at the call, not because it was from an author she didn't know on a day she wasn't working, but because she'd forgotten she even had the landline. "I had to pick it up," she said. "I haven't used the thing in months, maybe years."

I started with the fact that I was the person who had discovered Sunny's body in the closet.

"My god that was awful," she said, as if it had been her and not me who opened the closet door. "What a shock. And such a good writer, too. She sold a lot of books for us." That, in the publishing business, is the definition of a good writer.

"It's a great loss," I agreed, although my criteria might have been different. "It's very disturbing, and I'm trying to get some closure for myself. How long were you Sunny's editor?"

Carole made a show of thinking about it, hand to her chin. She wasn't much of an actress—Sunny had been an asset to her, not a friend.

"Oh, Julia and I went back to her first book, *Death Gets a Pedicure*," she said, making sure that I was aware she knew Sunny by her given name and not the one she probably took at the publisher's request. "She wrote such lovely deaths; it was truly a privilege to read her manuscripts."

I'd seen a piece of Sunny's latest on her computer and thought it was extremely rough. "I imagine she went through a number of drafts," I said. That wasn't exactly a question, but it would elicit a response, and that was all I needed.

"Not really," Carole (whose birth certificate probably didn't have the "e" on the end) answered. "I mean, she certainly took some editing, just like every other writer, but she was actually so well-tuned to the series that by the end, I rarely brought up a point that required much more than a quick polish. She was a real pro." Her voice got a little dreamy. "It's going to be hard to replace her." But no doubt they would. If Sunny's books had sold well enough, it might be possible to hire another writer to continue her series with Sunny's name in huge type on the front and the other writer's underneath in much smaller print.

Should I ask if that was being considered? I could probably . . . No.

Wait. The sample I'd seen on Sunny's computer was full of typos and misspellings. But of course what Carole was talking about was editing a piece for content, not form. The publisher would have copy editors to take care of grammatical mistakes and Carole (and her peers) to handle story problems, timeline issues, character incongruities, and cases where the author (in the opinion of the publisher) has gone too far and will upset some readers. One thing they absolutely hate is upset readers.

I guess that's more than one thing. "One thing" and "readers" disagree in that sentence. Hopefully my copy editor will correct the mistake.

"Was Sun . . . Julia at all difficult to deal with?" I went on. Maybe if she'd really pissed someone off royally, I could find a motive in this mess. But then I'd have to find the same one for the other three victims.

Carole's eyes got to the size of Oreo cookies, she was so amazed at the suggestion. "Oh no," she said. "She was a dream. Always polite, always helpful. She took revisions with a smile, and I never heard anyone around here say anything at all negative about her." Then she paused. "Why?"

"I'm just asking questions," I said. How could I say this honestly? "I'm trying to understand it for myself."

"Are you writing about it?"

The question caught me by surprise. "No!" Perhaps that was a little too forceful. "No, I'd never do that. I'm just . . . I know you can't make sense of it, but I guess as a crime writer, I need to understand the motive." Not bad.

Carole's face and voice were suddenly chillier. "Well I can't think of one person who ever said a bad word about Julia," she said. "Is there anything else I can tell you?"

I made a mental note to tell Adam not to submit anything to her for a while, until she forgot who I was. At least until Tuesday.

The ride back to Adamstown seemed longer than the drive to Carole's. Sunny was dead, and so was Julia. Finding out that her copy was considerably cleaner when it reached Carole's desktop via e-mail really didn't feel like much of a triumph.

When I got home, the incredibly concerned crew I had at the house was nowhere to be seen, so I dragged myself into Paula's office, but she wasn't there. She heard me from the dining room and called over. "Rachel! Your dad and I are in here." So I dragged myself there. Once you're dragging already, where you drag is not as much a concern.

They were sitting side by side with Paula's laptop, which I believe contains every piece of information known to the human race, accessible by Paula simply through thought waves, between them.

"We're comparing notes," she said. That seemed reasonable, so I sat down across from Paula. I didn't need to see the screen; she would tell me anything of interest that showed up on it.

"What have you got so far?" I asked.

Dad scowled a little. "Not much," he said.

But Paula shook her head. "We have some things. We don't know what they are yet, but I think there's information here that will help us."

"It's got to beat what I have," I said. "All I found out was that Marion Benedict didn't talk to her brother much and had too many typos in her work." Oddly, that seemed to amuse Paula, but she didn't say anything. "Sunny Maugham's editor seems to think I'm trying to profit from her death, but at least she sent copy in that was a lot cleaner than what I saw in the file I read on her computer."

They looked at me, apparently waiting for the tons more information they were sure I had. I looked at them in anticipation of clues that were at least clues. All three of us were sorely disappointed.

"There's something there," Paula said. She nudged Dad. "Tell Rachel what you found out."

"Not a whole lot," he repeated, sighing a bit. "I spoke to Missy Hardaway's publisher, Harrison Belechik. Seemed like a nice enough guy, but it took him a minute to remember who Missy was, since he has so many authors. You'd think the recently murdered one would be fresh in his mind.

"Anyway, he says she queried him cold and sent him the manuscript when asked, and he just responded to it, so he published that one and one more before she died. Said she was 'coming along' as a novelist."

"What else did he remember about her?" I asked.

Dad shook his head slowly. "Not that much. Said she didn't understand punctuation too well, but she knew how to write emotion."

Paula, I noticed, was grinning a little more broadly. That meant she was about to spring something on us that we had overlooked and she hadn't. Paula can be a little smug, but she earns it.

I decided to play out the string. "What about the other person you talked to, Dad?"

"Lance Galbraith. J. B. Randolph's agent. I thought he would know maybe what Randolph's real name was, at least. The cops obviously know, but they didn't tell us. Maybe he'd be able to talk about her financial situation, whether anybody would kill her for money and kill the others just to make it less obvious." Dad reads too many thrillers.

"So what did he say?" I prodded him.

"He didn't answer. I left a message."

Not a huge revelation there. "Paula?" I asked. She was doing everything but raising her arm, propped up by her other hand, and shaking it. Nothing Paula enjoys quite so much as being the smartest girl in the class.

"Well." She sat up straight and glanced quickly at the laptop in front of her. "First, I got in touch with Marion Benedict's boyfriend, a guy named Thad Claypool. He was distraught, as you might imagine."

"I didn't even know Marion Benedict *had* a boyfriend," I said. "Where'd you get that?"

"Facebook. Seems like Marion—her real name was Nancy Pantuso, by the way—was spending far too much of her money, in Thad's opinion, trying to get her books published. Then he said she had decided to self-publish and was spending all sorts of hard-earned funds on artists to design covers, ISBNs, formatting, and editing, which she farmed out."

"You think Thad was so annoyed by all this spending he decided to cram some rejection letters down Nancy's throat just to prove a point?" I asked. "That's kind of a harsh way to win an argument."

Paula checked out her computer notes a little more closely and pursed her lips. "No, I don't suspect Thad. For one thing, he doesn't appear to have any connection to the other three women at all. And he just strikes me as too gentle a type. He broke down in tears talking about Nancy."

Now *I* was getting a nagging feeling that there was a pattern I was missing; it was just past the thought I was having at this moment and would no doubt be making contact at any minute. "Who was your other call?" I asked Paula.

"Ah." She put on a pair of glasses she uses for reading; took a quick glance at her notes, perhaps for effect (Paula never forgets anything); and pointed at me with a pencil. "I think this is where I started getting an idea."

I knew it. I sat back in my chair and folded my arms. "You've been holding out on us," I said.

Paula looked aghast. "I would never! It's just that I'm not really sure. Duffy would say I don't have enough facts to reach a conclusion."

"I'm not Duffy, and neither is he. What did you figure out?"

She smiled. "I talked to Madlyn Beckwirth, who was J. B. Randolph's editor, or as she put it, 'the person who acquired her books for the publisher.' Randolph's real name was Claudia Skilowicz, and she had a real process, according to Madlyn, for getting a book ready. But she directed me to Claudia's assistant, Betty Field, and she and I formed a bond."

"You talking about me behind my back again?"

"I would never—!"

"I'm kidding. What happened?"

Paula huffed away her horror at the mock accusation I made and said, "Betty read all of Claudia's first drafts," she said. "She was the first reader, but far from the last. She said Claudia could barely spell, used apostrophes where they didn't belong, and had never actually understood the difference between a clause and a phrase."

"So how did she get acquired by Madlyn Beckwirth and published?" Dad asked.

"Well that's the thing, isn't it?" Paula stood up to make her point. "What's the one thing that all four of the murdered authors have in common?"

"They're all murdered authors," Dad tried.

But it was starting to come together for me. "They were all sloppy writers," I said. "Every one of them wrote copy that needed to be gone over with a fine-tooth comb before they could even consider submitting them to professional publishing companies." I realized suddenly that I was on my feet as well, pacing by the dining room table and wondering if what was left of Dad's sub was available to just anybody.

"So what?" Dad asked. He at least had kept his seat, but he still wasn't paying any attention to that sandwich. What had he ordered, again? "So they wrote books and they weren't great at all the p's and q's. So they had to get somebody to read their first drafts. Where does that get us?"

"There's only one kind of person who would be connected to all four of them in a professional capacity," Paula said. "It could be someone who didn't have to live near any of them; who didn't necessarily have connections to one publishing house, so all the authors could be in touch; and who would be passionately enough involved in the business to go off the deep end about something and finally snap. Someone who would actually think of all those ways to kill authors symbolically and then do it for real."

"A vindictive mailman?" Dad suggested, but I knew he was more baffled than serious.

I shook my head. "A freelance copy editor," I said.

Chapter 24

The first thing I did was to text Duffy (well, the first thing I did was hug Paula, but after that), but he didn't answer immediately, so I called Ben Preston.

He listened with what I took for awe at our deductive skills, then paused before answering. "You think somebody killed four women because he got tired of their bad punctuation?" It wasn't exactly the response I'd been looking for.

With my expectations damped down, I answered, "Well, it's at least worth checking out, don't you think? To see if they all needed a copy editor and hired one outside the publishing house. I mean, it would have to be a freelancer to cross over to all the authors."

"Well, that's the thing. Does it make sense that women like Julia Bledsoe, who had a long-standing publishing contract with a major house, would share a copy editor with someone like Missy Hardaway, who didn't have a contract at all? I mean, when you send in your manuscript, don't they have someone at your publisher who goes through it for all that stuff?" If this guy ever wanted to actually kiss me, he was going to have to be considerably more supportive of my wild theories.

"It's not likely they'd farm it out, but it's possible." I could lord my knowledge of publishing over him, if nothing else.

"Answer the question." That was it; next time, he didn't even get a handshake.

I rolled my eyes and huffed audibly (on purpose). "Yes. My editor reads it first for story issues and major changes. Then I revise it. Then my editor reads it again. Then it goes to a copy editor, who looks for typos and the like."

"So you see? Why would all four of them—I mean, we think this thing in Connecticut that Duffy's working on might pan out, and there's no copy editor involved. I'll keep you posted. I promise." But he didn't hang up.

What was Ben waiting for? A thank-you for completely ignoring the collective brilliance of Dad, Paula, and me (mostly Paula)? "So you're not even going to look into it?" I sounded like a five-year-old who'd just been informed that a dragon did *not* live under her bed. And I would know because I almost got a photograph of it when I was that age, but the thing was cagey, my flash misfired, and my father was in a grumpy mood.

"I'll get someone on it, okay? But sit tight. I'll get back to you when I hear from Duffy." And this time, he did hang up.

I made a low noise in my throat. "I'm definitely not going out with that guy."

"What's that?" Dad asked. Oops. Did I actually say that out loud?

"Nothing. I don't think he's going to look into it. They think this Connecticut lead might be the one."

Paula, who usually questions authority as often as she flaps her arms and flies to Cincinnati, scrunched up her face in a skeptical expression. "Well, just because the cops aren't following this lead doesn't mean we can't," she said.

"I like the way you think, but I don't want to call Carole Pembroke back," I told her. "She sounded like she wanted to forget I'd called, and I wouldn't mind if she did."

Paula shifted from one leg to the other, which meant she was thinking. "If you were going to look for a freelance copy editor, where would you look?" she asked.

"I'm not looking for one," I said. "I'm trying to keep one from looking for me."

"But you're an author like them, and they found a copy editor, maybe the same one," Dad said, picking up on Paula's train of thought. "If we can trace how you'd search for him, we might figure out how they did." He turned to Paula. "Right?" She rewarded him with a thumbs-up.

"I'd tell you to find me a copy editor," I said to Paula.

She looked sheepish. "Actually, that's true. You would. So I'd run some simple searches first, and one of the things I'd look for would be previous clients. A freelancer's website would list people who have worked with him so other authors would be impressed with some of the names and consider his services." She sat down and started banging away on the keyboard.

I was circling the table to look over her left shoulder (Dad had the right covered) when my cell phone rang. The caller

ID was unfamiliar, but I picked up anyway. If it *was* the lunatic who'd been e-mailing me and killing off other authors, I might be able to ask questions that would corner him into pitching me on his proofreading service. It's a funny business, publishing.

But a cold feeling did grip my stomach; I won't deny that.

No such luck, depending on your definition of "luck." The voice on the other end was female and perky. "This is Marcie from Beverly Hills Productions," she said. "I'm looking for a Ms. Goldman?" People from California have a way of taking declarative sentences and making them sound like questions?

(*Now* who was obsessed with punctuation?)

"This is she," I said, syntax perfect as ever.

"Mr. Waterman is hoping to meet with you tomorrow," Marcie said. "Is nine AM possible for you?"

Adam had said Waterman wouldn't let him go to the meeting, but it was still odd. I had to make sure he knew what was going on. "Have you called my agent?" I asked.

"I have, but Mr. Waterman likes to contact writers directly. After I spoke to Mr. Resnick, he wanted to make sure you were available, so I'm calling directly," Marcie said. "I'll get back to Mr. Resnick and let him know the details."

To get into New York City by nine in the morning on a Monday requires the stamina of a bull, the courage of a lion, and the bus of a Greyhound. "Of course," I said, possessing none of those things. "Where in the city does he want to meet?"

"Oh no," Marcie said, a light chuckle in her tone. "Mr. Waterman would like to come to *you*. He feels that the atmosphere in your novels is so strong, he'd like to see you in your natural habitat. Can he pick you up for breakfast at your home?" California people also think you have to drive everywhere. Come to think of it, that's one trait they share with New Jerseyans.

Even in my state of excitement over my novel being turned into a movie, I was not going to give out my address to a stranger. "I'll tell you what," I said. "There's a lovely place for breakfast right in my town, the English Muffin. I'll give you the address, and I can meet him there. We can sit outside in the morning." Before the heat and humidity make you want to donate your skin to science.

"Fine," Marcie said pleasantly. I gave her the address, and we confirmed the time and place. She thanked me very efficiently, and we disconnected.

I went back to looking over Paula's shoulder, but now I was a little distracted. A movie deal! This was the kind of thing that took a midlist author like me and turned her into a great big *New York Times* Best Sellers list favorite. It could be the end of worrying about the mortgage. It could mean that I'd be set for life. It could mean that I could write Duffy when I wanted and do something else when that appealed to me. It was a life changer.

Assuming I still had a life. That was something to consider. We did have that little matter of finding out who was killing mystery authors and whether or not I was the girl most likely to be poisoned with printer's ink.

"Got anything?" I asked Paula. The truth was I could see the screen in front of her, but I didn't recognize it and didn't want to get so close I had to literally breathe down her neck.

"Maybe," she answered. "I've found a couple of freelance copy editors, none of them around here or in New York, which doesn't mean that much because the killer clearly travels around. A few websites for copy editors. And I'm checking to see if there are any previous clients listed who have since turned up dead."

She was clacking away as I turned to look at my father. He had never looked quite so worn and old to me; his face was tired and a little wrinkled. The light that usually shown in his eyes was dim. He stared at the screen on the dining room table and looked very worried until he must have sensed that I was watching him. He turned, met my eyes, and smiled a reassuring and unconvincing smile that just about broke my heart.

My predicament was killing him, and he was compensating by being a tough, gruff man doing all he could to protect his little girl. That was why he was so difficult with Duffy and why he hadn't been hungry. He was too scared.

And that made me even more terrified than I had been before. If the rock of my life, the guy who could always make everything okay, looked that tense, things must be *really* bad. I started to wonder seriously what it was like to be dead and caught myself gasping just a little.

"You okay?" Dad asked gently.

I nodded, because speaking would have belied the message of the nod. Sure. I was fine. What was there to worry about? I reached over and took his hand. He squeezed mine and nodded.

"It'll be okay, Rache," he said. "I'm here."

"Here," Paula said. She can gain the power of tunnel vision when she's intent on a task and either hadn't noticed the exchange between Dad and me or had decided not to say anything as a way of preserving our privacy. Paula is a good and moral person. "This might very well be our guy."

I looked at the screen, which showed the website for Shana Kineally, a freelance proofreader/copy editor based in Racine, Wisconsin. The home page, as plain and cheap as could be imagined, was bathed in a rather nauseating green with large pink lettering.

"That's not a guy," I pointed out.

"Nonetheless. Take a look here." Paula moved the cursor toward a paragraph—and all the copy was immaculate, for the record—near the bottom of the page and circled it. "List of satisfied clients."

I scanned the list. "Sunny Maugham," I said. "But that's not—"

"And J. B. Randolph," Dad said, pointing. "That's two of the four."

"It's only two." I don't know why I was so desperate for Shana Kineally not to be the killer. It's possible I was still trying very hard to believe that there was no killer, that this was all some strange nightmare from which I was sure to wake at any minute, or that Sunny Maugham was exercising a truly macabre sense of humor and would be walking in the door momentarily, doubled over in laughter.

"Well, Missy Hardaway was a pretty new author, not very well known at all, with only two books from Ballmer Press, a company not exactly rivaling the big New York houses," Paula pointed out. "And Marion Benedict was unpublished. Those are not names that are going to be especially helpful in attracting new clients."

"It makes sense," Dad said. My father, rational businessman and doting dad that he is, was taking the opposite approach to mine. Instead of denying the whole situation, he was taking great pains to be sure this Shana Kineally really *was* the maniac on the trail of crime fiction writers so the police could catch her and this whole business could be over quickly. He could go back to his barn, and I could keep breathing. Win-win.

"We need more than this to go to Ben Preston and demand this Kineally person be arrested," I pointed out. "We need some evidence tying her to the crimes, not just the victims. Maybe the killer is someone with a real grudge against poor Shana, taking out his revenge on her by bumping off her best clients and smearing her name."

"You really have been writing mysteries too long, haven't you?" Dad asked.

"I don't think so," I said. Four books—five, really, once I finished the revisions—wasn't too long. What was he implying?

"There are no pictures of Shana Kineally on the web," Paula, who had clearly not been listening, said. "That's weird."

I shrugged one shoulder. "A copy editor doesn't need to have a portrait on her website," I said. "Authors always have official pictures because we're supposed to look like people our readers would like to hang around with, but copy editors aren't trafficking in personality; it's results that matter with them."

"You don't understand," Paula insisted. "It's not just that there's no photograph on her official website—there are no pictures of Shana Kineally on the web *anywhere*. It's as if she really doesn't want anyone to know what she looks like."

"Is that even possible?" I asked. "I mean, hasn't somebody posted a picture of old Aunt Shana somewhere?"

"Maybe on a personal website with protection or just through e-mail, but there's nothing I can find in the public areas," Paula said, frowning.

"I don't know about you, but I'm suspicious," Dad said to no one in particular.

"First thing's first," I said. "Duffy would say we have to confirm our facts. We have to confirm with Marion Benedict's boyfriend, Thad Claypool, that she was working with the copy editor and see if he can confirm the name Shana Kineally."

"Why Thad?" Dad asked. "Why not Marion Benedict's brother?"

Paula and I exchanged a glance. "Two reasons," she told Dad. "First, because Thad was annoyed at Nancy for spending all the money on her books, so he'd remember the expense if it happened."

"What's the second reason?"

Paula looked a little weary. "Because I was the one who got in touch, and Rachel knows she can get me to make the call." I nodded with empathy. The poor woman. So glad it wasn't me.

Paula called Thad Claypool while I stretched my legs and daydreamed about a Hollywood premiere of *Little Boy Lost* with maybe Paul Rudd as Duffy. Or Ryan Reynolds. As Duffy. Not Paul Rudd as Ryan Reynolds. That'd be weird.

Dad went into the kitchen to get himself a bottle of spring water. Dad is getting back to nature, only in plastic bottles that need to be recycled filled with water from a spring apparently so large, fifty thousand quarts of it can be bottled each and every hour. Dad believes in doing what he can, as long as it's convenient.

I decided not to be in the room while Paula called because she'd just want to tell me everything that was said anyway, so I took a tour around my downstairs (upstairs was mostly storage space) and tried not to think that some nut job was out there, possibly watching my house as I tried not to think about him. Her. If we were right, her.

Wandering back into the dining room after a few minutes, it was clear Paula was wrapping up the call. I could hear her thanking Thad two or three times as I approached, and she was already typing with both hands, phone on the table, when I reached the entrance to the room.

"Thad asked how I knew about Shana Kineally," she said. "He even got out the bank statement with the cancelled check from seven months ago. Marion was definitely a client."

"Do you think we can tie in Missy Hardaway?" I asked.

"Give Harrison a call," she said, grinning. So it was my turn.

Or not. "He's her publisher. If she were using a freelance editor, she might not want him to know."

"You're stalling," Paula said, teasing. "You don't want to know, do you?"

"Of course I want to know." I'd show her. I got out my phone and called Harrison Belechik. And he sounded surprised.

"No, Missy didn't call Shana Kineally," he said flat out.

She didn't? What could *that* mean?

But Harrison wasn't finished. "*I* called Shana Kineally," he said. "Ballmer Press is too small to have its own editors, and Missy's books were very imaginative and well written, but . . ."

"But she couldn't spell to save her life, so you got her a freelance editor."

"Something like that," he said. "Why do you ask?"

I gave him a nonsensical excuse, something about wanting to clean up my next book, and hustled him off the phone. I looked at my father and my assistant, who I knew had been a philosophy major in college. This was the crack investigative team that had busted the serial killer case wide open? We probably needed a little help.

"Who can we call?" I asked.

Dad and Paula looked at me. "Duffy." In unison.

I tried his cell, but it went straight to voice mail, so I left a message. "Duffy, we think we might have found something. The person's name is Shana Kineally." I spelled it for him. "She's a copy editor and proofreader who works freelance and appears to have a connection to at least two of the four authors. Give me a call back."

Disconnecting the call, I looked at Dad. "Okay, maybe I'm crazy . . ."

"Maybe?" The man's a laugh riot.

I went on. "But I know Duffy Madison. He has his cell phone on vibrate, and he's not taking anything but urgent calls because he's on a case. I'm not going to hear back from him soon if he's on his way to Connecticut, especially if he's driving. He'd have to pull over, and he thinks that his mission is absolutely a matter of life and death, which it probably is."

"He won't pull over to call back?" Dad asked.

I shook my head. "If Duffy sees I'm calling, he knows I'm still alive. He can put it off or assume I'm talking to Ben Preston, because that's what he told me to do."

"So call Ben," Paula said.

"I did call Ben. He thought I was a nut and dismissed our theory as silly."

We sat silent for a moment because we were all thinking the same thing, but none of us wanted to say it. Finally, Dad broke the silence.

"The FBI's in charge of the case," he said. "Call the FBI."

I heaved a sigh of—what's the opposite of relief?—and dug Special Agent Eunice Rafferty's business card out of my back pocket. Sure, she'd been dismissive and condescending when we'd met, but she liked my books, right? So why not give the feds a call?

She answered the phone on the second ring and was anything but dismissive and condescending when I told her about

Shana Kineally and the idea that she'd somehow linked all four of the murdered authors together, the only such link that had been discovered so far. In fact, she sounded impressed.

"That's very good work," Rafferty said. "It's a real lead. I promise you, we're going to follow up on it right now." She assured me the local police would be driving by my house more often because Ben Preston had requested it and said she'd call when she had something to tell me.

"I don't know," Dad said when I hung up. "She doesn't sound all that bad to me."

"She's not," I answered. "Cops don't like it when cops from other bureaus come in and tell them what to do. So Ben and Duffy don't like the FBI. The FBI probably doesn't like the CIA. The CIA is probably not that crazy about the military. And on it goes."

"I just hope they can find Shana Kineally soon," Paula said, standing. "I don't usually work weekends." She smiled to let me know she was kidding; Paula thinks I take everything she says seriously.

"Go home," I said. "You've earned your time and a half today."

"Double time." She wasn't smiling quite so broadly now. I walked her to her car and watched her drive off.

Back in the house, I flopped onto my living room couch and watched Dad drink a beer. I had already made sure all the doors were locked.

My father knows what kind of household I run, so he put his feet up on the coffee table without a thought. Now that I thought about it, he was one of the people I'd learned to run a household from, so it made perfect sense. My mother would no doubt have been appalled; she'd also have been outvoted.

"Should we call Mom?" I asked.

"What's this 'we' stuff, kemosabe?"

"Maybe I'll wait until you go home, then." I lay back deeper into the cushion. "This being the target of a mad killer is incredibly tiring."

"Imagine how I feel," Dad answered. He sat back on the easy chair and closed his eyes. "Want to watch a movie?"

We settled on *The Philadelphia Story* because Dad was being nice. He's not a huge fan of the movie, in which a father cheats on his wife and everyone looks the other way, and he has his reasons. But movies made after 1960 tend to have sex in them, and watching those with your father is a little awkward. A lot awkward. Incredibly awkward.

We'd gotten to the part where Jimmy Stewart is starting to think he's in love with Katharine Hepburn (he's wrong) and she's letting him think so when my phone buzzed. A text. From Duffy.

> Nothing in CT. Rafferty wrong. Coming back tomorrow. Do nothing. Hear from me.

"What is it?" Dad asked.

"Duffy. He's texting me but he thinks he's sending a telegram. He'll be back tomorrow."

But before Kate and Jimmy could realize they belonged with Cary Grant and Ruth Hussey, respectively, there was a jarring crash outside my house. I jolted up—I'd been almost asleep on the couch—and woke Dad, who was all asleep on the easy chair.

"Did you hear something?" I asked.

"Rabbit," he said. That didn't help. But then he woke up completely and said, "Why? Did you?"

"Yeah." I got up and walked to the front hall to turn on the outside lights; it had gotten mostly dark while we were watching and dozing. I reached for the chain on the door, but Dad put his hand over mine.

"I'll go," he said.

I didn't argue, but I was going to watch carefully from inside. Our pal Shana Kineally might not be after Dad, but I was a crime writer and knew what "collateral damage" meant. I was not interested in my father becoming that.

He took a flashlight from a shelf at the top of the basement stairs and went out the side door. "Anybody would expect me out the front," he said. "Lock the door behind me. I'll text you when I want to come back in. Make sure every door is locked. Every window, too."

With that, he was gone.

I did indeed lock the side door behind Dad and checked the back door in the office and the deck door. The front door was definitely locked, and the windows . . . well, I wasn't going to check the windows. If someone was in the house already, checking the windows would just make me feel stupid.

Just to make it harder for my predator, I started turning the lights off in each room I walked through. There weren't enough windows to watch Dad as he walked around the house, and I wasn't nearly wealthy enough to have considered outside security cameras; until now, I'd always figured that anyone who was so hard up to steal my stuff probably needed it worse than I did.

I couldn't hear Dad outside the house, and it was working on my last nerve. I ran to the window in the office, the best vantage point for the back of the house and the rear left side. He wasn't there. The front window was problematic; if I raised the curtain there, I might as well be wearing a target on my forehead. I peeked around the edge of the curtain, then went to the other side of the front window and peeked around that edge. No Dad.

When I was just about to open the side door and go out myself, my phone buzzed. A text from Dad: *Coming in the back door.* I ran to the back door in my office and unlocked and opened it. Dad walked in, but I couldn't read his face. Worry? Relief? Bemusement?

"There's no one out there," he said. "A garbage can got knocked over."

My trash bins are plastic; they would make noise, but not enough to wake me up from even a light drowse. "A cat or a raccoon?" I asked.

"Not unless one can type," he said. He handed me a piece of paper. "This was sitting on top of the heap."

The wrinkled paper, smelling only slightly of trash, held a disturbingly familiar sort of note: the typeface varied as usual, and the message, while on a slightly different subject, was no less worrisome than the ones that had come through my e-mail:

Don't *trust* DUFFY **Madison**.

Then, underneath, almost as an afterthought:

I know **where** *you* live.

Chapter 25

I called Ben Preston this time—I figured that knocking over my garbage cans, however much it led to finding a threatening message, was not a federal crime. Ben took this situation seriously (which was refreshing), and Adamstown police officers were at my door in a matter of minutes. Forty minutes. Ben got there considerably faster.

He looked rumpled, like I'd gotten him out of bed, when he arrived. Somehow that made him more sympathetic than the guy who had essentially brushed me off only a few hours before because my theory about a mad copy editor had seemed unworthy of a follow-up to him. This guy seemed sincerely concerned for my welfare.

After the introduction to my father, during which the two men shook hands and exchanged significant looks of manliness as if to prove to each other that they could protect me (men!), Ben sat down with us in the living room and got out a reporter's notebook and a pen from his windbreaker. He hadn't needed the jacket; it was still pretty hot and humid out, but this was one of those moments that proves men should be allowed to carry purses. Wake up, civilization.

The fact that the windbreaker was also covering Ben's shoulder holster was another matter altogether.

"Where was this found, exactly?" Ben said, indicating the note, which we'd left on the coffee table, so as to better scare the crap out of me.

"It was on top of the overturned garbage can," Dad told him. "In fact, it was taped to the lid, so that when I went to put everything back the way it was, I couldn't miss it."

Ben looked; the tape was still attached to the top of the note. "What did you touch?" he asked Dad.

Dad thought carefully. "The handles on the trash can," he said, closing his eyes to remember more completely. "The one full trash bag that had fallen out, so I could put it back in. The ground around the trash can, when I knelt down and when I stood up, for balance. The top of the trash can, by the handles, so I could replace it. And that's when I saw the note."

"You touched the note, obviously, because it's here," Ben said.

I nodded. "And so did I, when Dad handed it to me."

"Did either of you touch the tape?" Ben was already placing the note, tape intact, into a plastic evidence bag he'd retrieved from the windbreaker. That jacket had more equipment in it than a pro athlete's locker. I'm told.

Dad looked at me, and I returned the look. We both shook our heads.

"Good," Ben said. "If there are prints on the tape, we know they're not yours."

That was nice, but it wasn't really getting me anywhere. "This killer isn't stupid enough to have touched anything we were going to find," I said. "Not unless she was wearing gloves first."

"She?" Ben echoed.

"Yeah. Shana Kineally."

Ben had the good taste not to roll his eyes. "The mad copy editor," he said. "We're back to that one?"

I told him that Special Agent Rafferty had not shared his amusement at the theory and was investigating Ms. Kineally as we spoke. "Just because it sounds goofy doesn't mean it isn't true," I said. "Half the stuff I make up is toned down compared to stories real cops tell me."

"Are you saying Rafferty is a real cop and I'm not?" Ben demanded.

I did not have the good taste not to roll my eyes; fine, so I'm not as classy as Ben Preston. "Oh, calm down," I said. "Nobody's casting aspersions on your manhood." I noticed Dad and Ben took pains not to look at each other at that moment. "Can we stick to the subject? What about the message on the note?"

Ben cocked an eyebrow. "It seems a little strange," he said. "Be interesting to see what Duffy makes of it."

"It tells me not to trust Duffy Madison," I reminded him.

He looked at me with the same incredulous look Dad suddenly had on his face. "And what do you think that means?" Ben asked.

"Rache, at this point, I think it's clear that if this maniac tells you not to trust Duffy Madison, you should immediately trust Duffy Madison more," Dad said.

"You don't trust him," I said. "You think he's a nut."

"He *is* a nut. He thinks you created him out of the air; he thinks he's a fictional character." I glanced at Ben, because what Dad was saying was technically a lot more than I'd told Ben about Duffy's delusions (which would make a great band name, by the way). "But he's been right about almost everything since this nightmare began, and the fact is, being crazy doesn't necessarily disqualify him from being trustworthy."

"Duffy doesn't think this whole character name thing is a coincidence?" Ben asked. "He actually thinks he *is* the character?"

I did that thing where you sort of bounce your head from one side to the other in a *yeah, well* sort of gesture. "More or less," I said. "I'm not sure what he thinks." Ben didn't say anything else about it, but he did write something in his notebook.

That's the moment when the doorbell rang, heralding the arrival of the local cops, who spent the next two hours asking me about my garbage, taking pictures of my garbage, and trying very hard not to make fun of me because I'd called them about my garbage.

By the time the cops left, it was beyond late; I was hungry but didn't feel like eating; Dad was yawning; and Ben, who no longer was giving off any particular kissing vibes, had told me in no uncertain terms to look into private security, lock all my doors, and "next time, call *before* your dad goes out and possibly gets himself in trouble."

"*Next time*?"

"Forget I said anything." He looked me up and down and exhaled. "You've had a long week."

"What are you going to tell Rafferty about this?" I asked. At the moment, I wasn't interested in being looked up and down.

He laughed. "This? I think I'll refrain from telling the FBI your trash cans were knocked over."

"The note," I pointed out.

"It's not the first one you've gotten, and it won't help Rafferty find anyone. I don't want her to see Duffy's name dragged into it from that angle, to tell you the truth."

"It's hard to know what to do," I said. "I go back and forth between being terrified and being pissed off."

"Stick with pissed off; it helps you think."

But Ben left right after that without offering any further advice. I don't suppose there was that much to offer: *Try not to get killed before I see you again, okay?*

I convinced Dad to go to bed soon after, even though we never really caught the end of *The Philadelphia Story* (I'd seen it before once or seventy-six times). I sat down on the sofa with an ice cream sandwich I'd "discovered" in my freezer and kept looking at the note left on my coffee table.

Why on earth would the killer want me not to trust Duffy Madison? Why go to all that trouble to leave the message there and make sure I'd find it? As Ben had said, if this nut wanted me to have doubts about Duffy, it was probably a great reason to trust him even more. But what difference would it make to someone who would stuff a woman's throat with rejection notes? And what could she possibly have in store for me? It was best not to think about that.

On impulse, I texted Duffy with the name Shana Kineally and waited for a reply. He was either asleep—unlikely, since

Duffy only slept about three hours a night, I had decided in *Little Boy Lost*—or back in his ruminating mode, probably driving back from Stamford and brooding over the wild goose chase he'd been sent on by the FBI. Duffy takes things personally.

It was time for me to go to bed, but I didn't. Instead, I sat down at the computer in my office and started writing some revisions. But I didn't do it my usual way, picking up from the page I'd last rewritten and then moving on. This time, I started with the last chapter. Duffy had punched holes in my ending, and that was bugging me. I'd find a way to make it closer to the man himself. After all, he should know how he'd act.

Now he had me thinking like that.

It was two in the morning when I stood up, still without a satisfactory ending but on my way to one, and headed for my bedroom. I wasn't even scared walking through the dark house. I'd just spent time in my head with Duffy Madison, and he always kept everyone safe.

Except Sunny Maugham (and some unnamed people I'd been told about), but I wasn't thinking about that. To be honest (and this doesn't paint me in a flattering light), I was much more engrossed in thoughts about the meeting the next day with Glenn Waterman. I'd Googled him (I didn't want Paula to know about the movie deal yet, in case it went south, which almost all of them do) and found some movies his Beverly Hills Productions had made. If he really was interested in *Little Boy Lost*, I would be in classy company. I started to wonder seriously who would play Lt. Antonio.

Such thoughts distract when there is danger lurking around the corner. And distraction is not always a good thing.

* * *

Dad wanted to come to the meeting at the English Muffin. "You're being stalked by an insane killer," he reminded me, because that thought hadn't crossed my mind for at least three seconds. "It's not safe to go out all by yourself."

"I'll be in broad daylight," I argued. "Outdoors where everyone can see me. You can check the car before I go and make sure no one is lurking in the trunk or the backseat, okay? But you're not coming to my option meeting."

"I *am* coming, but I'll certainly check the car before *we* leave," he countered, and grabbed my keys that were hanging off a hook by the office door. He was out through the mudroom before I could protest again that one does not generally take one's daddy to a high-stakes business meeting with a Hollywood producer.

I took another look at myself in the mirror, sighed (I'll bet even Beyoncé groans when she looks at herself in the morning, unless she pays someone to do that for her), and touched up my lipstick for the seventh time. If I actually could calm my stomach to the point that I bit into a muffin, I'd probably leave about an ounce of Pink Cognito on the top and the bottom. I could kiss Portugal and still have my mouth covered.

When I couldn't put it off any longer, I went outside. The tropical heat was just getting its act together at this hour, but it had some game. Maybe this outdoor meeting wasn't such a great idea. Dad was closing the trunk of my car as I approached.

"How do you want me to dress?" he asked.

"Like a man who's staying home," I said. "This is a business meeting, Dad. How would you look at someone who brought a parent to discuss investing in a new IPO?"

"I'd probably say, 'Is there a murderer coming after you?' and if they said yes, I'd ask why it was only one parent and not the local division of the National Guard."

"I'm not expecting that question to come up here, and I'm not volunteering the information," I told him. "Look, I have my phone with me. You can call or text every twenty minutes. If you don't get a message back, call Ben or Duffy; I'm sure he's back by now. Call the cops. Hell, go ahead and call the National Guard if you want, okay? You can check in every twenty minutes, and I'll only be gone an hour, tops."

He chewed over the idea. "Every ten minutes," he said.

"Fifteen."

"Twelve."

"Done." I hugged him tight. "Don't worry about me, Pops."

He held me very close, like he thought letting go was a mistake. "If I don't worry about you, how will I fill my day?" he asked.

"Chess?"

I got into the car, waved my cell phone at him, and drove without incident the grueling mile and a half to the English Muffin. Dad didn't look happy in my rearview mirror.

The English Muffin is a little café so adorable, you want to buy it some chew toys and adopt it. There are exactly four tables outside, each with an umbrella made of cast metal of some kind that's supposed to make the place look like New Orleans, which belies the whole "English" thing. But Danielle St. James, who owns the place, is a warm, lovely person and, better, a terrific baker. Glenn Waterman was certain to be dazzled by the fare, if not by me.

Except he didn't show up. Not for half an hour. I sat outside at the table watching the temperature and humidity levels rise, checking my phone for texts—only two came, both from Dad—or missed calls. Nothing.

It wasn't really a long enough period of time to call for clarification, and I was just about to give up without even having anything to eat (disappointment doesn't generally kill my appetite, but despair brings it down a notch for sure) when I heard a slightly familiar voice from behind me.

"Ms. Goldman. Who else knows you're here?"

I stood up and turned, my stomach doing calisthenics the whole time. Then I let out a sigh of relief. Behind me, reassuring in all her Amazonian largeness, was Special Agent Rafferty.

"Just my dad," I said. "How did you know I was here?"

"I've been running checks on the calls you got from this movie producer you're supposed to be meeting," she answered. "Something sounded a little weird about it. I mean, I like your books, but have they ever even heard of you in Hollywood?"

Everybody thinks they know the book business. "They're interested in the Duffy Madison books as a possible TV series, as a matter of fact," I said, wondering why I was defending myself all of a sudden. "So what about Glenn Waterman? I checked him out; he's real."

Rafferty nodded. "Yeah, but the calls you got weren't. They didn't come from Los Angeles, and they weren't from that company. Someone wanted to lure you—" She turned her head suddenly, seemingly alarmed. "Did you hear that?"

I hadn't heard anything and told her so.

"Stay right there a moment. Don't move," Rafferty said. She patted her side, no doubt looking for her weapon, and walked, quickly but cautiously, around the side of the English Muffin. There was an alley there where I knew Danielle could receive deliveries and sometimes park her car when there wasn't a space nearby. But Rafferty didn't seem interested in that; she looked really intense. Then she disappeared around the corner.

After a second, she started to laugh. "Oh, sorry about that," she called from around the corner. "Didn't mean to worry you. It's just . . . it's too funny."

I snorted at the sound of her amusement and walked around to the side to see what was so damn hilarious. But when I got to the alley, all I saw was a pretty ordinary four-door car, a Ford or a Nissan or something. I'm not great with cars.

"What's so—?" That was as far as I got.

I felt a sharp pain in my right hip, a pinch, really, and heard Rafferty say, "You just go ahead to sleep, now," as she caught me under the arms. I tried to protest, but my head suddenly weighed sixty-five pounds and my eyelids were gaining weight equally fast.

The last thought I had before I blacked out was "TSTL."

Too stupid to live.

Chapter 26

Honestly, I don't remember much for the rest of that day. Whatever had been injected into my hip did its job with some high level of efficiency. I can't remember being put into the car, although I surely was, or riding for hours (and I'm sure that's what happened), and I don't remember being taken out of the car and dragged into what appeared to be a very large, mothball-scented attic.

Whoever had done this to me must have been remarkably strong or had help, an elevator, a hand truck, or some combination of those things. That really didn't matter much to me at the moment.

I'll confess it: my first coherent thought after quite a while of not wanting to wake up at all was, "I guess this means I'm not meeting with Glenn Waterman."

Yes, that is precisely how crazy I am, and I was willing to bet I'd be the sanest one in the room the minute that hatch in the floor next to me opened up and someone climbed into my loft. I'd decided it was a loft because "torture chamber" was just a little too bleak.

To be fair, there wasn't anything in the room that would indicate I was in line to be physically abused. There were blue, probably room-darkening blinds on the one window, so I couldn't really see out to determine where I might be located. There was an area rug in the center of the room, but I was not sitting on it and the hardwood floor was living up to its name, so my butt was falling asleep rapidly—or maybe it just hadn't yet woken up.

I sincerely can't tell you why I wasn't in the panic attack to end all panic attacks. I should have been crying, screaming, gasping for breath, and pleading for my release. Of course, there wasn't anyone there with whom to plead, so that last part was simply a matter of practicality. The rest? No idea why I wasn't doing it.

I was thinking along with the character. I must have decided somewhere along the line that if I was going to be in this terrifying position, I'd pretend it was a scenario I was concocting for a new book and that I was somehow just doing the research to see how it felt to be kidnapped and held against my will.

It sucked, for the record.

My hands and feet were not bound, which I had figured, since Sunny Maugham's arms and legs—and I was sure, those of the other three members of the exclusive club I'd just joined—had not shown any bruises. But there was clearly no way out of this place except the hatch, and that was clearly locked from underneath. I suppose I could have tried the window, but jumping to my death wasn't really all that much an improvement over whatever hideous plan my captor(s) must surely have in store for me.

I walked over to the window, giving my behind a chance to work out the pins and needles. I was walking slowly, my head in a fog still. Stumbling was not a fantastic option; there was no furniture to break my fall if I fell, and there was that window, which undoubtedly was very high off the ground.

But I'd never really get to know, because when I moved the blinds, I saw the window had been boarded up from the outside. Touché, complete maniac who had taken me away from my friends and my father.

Dad must be frantic, I thought. He'd been right all along, and even if I managed to do what none of the other authors had done and survive this ordeal, I'd have to admit that to him and hear him tell me exactly how I didn't listen to his warnings for the rest of my life. It almost made being murdered by a nutty copy editor seem preferable.

Almost.

In one corner behind me, there was a steamer trunk from an era when luggage was big enough to take with you on a ship to Europe and stay six months but before they'd figured out about putting wheels on suitcases. Next to it was a carpenter's toolbox, probably built by the carpenter himself (or herself; what did I know?) out of wood, with a drawer on top and an open section, about the size of two kitchen cabinets, below it. I walked over. The whole toolbox was empty; the steamer trunk smelled of mothballs but had no clothing in it. No weapons there.

There was a lamp in the far corner of the room, which was why I could see anything in here, I realized. It was a pole lamp with three bulbs, but it wasn't exactly making the place look cheery. There was no furniture, no chairs, no table, no bed.

Whoever was keeping me here certainly didn't intend to be doing so for a long time. I wasn't sure whether I was glad about that, but I was guessing I wasn't.

I looked around for something I could use. As a novelist, you have to mentally put yourself into the scene you're writing. That means you imagine where the fake incidents are supposed to be happening, you furnish it with things that would be logical for the surroundings, and then you decide how your characters would use those things, either furniture or objects. The better you imagine, the more real your scene will be.

The person who had dreamed this scene up appeared to have a very sparse imagination. Besides the lamp and the rug, there was a collection of paperback novels—all crime fiction, of course, and many of them by the murdered writers—in a bookshelf that was built into the wall and couldn't be shaken loose. Believe me.

The worse part was that the maniac didn't have one of my titles on the shelf. Not one. I was going to die at this person's hand, and I couldn't even be sure it belonged to one of my readers.

Don't worry; the fact that you think that's crazy indicates you have a normal mind.

There was no gun rack, no straight razor, no hunting knife, no bow and arrow, none of the conveniently if unrealistically placed weapons authors like me are always placing in rooms like this one. There were books and a lamp and a rug. I supposed that when Shana Kineally showed up in the attic—I'd decided it was an attic and not a loft because *loft* seemed too grand a word now—I could throw some paperbacks at her, but it didn't really seem the best possible escape plan.

On the other hand, it was the only one I had right now.

Despair is an interesting thing, as long as you're not experiencing it yourself. The notion that nothing is possible, all is lost, you're out of options (stop me if you've heard these . . .), there are no possibilities—it is supposed to lead to a nothing-to-lose attitude, a sense of freedom, almost. That's if you like popular fiction or TV.

What I can tell you about the emotion of being trapped in an attic is that more than anything else, it pisses you off. Everything you think you might try is a dead end, but you don't realize it until after that adrenaline rush of hope, almost immediately dashed. After this happened three or four times, I was nail-spittin' mad.

And that was the bad luck of the person who unlocked the hatch in the center of the room and pulled down the stairs to climb up to my level. Because even if my head was still a little woozy, I had been abducted, my life was no doubt in some jeopardy, and worst of all, I now had to apologize to my father. When Shana Kineally appeared, she'd have the devil to pay.

I couldn't arm myself with anything, because there was nothing there. I suppose it would be possible to threaten someone with a rolled-up area rug, but I hadn't given that enough thought and left the thing on the floor, flat and the opposite of dangerous. I did find myself, without conscious thought, curling my hands into claws and mentally sharpening my fingernails.

When Special Agent Eunice Rafferty emerged from the lower floor of wherever I was, it was less a surprise than a disappointment. I had probably already registered in the back of my sedated mind the information that brought with it.

"You," I said. "You're Shana Kineally."

"Big reveal," she answered. "Somewhere around page two fifty, no? Or is this a mystery novel, and I don't get exposed until the last chapter?"

"I didn't write this one," I said. "You're the author of this sick story."

Her eyes met mine. "Ooh. A feisty one." She held out her right hand and then opened it to show two tablets and reached into her cargo shorts to pull out a plastic water bottle. "Take these," she said. "Your head must be pounding."

I took the pills from her and put them in my mouth, then gratefully took the water bottle and sniffed it before drinking.

"Don't worry," she said. "There's nothing in the water. I don't intend to poison you."

Be that as it may, I still stashed the pills in the corner of my jaw between my teeth and my cheek. I wasn't swallowing any "medicine" she gave me. This was blood sport.

"What *do* you intend to do with me?" I asked. "How long has it been since you knocked me out and took me away?"

"Only about eight hours," she said. "You're not even officially missing yet." I was sure that was wrong, since Dad would have called Ben or Duffy almost immediately after I failed to answer his text. "Still, I'm sure your pals down in Bergen County are already looking for you. They won't find you."

Down in Bergen County. That meant we were north of there, probably in New York State or Connecticut, based on the time. If Duffy's candy wrapper was right, we were in or near Syracuse, best bet. I couldn't be sure how long I'd been in the room; the drive could have taken an hour or seven. But any information I could get might prove useful later.

"You didn't answer my first question," I said. "What are you going to do with me?"

A really chilling smile arranged itself on her face. "You saw the others," she purred. "What do *you* think I'm going to do?"

I braced myself emotionally; showing fear would do no good, and it wouldn't even make me feel better. I decided to concentrate on being angry. "If you think I'm giving you creative ideas, lady, you have snatched yourself the wrong author. You want to know how to treat me? Read some Dr. Seuss."

"He's dead," Kineally answered. "And I didn't even kill him."

"That's a relief. But I'm going to be up here in your little cage for a few days, aren't I? Isn't that your pattern?" The pills next to my gum were starting to chafe; they'd probably dissolve and my efforts not to take them would have been for naught. It was a bitch being a modern damsel in distress; cowering and waiting for a man to come save me would have been so much less stressful.

"I don't discuss process," she said. "It ruins the surprise."

"So you came upstairs to give me a couple of Tylenol and act like Catwoman?" I sat down next to the wall and leaned back. "What's the matter, by the way—a chair would have put you in bankruptcy?"

"I came up here to establish the rules," she said, barely an inflection in her voice.

"Yeah, because if I don't follow them, you'll do what? You're going to kill me either way."

"True." Kineally began walking the perimeter of the room, perhaps daring me to make a break for the stairs in the center, but I knew that was a sucker's move. Instead, I faked a cough and ejected the two slobbery pills into my left hand. Which had seemed like a good idea at the time. "But how . . . unpleasant your time might be is determined by how closely you follow the rules."

"That's a hell of an incentive," I shot back. "Please. Tell me what I must do to die pleasantly."

"No escape attempts," she answered, as if I were serious about the question. "The first time I catch you trying to get away—and believe me, I will catch you—I will make sure to cause you great suffering. There won't be any attempts after that." Okay, that was pretty ominous, so I tried to think of things to make me angry instead of scared. No movie deal. That was it.

"You know that by snatching me up this morning, you cheated me out of a movie deal for one of my books?" I spat at her. I have no idea why I thought that would be a useful weapon, but it did piss me off again, and that seemed the right way to go.

But from Kineally's mouth came the voice of the receptionist Marcie I'd heard on the phone. "You mean the meeting with Mr. Glenn Waterman of Beverly Hills Productions?" she teased, then switched back to her real tone. "Honey, that wasn't ever going to happen. It was a way to lure you out, is all. Glenn Waterman's never heard of you."

"You called my agent? How did you even know about the manuscript?"

"Thank your pal Duffy Madison," she said with a brittle, cold laugh. "He was talking up that book *Little Boy Lost* with Hollywood producers and made some phone calls. Word got to me through a connection in Hugh Ventnor's office at Parthenon, maybe to see if I'd edit a new series from you if the movie deal went through." She sneered. "Which it's *not*."

"But my agent didn't know, and he didn't show up at the supposed meeting this morning." Go ahead; prove the movie deal was real to the woman who'd made it up.

Her voice took on that of "Marcie" again. "Hello, Mr. Resnick? Ms. Goldman and Mr. Waterman decided to make the meeting tomorrow at his hotel. Yes, I'll get back to you with the details." Rarely have I felt more stupid.

"Duffy," I said to myself. She'd mentioned his name, but I was almost trying to summon him.

"I told you not to trust him. But then, we were talking about the rules. I said not to try to escape."

"Why would I want to, as hospitable as you're being?"

She ignored that. "I've taken your cell phone; you probably realized that already. When it's time for people to find you, I'll make the call. Not to worry. You won't have to pay your cell phone bill this month, anyway." Now I was pissed off *and* afraid.

"If I knew you were paying, I would have gotten the more expensive data package." It wasn't much, but the circumstances were playing against my quick wit.

"I'll give you food and water when I feel it's time. You may not come out of this space to use the bathroom unless I bring you downstairs myself. Otherwise, you're on your own."

"What's the point of keeping me here for however many days?" It had been bothering me for a week now. "You take these authors and keep them here for a while, and then you kill them and take them back to where they live. Why not just kill them right away?" Talking about the other victims made it seem less like I was becoming one of them. Reality was not my best friend right at the moment, so I was denying it.

"In your case, the point is to get your pals looking for you in the wrong direction," she said, eager to show off her brilliant technique. "The others were for different reasons. You're a special case."

Somehow that didn't make me feel better. "You're a major nut job, you know that?" I yelled. "What's your problem, anyway? You had to kill all those authors because you didn't like their syntax? Their misuse of apostrophes finally put you over the edge?"

For a moment, I thought Kineally was going to rush me; her eyes took on a red, mad quality and her teeth clamped shut with her suddenly outstretched jaw. But she caught herself and stopped, standing just in front of the pull-down stairs. If I could make a move at the right time, I might be able to push her down the way she came. But if she wasn't completely immobilized by the fall—killed would be best—she'd be standing between me and freedom, and she'd be injured and furious. Probably not the best plan.

"That would be the cliché, wouldn't it?" Kineally shouted. "That's what you'd write into your novel, isn't it? That the crazy copy editor, the defender of the English language against abuses that would have been considered signs of a mental deficiency twenty years ago, just snapped one day? You'd write a copy editor who went around killing people in creative, macabre fashions tied to their writing because she couldn't stand bad punctuation? That character would probably be a frumpy, sexless, middle-aged spinster whose only pleasure was the proper use of sentence structure, wouldn't she? Well, that's not me, lady. Not by a long shot." Great. So now I knew she wasn't sexless.

"Then why?" I said in a more normal conversational tone.

"None of your damn business," she said. She turned and stomped down the stairs, and before I could rush the opening, she pushed them back up and locked the hatch beneath me.

"Well, that went well," I said to myself.

I sat down. No bathroom breaks without permission? This was truly Purgatory. There had to be a way out. And thinking that none of the other authors, at least one of whom must have been smarter than me, had found it was not encouraging.

But someone I knew was much smarter than me and would easily see the openings, the opportunities for escape, no matter what my archnemesis downstairs might think. Someone who could assess the situation coolly and calmly, take in all the possibilities in the room and the predicament, and discover the one method of extraction that no one else would possibly see.

Duffy Madison.

And since I had created Duffy out of nothing, since he was unquestionably a product of my imagination, it followed that the capacity to get myself out of this particular cage was in my brain, waiting to be unleashed. All I had to do was put *Duffy* into this attic mentally, see things through his eyes, and the answer would surely be revealed.

Yes, writers are crazy. But we perform a public service: we think up this wacky shit so you don't have to.

I let Duffy take over my head and thought in his voice. It's something I do to get the character right, and if I could think of this as a fictional situation, I could control it.

In *Olly Olly Oxen Free*, I had Duffy locked up as a potential suspect in the kidnapping case he was investigating. (It's a long story—go buy the book; it's in paperback.) And I wanted it to be realistic, so I actually got Marty Dugan to lock me up in a municipal holding cell in Pequannock. I looked at it through Duffy's eyes, thought logically, and noticed everything I wouldn't have noticed as myself.

I couldn't bust myself out of the cell, but I could come up with a scenario in which Duffy managed to fool the officer on duty into thinking he was no longer in the cell so he would come in for a look and Duffy could sneak out. It was partially because of the research and partially through a very sophisticated literary technique we authors refer to as "fudging it."

Now I looked around the dark attic with Duffy's voice in my head. *Look for light*, it told me. *Light means a crack in the armor. It is a pathway to freedom.* That seemed logical, so I sat down in the center of the room and looked for shafts of light. There was a dull glow from the window, but it was mostly boarded up and curtained, so that wasn't much. Getting through the plywood and nails holding it would have been difficult if I'd had tools. There were none, however—not even in that damned huge toolbox. Without any, I was helpless on that front.

Still, I could see in the room, and there was just the one lamp, and that was in the far corner. No candles. So by rights, I should have seen only the area around the lamp well; everything else should have been in close to total darkness.

It wasn't. Where was the light coming from?

A careful view of the room made that question easy enough to answer: the light was coming from the ceiling. There was no skylight installed (that would have been too easy), but there were areas where light was coming through. This building must have had a remarkably old and battered roof. I lay on the floor and looked straight up. There were several points of light coming through the ceiling, but mostly pinpoints, far too small to be of much use.

Except one.

A little to the left of the ceiling's peak was a light area in the weathered plywood. It wasn't a hole exactly; it was more in the area of wear. It was like that section, about a square foot, of the ceiling was glowing. That meant there was very little roofing material over it. And *that* meant it could be punched through pretty easily, allowing access to the roof.

There were only two problems with that: I had no way to get that high up in the room to punch through, and even if I did, I was horribly afraid of heights. Being out on the roof didn't seem all that much better than letting Kineally come in here and kill me in a witty literary fashion.

Come on, Duffy. What else? *Examine the drop-down stairs on the hatch. How are they hinged, and how are the stairs attached to the floor?* Making it down the stairs would be risky, but a heck of a lot less terrifying than trying to Spider-Man my way up to the ceiling and then walk out onto an obviously unstable roof. Maybe there was something here.

The stairs were a standard-issue Home Depot kind of contraption. When they were folded up, like now, the stairs were flattened into an accordion-style configuration, but what the Duffy in my mind was telling me to examine was the edges of the board to which they were affixed.

The metal stairs, folded, were bolted to a heavy particle board material that was probably finished on the underside with drywall to look as much like a regular ceiling as possible. But in order to open down when the stairs were to be unfolded, there were hinges on the edge closest to me, screwed on one side to the particle board assembly and on the other to the floor of the attic.

So if I could find a way to detach the hinges, at the very least I could keep Kineally from coming upstairs. Best-case scenario had the stairs dropping through the hole in the floor and giving me a somewhat treacherous but possible escape route.

Problem: I had no screwdriver to remove the hinges. I had, in my estimation, a grand total of nothing.

One more time, Duffy; you've gotta come up with something! *In the absence of an escape route, find a way to signal someone outside or get a message to me.* He would say that, but he wasn't offering a concrete possibility.

There is an electric lamp in that corner. That means there is a power outlet into which the lamp is plugged, no? There was. *Good. Find a way to short out the outlet and turn off the lights in the attic. Your eyes will adjust. Kineally's won't. Make a great deal of noise, and when she comes upstairs, you will have the advantage.*

Couldn't I just unplug the lamp for the same effect? *Yes, but shorting the outlet opens up the possibility in an old building like this one that the power will fail in other areas as well. That gives you more of an advantage.*

It wasn't much, but that appeared to be the best Duffy could do. There wasn't anything lying around the attic that presented itself as a useful electrical disruption tool. I supposed a paper clip or something metal would do well, but of course there was the possibility that I'd electrocute myself and spare Kineally the time and trouble of killing me. Still, the average home's power supply probably wouldn't kill me if I stuck some metal into a power outlet. Probably.

Aw hell, it was worth a shot.

I went through my pockets. Naturally Kineally had taken my cell phone, but I still had my keys; I guess she figured I couldn't unlock something and get away, and gouging her eyes out with the key to a Toyota Prius c seemed unlikely and difficult. For my purposes, the keys would do, however unpleasantly.

Without any further messages from my mental Duffy, I was resigned to the unpleasant task ahead. I heaved a heavy sigh and dragged myself over to the sole source of light in the room. I followed the cord from the base of the standing lamp to an outlet about midway in the far wall.

I took the keys out of my pocket and selected the one from my car, which was the longest, to insert into the socket. If I'd had a paper clip, I could have wrapped it around the prongs of the lamp's plug and pushed that into the socket. I wasn't sure if that was a proper way to make the lights go out, but it had worked for Walter Matthau in *Hopscotch*, and he was playing a really smart CIA agent.

Now you have to understand, I am seriously squeamish about electricity. So that simple move—pushing the key into the socket—was requiring a lot more determination that I wanted to muster. But the thought of Kineally coming up those stairs again, coupled with the memory of Sunny Maugham in her supply closet, a pen sticking out of her neck, drove me forward.

I picked up the key again, aimed it at the left hole in the outlet, and took a deep breath. And just as I was about to thrust forward, Duffy's voice came through once more time: *Wait! Put a key in each of the vertical receptacles. That will complete the circuit and cause the breaker to trip, which will help to prevent electrocution*. Who knew I had that knowledge buried in my brain?

For fifteen minutes, I tried to push the two keys—to my car and my post office box—into the socket by getting them close, and then pushing them in using the sole of my shoe, assuming that would provide some insulation, or grounding, or something. But the keys kept falling out before I could move the shoe in place.

Fighting nausea, I decided the only way to do this was to do it. I took the two keys, one in each hand, positioned them as they had to be, and pushed hard.

Zap!

Sparks flew from the receptacles. But oddly, I didn't feel any current run into my hands. I'm not complaining, believe me, but it surprised me, making me think I'd somehow done this incorrectly.

Except that the sparks were followed by the lamp going out and a crackling sound that, it seemed to be, was not confined merely to the attic. I could see very little now, but within seconds, my eyes adjusted to the new condition. The tiny pinpricks of light from the ceiling that I'd had to search for before were now much more visible, but I trained myself not to look directly at them. *Make sure your pupils dilate. See as well as you can in the dark. It gives you an advantage over your captor, but it won't last long.* Thanks for the reminder, Duffy.

It also occurred to me that freed of its light-diffusing responsibility, the floor lamp would make a dandy blunt instrument. Which was a good thing to know in this dark room, because I was already picking up sounds of someone on the floor below—and the lock on the ceiling latch being pulled back.

Kineally was coming.

Chapter 27

I had to operate on a few assumptions. First, it was fairly clear that my socket escapade had had some effect in the building's lower floors, or Kineally would not have known anything was the least bit amiss. So it was possible that things were just as dark below as they were up here. Which meant I wouldn't have any edge in the seeing-in-the-dark competition that was about to begin.

You might have mentioned that, Duffy.

The difference might lie in the idea that she would have a flashlight or something, and that brought the advantage back to me if, upon opening the hatch (as appeared to be happening now) and climbing the stairs, Kineally did not find me in the spot where she would expect to do so. That might give me the second I needed.

Besides, it was the only thing I could think of.

I positioned myself, lamp in hands, behind the hatch opening. There was a light coming up from beneath, but it was indeed a flashlight, and I was thrilled to see it was pointed ahead—that is, away from me. And even as she ascended, Kineally was already spitting nails.

"What did I tell you about escape attempts?" she growled in my general direction as she rose, moving the flashlight back and forth in an attempt to locate me.

It's really hard to stand absolutely still when you're holding a floor lamp, watching a deranged killer come toward you raging mad, and feeling like the pounding of your heart could undoubtedly be heard in a parking lot two blocks away. So give me some props for not collapsing to the floor and begging for mercy.

"You're going to pay dearly for this," she continued, apparently attempting to go through all the moustache-twirling clichés in one fell swoop. "I tried to deal with you fairly, but you had to break the rules. Now you'll feel pain."

Was it better to smash her in the back of the head or the face? *The skull is much thicker in the back than any bone in the face. But be careful to aim low enough, because the forehead is not a thin piece of bone at all.*

Thank you, Dr. Duffy.

"Sorry for spoiling your plans, bitch!" I screamed as Kineally's foot hit the attic floor, and sure enough, she turned toward the sound of my voice. I had ducked down, anticipating her shining the flashlight in my face and that worked, too, as the beam went over my head and not into my eyes. I swung the lamp like a baseball bat and hit my target.

But I had swung too low. The lamp impacted with Kineally's shoulder, not her face. Hey. It was a heavy lamp. You try it sometime and see how it goes for you.

She moved and grunted, but she didn't fall down the stairs, which was a disappointment, and she did not become unconscious, which wasn't surprising but was a considerable setback. So I swung the lamp again, but this time Kineally could anticipate the movement and ducked. The element of surprise was completely gone.

Advantage, Kineally.

Two elements made me drop the lamp: first, it clearly was not going to be the instrument of liberation I had hoped for, and second, it was getting really heavy. But, sorry, did I say *drop the lamp*? What I actually meant was *throw the lamp with all my might at the window and hope it would break through so I could scream and someone would come rescue me.*

Alas, the lamp base hit the plywood blocking the window and bounced off, falling harmlessly to the floor. They don't make lamps like they used to, or they make plywood better. Either way, I was screwed.

"You *idiot*!" Kineally hissed. "I told you there was no way you could get out!"

"Yeah, you told me you were an FBI agent, too. Why should I believe anything you say?" You can say what you want about Jersey girls, but if you knock us out and lock us up in an attic with a clear intention of killing us, you should definitely expect to get back a decent dose of attitude.

Wait. Was that a doorbell I heard? Nah. It was too far away. Nobody was coming for me.

"You made all the power in the house go out!" I was being scolded like a naughty child. There was a certain absurdity to her giving me a hard time about it that I couldn't decide whether to laugh or kick her. She was too far away, luckily, to kick, and I didn't think it was all that funny, so I passed on both.

"Yeah, excuse me for making it harder for you to imprison and murder me; I don't know what I was thinking." I backed up a little bit farther, feeling for the wall with the soles of my shoes, to get a better feel for my position in the room. I had to keep both eyes on Kineally, who was circling around the open hatch and toward me. She was still holding the flashlight, which was doing nothing for my vision at all, but did not appear to have a weapon in her hands. What is it they say about small favors?

Maybe if I kept her circling and reversed our positions in the room, I could lunge for the stairs and lock *her* in the attic! There was a delicious sense of justice in the notion; I was careful to keep my steps small and my movements slow so she wouldn't understand my intentions until it was too late.

Okay, so my hands tingled a bit from the electrical interlude, and my legs still were a little stiff from having spent a good number of hours lying drugged on the attic floor, but adrenaline will do a lot for your body for a short period of time. I was counting on that.

Distract her, keep her talking. My inner Duffy was still trying to help, the dear thing. "Why on earth does a person do something like this?" I demanded. "You killed four authors."

"So far," Kineally intoned. She took a step toward me; I moved a bit to my right while I backed up.

"Fine, if you're going to kill me, can't I know why? How will I learn otherwise?"

She didn't even pick up on the absurdity of that notion; the woman was so far into the bonkers category, she probably thought I was making sense. "You're different. You aren't like the others; I didn't plan for you. It's because you became an irritant. You sent me back rude e-mails, and you helped with the investigation to find me. You are a *pest*, Ms. Goldman."

So that meant that everything that was about to get me killed was something I wouldn't have done if it weren't for that tall, rangy lunatic who ambled into my life and told me he was my own fictional creation. He made me come along to Ocean Grove. He made me send the e-mails that pissed off the killer. He caused me to discover Sunny Maugham's body.

It was Duffy's fault I was going to die.

Don't get mad at me; keep her talking.

Yeah, an obvious dodge, you jerk. But it was all I had left as I moved with sickening stealth toward my goal. "Why the others, then? What did they ever do to you? They all paid you for your work, didn't they?"

I couldn't really get a good look at Kineally's face, but her inflection carried enough hate for me to grasp everything I needed to understand. "Oh, they paid me, all right," she said. "They paid me to clean up their ridiculous spelling errors—they didn't know 'your' from 'you are.' And they made sure that I was there to repair their torturous mangling of punctuation. Apostrophes! What did they have against apostrophes?!"

Four more steps and I'd be in jumping range of the hatch. "But you said you didn't kill them because of proofreading errors," I reminded the homicidal maniac.

"I didn't!" Her voice had crossed the line from irritated to raving. "I fixed their asinine errors, and I took their money. But when I tried to lay it all out, neatly and perfectly in a volume that would explain to everyone in a generation why grammar and punctuation matters, did they help me? I couldn't get one of those bitches to pick up a phone."

So that was it; I should have seen it coming a mile away. "You wrote a grammar book?" Had I said that out loud? Two more steps . . .

Apparently so. "It was a grammar *bible*!" Kineally screamed. "It was going to change the way every writer in the country operated. It would have done so much good, but every time I asked, it was, 'Oh, I don't deal in nonfiction,' and 'Didn't *Eats, Shoots & Leaves* take care of all that?"

I moved toward the hatch but too fast. Kineally saw what I was doing. "Stop!" she screamed. "Don't even think about it!" And she leapt into the space between us to block me from my escape. For an unhinged, unpublished writer, she could jump; I'd give her that.

"That's a reason to kill people?" I said. "Because they didn't help you publish your"—I looked at her and changed course midstream—"grammar bible?"

"Don't change the subject—you were about to rush down those stairs!" The flashlight dropped from her hands, and the only light in the room now was from the cracks around the window and the holes in the ceiling. It wasn't much, but what I could see was enough to make me wish it was darker.

Kineally was reaching into her pocket and pulling out a weapon. "I was going to wait two more days, but you've made it impossible," she said. "This is your last moment alive." And she produced from her pocket—

"A *letter opener*?" I shouted at her. "You plotted and planned all those over-the-top deaths for those other writers, and I get a *letter opener*? That's the best you could do?"

She looked contrite. "I told you," she said. "You were a rush job." And she raised the dagger, which did indeed look sharp.

This was so Duffy's fault, I thought. He'd gotten me killed and I hadn't even revised his latest adventure. I was beyond irate. The only thing that man could possibly do to redeem himself in my eyes now was . . .

There was a sound from downstairs, and Kineally stopped her motion and looked down into the hatch. It sounded like a door opening, or wood splintering, or both. And in seconds, a voice screamed into the blackness below me, "Rachel?" More authoritative. "Rachel!"

Duffy.

Kineally's face took on an expression of such anger, you would have thought someone had broken into her home and threatened to ruin the rest of her life.

Oh, yeah. Never mind.

Before I could twitch a facial muscle or vibrate a vocal cord, she had grabbed me and put a hand over my mouth. "How did they find you here?" she hissed. It was a good question, but even if I knew, I don't think I would have volunteered an answer. Which was just as well, because there was that hand on my mouth. Kineally started pushing me away from the hatch and back toward the wall.

"Rachel?" came the voice from below. Was that Ben Preston? Was it weird that, though he sort of asked me out, I couldn't immediately recognize his voice, yet I could pick Duffy's out of a lineup? Was that because I'd had Duffy's voice in my head for years?

Maybe this wasn't the time to ponder that.

"So you didn't care for the letter opener?" Kineally whispered in my ear as she dragged me into the darkest corner of the attic. "I can respect that. How's this for creativity? If they haul me off, you're going to die the worst kind of death: slow and agonizing from starvation and dehydration, because you'll be locked in this attic, and they won't find you until someone complains about the smell. And if they don't figure out who I am, I'll come back for something more inventive. Assuming you don't suffocate first."

I fought against her shoving a little harder after that, but the woman was big and strong, and I was, you know, not. She struggled with my resistance, but it didn't stop my momentum. And I could see what our destination was going to be.

The steamer trunk in the corner.

Under normal (for a crime such as this) circumstances, that would be the best possible place to be stashed away. It was the first object an observer would see that would be large enough to store a body—even a live one. If I could count on Kineally not dosing me up with another shot of her sleep juice, and if it didn't have padlocks on it the size of hubcaps, and if I wasn't petrified at the idea of running out of air in that little thing, and if *Duffy Madison wasn't going to assume this criminal would never put me in something that obvious*, I'd have hopped happily into the trunk and awaited my rescue.

But that was a lot of "ifs" to consider, and the last one was the—you should pardon the expression—killer. Duffy would see the trunk, figure Kineally was an evil genius who would never use such a trite storage receptacle, and look for something less pulp fiction and more Hannibal Lecter. By the time he realized that he should be thinking more conventionally, I'd be deprived of air for too long, and it wouldn't matter. To me.

I increased my resistance as we reached the trunk. I needed to instantly flash upon a more creative alternative and then convince Kineally that the change in plan was her idea, because if I showed too much panic at being stuffed in a trunk, that would become much more attractive to this sadistic maniac.

First order of business: figure out what Duffy would flash on. I had to think back on what I'd seen when I'd scoped out the area before. What was the opposite of a place the average deranged criminal would stash a victim?

Oh, no.

The small wooden toolbox, which on first glance didn't appear large enough for a human being to exist in, was exactly the kind of thing Duffy's criminally attuned mind would latch onto. It was just the right place to get Kineally to store me. And I hated myself for thinking of it. I'm not overly claustrophobic, but a big dog would feel a little cooped up in that thing, and I am somewhat larger than a collie.

Damn it, it was perfect.

Now to convince her to do it. I fought against her pulling, which was still the best option but least likely, and forced my mouth open between her fingers. "What are you *doing*?" I asked, muffled but audible. As if it weren't crystal clear exactly what she was doing.

Kineally didn't answer. From downstairs, but closer now, I could hear Duffy's voice. "Is anyone here?" he called. He'd never yell, "Police!" It wouldn't be accurate. Still not close enough to see the pull-down stairs, he was definitely on his way in the right direction.

When we were (finally) near enough to both objects, I dug in my heels, looked at the toolbox, and widened my eyes with not-very-feigned fear. "You're putting me in *that*?" I gasped. "No, please. Not in there! It's too tight! I'll die!"

Okay, so I stole my tactic from Br'er Rabbit. That doesn't make it bad.

Kineally, clearly not having considered the toolbox before, looked at it, sized me up, and grinned with evil glee. "That's exactly what I'm doing. And if you so much as make a squeak to signal your pal downstairs, I'll leave you in there until you're dead. Is that clear?" Then she reached into the one drawer in the toolbox and pulled out (it figured) a roll of duct tape. She ripped off a piece and slapped it over my mouth.

Before I could reach for it, she had taped my hands at the wrists like handcuffs and punched me in the stomach, making me double over. After that, stuffing me into the open doors of the toolbox was, I imagine, relatively easy. I was too busy watching the twinkling lights falling from the sky and feeling like I was going to vomit to take note. I fought the impulse. Successfully. For now.

In a nanosecond, the doors of the toolbox, made well (damn that good craftsmanship!) of heavy wood, were shut. I heard a lock click on the other side. And then I heard Kineally's footsteps head for the pull-down stairs. Then the groan of the springs as she began to push the steps back up into the attic. But there was no snap at the end, no report that indicated the stairs were back in place.

I'm sure that if I'd had the time, I would have panicked. My knees were practically in my face, it was pitch black and hot, and I had no idea how long the air in this disgustingly well-built box would last. If I'd misread Duffy, or if—worse—he never made it up to this space to search for me, I was doomed.

But luckily, there wasn't the time to think about that. Within seconds of hearing that lock snap shut, I started to hear voices. First, it was just snatches of a sentence: "Special Agent Rafferty," "already searched up there," "fresh pair of eyes." Then there was the sound of feet on the pull-down stairs, and the voices got louder.

"It's not much to look at," Kineally was saying, and even though I knew what she was saying was a lie, I had to admit it was being played convincingly. "I think we have a better chance trying to figure out where she might have been taken after she was here."

"I'm not clear on how you beat us here." That was Ben Preston's voice. "We've been tracking the GPS Duffy put in Rachel's cell phone when they drove to Ocean Grove, and it led us here. But you obviously knew about this Kineally woman that Rachel mentioned because her ex-husband's name is on the deed to this place." Oh yeah, like you had really been following up on Shana Kineally, you liar! Ben would really have to rescue me all on his own to get past first base now.

"I've been following up on the only connections the authors all had, and Kineally showed up pretty early," said the "special agent." It was amazing how she could talk about herself like a stranger. "She showed up on Sunny Maugham's hard drive. The computer spat out this address as a property owned by someone with that name. It fit."

"You thought that Rosemary Cleland was missing and sent Duffy to Connecticut when she was just off on a weekend with her boyfriend," Ben reminded her (as if she hadn't done that on purpose). "Not only did you get her husband mad at her, you wasted Duffy's time and maybe got Rachel kidnapped. So let us look around a little, okay? Your eyes aren't the only ones that see things."

"Why would the window be boarded up?" Duffy Madison was already punching holes in the idea that the attic was a dead end. Atta boy, Duffy! "I saw from outside that the glass is still intact. There is no safety element involved. It seems to me that the only rational explanation under these circumstances is that the owner of the building didn't want someone to be able to leave this room. Rachel was being held here."

"That's my point," Kineally said, trying to punch holes in Duffy's holes. Maybe I was already starting to get a little woozy. I knew for a fact that my left buttock had fallen asleep, and the rest of me wasn't far off. "She *was* being held here. She isn't being held here now. I think we're losing valuable time investigating a place that is no longer relevant."

"Maybe so," Ben said, pondering. "Her father is frantic, and I don't blame him. We might only have a few hours now before we find Rachel murdered in some bizarre way. Maybe we should try to pick up the trail."

"That's what I've been saying," Kineally reiterated. I realized I was closing my eyes. When it's totally dark in your environment, closing your eyes is either an acknowledgement that you can't see anyway or a sign that your oxygen supply is starting to dwindle and your brain can't necessarily be trusted. I forced myself to stay awake. Maybe I could make the toolbox move or fall over. That would get their attention. "If we leave now, we might be able to get to Ms. Goldman's house before this Kineally person manages to kill her."

I was definitely not fond of all this talk about me being murdered, particularly when the person who did the murdering around here was one of the people saying it. I tried to shake myself from side to side, to get the big wooden storage unit moving. Nothing. For all I knew, it was bolted to the floor. And there was barely enough room inside for me, let alone for a swaying motion. My muscles were crying out from effort and there were no results. Worse, I was breathing harder through my nose because my mouth still had the duct tape barrier on it. Air was at a premium, and I was using it up faster. That couldn't go on. I stopped trying.

I had to count on Duffy.

There was the sound of footsteps moving away from me. They were heading for the stairs! If they left and got in a car to drive to my house, which had to be at least an hour and a half away (judging from Ben's comments), I'd never get out of this toolbox. I tried to yell, but the small squeak I managed wouldn't have attracted the attention of a really astute Labrador retriever in an otherwise silent room.

"I don't think so," Duffy said, and I think I might have held my breath, which wasn't a really strong survival tactic. My head got fuzzier. "I believe there is a possibility we are giving up too easily."

"What are you talking about?" Kineally demanded. "We have very little time, and you're wasting it on a cold lead." Now that I knew she really wasn't with the FBI, that sounded like something a woman would say if she'd watched too many CBS crime dramas. A cold lead. Really.

"Everything in this room, even though it is dusty, is in place," Duffy began. I knew this technique. "The furnishings are sparse, but they have been arranged with a purpose. There are spaces on the floor that have no dust, as if someone has been sitting down. And that lamp over there, which clearly was the only source of light in the room, has been unplugged and left on the floor, discarded, not neatly standing in a corner, like the rest of the room would suggest."

"Nobody's saying she was never here," Ben argued. "Why is the lamp so important?"

"I'm collecting data," Duffy said, but his voice was gaining urgency. "And I am developing a theory."

Forcing my eyes open, I found myself hoping that Duffy's theory would develop into a concept, become an idea, and solidify into a course of action in a very short time. I felt the need to gulp air and fought the impulse, realizing that each gulp would use up more oxygen than I had to spare at the moment.

"A theory?" Kineally echoed.

Duffy didn't answer. I heard footsteps; if I were writing him, he'd be walking the perimeter of the room. "There is no evidence of physical abuse, no blood, no areas where blood might have been cleaned from the floor. There *is* evidence that someone was being held here, and footprints in the dust would indicate more than one person. This is not the first time this attic has been used for housing victims."

"You're wasting time," Kineally said.

"No he's not," said Ben. "Duffy never wastes time." That was true; I was planning on revealing in a later book that he suffered from undiagnosed ADHD. Maybe I could think about that while I slept right now . . . *No!* Wake up! The duct tape on my hands was especially irritating; my feet were unbound but had no room to kick.

Why didn't the genius who built this toolbox put in a window? Or an air conditioner?

"There is no evidence of someone being taken out of this room," Duffy announced.

Kineally's voice dropped an octave. "What?"

"It's true. The only physical evidence I can find speaks to a woman, mostly likely Ms. Goldman, being brought into the attic by someone very strong and placed on the floor and then walking around the room. And a struggle. Two people, probably women. I would guess they were Rachel and Shana Kineally."

"So what does that tell us?" Ben was great at feeding him straight lines. Suddenly, this conversation had more interesting features. I didn't need to work quite as hard to stay awake. But it was starting to feel like I was working on a story; it wasn't like they were talking about me so much as a character I had written.

Wait. If I could make Duffy real by writing about him, did that mean I had made myself up, too?

"It tells us there's a good chance Rachel Goldman is still in this attic," Duffy said.

Wow. That would be really cool. I wondered if she *was* up here! If only I could look around, I might be able to help them find her!

"That's ridiculous," Kineally said. "This killer has always abducted the victim first and then taken her back to her home to kill. They've already got a head start on us; let's *go*!"

Her footsteps were clearly the only ones I heard next. The two men must have been standing still, looking either at her or at each other.

"Gentlemen," she said. "Think of Ms. Goldman. Her life is very much in peril right now. You saw the note that was left on her trash can. The killer is targeting not just her, but you, too, Duffy. We need to get down there while she's still alive."

A long silence. Or maybe it just felt like a long silence. When Duffy spoke, it was quietly, and I was a mile and a half past drowsy, so I can't be sure my account is completely accurate.

"How did you know that, Special Agent?"

Kineally took a while, maybe two seconds, maybe three days, to answer. "Know what?"

"The incident at Ms. Goldman's house involving the note on her trash can. That was never reported to you. How did you know about it? How do you know what was written on the note?"

"Yeah," Ben's voice said, coming from somewhere around Michigan. "And the previous victims were brought here for days before they were discovered. They hadn't been killed in their homes; they were brought there afterward and staged."

I might have missed a few seconds there; I think I might have heard the sounds of a scuffle. But I knew Kineally was armed with a letter opener, while at the very least, Ben had his service weapon. It couldn't have been too much of a battle.

When I heard Duffy's voice again, it sounded panicky and a little breathless; the man needed to work out more and build up his wind. It was a condition that, now especially, I could empathize with. "She's up here somewhere! And she has to be running out of air!"

Kineally started to yell something but was told to shut up. That must have been Ben. "Tell us where you put her!" he added. There was silence, and Ben sounded disgusted when he shouted, "Officer, get her out of here!" Scuffling, feet dragging. I didn't hear steps on the stairs and wondered for a moment if they were lowering Kineally out of the window.

"The only place large enough to hide a person is the steamer trunk," Ben told Duffy. "But it's locked."

"It's the toolbox!" Duffy shouted. "That's the one we wouldn't expect! Rachel would know." I heard more running around, and after that, I don't remember much except that I had started taking those gulps of air.

And coming up short.

* * *

The next thing I remember—and since I was alive, it couldn't have been long after that—was something big, black, and round breaking through the ceiling above me. There was a very loud cracking sound, and then it came in. When it was pulled out again, air, which I would never take for granted again, flooded in. There was a fairly substantial hole in the top part of the toolbox. That was it—I was in a toolbox! And then the black thing came down again. And again. Maybe a few more times.

Then the ceiling over me was gone, and there was Duffy Madison's face. He put down the lamp I'd thrown across the room, the base of which he'd used to break through the locked doors of the toolbox, and removed the duct tape from my mouth. "Rachel," he said.

"Are you real?" I asked. My voice was raspy.

Duffy smiled. "Depends on who you talk to," he said.

Chapter 28

"Damien Mosley," I said.

Four hours later, we were driving back to my house in Duffy's car. I'd been questioned, requestioned, and then questioned again. I didn't think they had asked Shana Kineally that many questions, and she was being driven back to New Jersey—it turned out we *were* in Syracuse, New York (home of caramel candies), at Kineally's ex-husband's house, an abandoned rental property—in the back of a police car, and she was wearing zip strips on her wrists, which were behind her.

Ben Preston had offered to drive me back, but I had opted to ride shotgun in Duffy's car. Somehow the "Don't trust Duffy Madison" note, which had in an indirect way been Kineally's undoing, had done exactly what Ben and Dad had said it should do: it had made me trust Duffy that much more.

I'd called Dad on my cell phone—the one they'd found in Kineally's back pocket and in which Duffy had apparently slipped a GPS device when I'd left it in his car at Ocean Grove—as soon as I could breathe normally again.

He sounded incredibly relieved, refused to even hint at an I-told-you-so, and must have been so happy that he'd lost his mind, because he offered to call my mother and fill her in on what had been going on.

Personally, I just wanted to go back to my house and sleep for a few days, and then revise my novel with a new ending, in which the girl Duffy is searching for actually takes an active role in helping him locate her. She would not be TSTL if I had any say about it, and it looked like I would.

"Who is Damien Mosley?" Duffy asked, not a hint of recognition, even to the point of an eyelid flutter, on his face.

"You don't remember him?" I asked sweetly. All right, manufactured sweetly. High fructose corn syrup sweetly. "He went to high school in Poughkeepsie, just like you. Went to Oberlin, just like you. Right about the same time, too."

"Coincidences are interesting but by definition meaningless if there is no pattern or intent," Duffy said. I didn't have time to analyze his sentence structure, but I thought he was asking me exactly what the hell the point of my exciting Damien Mosley story might be.

The highway was not crowded, unusual for any time of any day on Route 17. Maybe my luck was changing. I looked through the windshield at the road and saw nothing but open space, which admittedly was crowded with strip malls and office buildings. It still looked like an unlimited source of possibilities.

"Damien Mosley vanished about four years ago," I said. "He left his job, his apartment, his mother, and his life. Nobody's heard from him since."

"What is the significance?" Duffy asked. "I have no recollection of a Damien Mosley."

I sat back and rested my head, closing my eyes for a refreshing moment. "Don't you see any interesting parallels?" I asked Duffy.

His gaze never left the road. "Parallels?"

"Damien Mosley left New Rochelle, where he lived at the time, and never came back. At almost exactly that moment, a man shows up at the Bergen County Prosecutor's Office with no background, no history, and no memory, except that he calls himself Duffy Madison, oddly the same name as the character in my novel."

Duffy smiled slightly and let out a small sigh. "Are we back to this?" he asked.

"You don't think the facts fit the theory?" I asked. I can speak his language. I invented his language.

"I'm saying that I'm not Damien Mosley," he answered. "I am Duffy Madison."

"And you leapt to existence from my tortured mind?" I closed my eyes again. I thought the sedative Kineally had given me, coupled with my time inside the wooden toolbox, had not entirely worn off.

"I did not leap to existence from a man who happens to share my initials," he contended.

"You're right. Your explanation makes way more sense. By the way, nice not checking on some woman who marches into your office and says she's an FBI agent. Excuse me, *special* agent."

Duffy's eyes never left the road. "There *is* a Special Agent Eunice Rafferty in the Newark office, but since the photo on her credentials, which she never reported stolen because she was embarrassed, was taken when she was a rookie ten years ago, there was no reason for us to suspect the woman we were checking on was anyone but who she claimed to be."

Oh.

We drove in silence for a while. I might even have fallen asleep at one point; the next thing I knew, we were on Route 78 in New Jersey. Duffy had turned on the radio because there was a baseball game being broadcast. Duffy is a Mets fan. They were losing, the sportscaster said, four to two.

"Why did you talk up my book to publishers?" I asked him. I think I must have caught Duffy by surprise; his mouth twitched a little when I spoke.

"Because I believed it was obvious that the killer had some connection to the publishing industry," he answered. He had missed a beat and was trying to compensate by talking too fast. "No matter what anyone was saying, the link among the victims, including Ms. Bledsoe, had to do with crime fiction publishing."

"I don't see how—"

"If the publishing business was buzzing with word of your work, it could have the possibility of shaking loose someone who was already involved in the industry but had another agenda. It was the same principle as the e-mail I had you send back to Ms. Kineally when she threatened you."

My lips pushed out, I think without my consent. "You were using me as bait."

Duffy did look a little flustered at that; he actually broke eye contact with the road for a split second and looked at the radio. "Fly ball scores a run," he said quietly.

"You heard me," I said.

"Yes. I suppose I was making you a target. I had determined that I could track you using your cell phone, and I thought that even if something were to go wrong and you were taken, we would be able to find you in time."

"You almost didn't," I said.

"I know. I apologize."

I should have been furious with him. A day before, I probably would have been. But spending some time inside a dark box with your kneecaps in your eye sockets can change your perspective. In this case, it made me a little more tolerant of the man who had worked so hard to get me abducted and then harder to get me out of danger.

I waved a hand at him. "Could happen to anyone," I said.

We didn't say anything more on the drive home. The Mets rallied and won, six to four in ten innings.

* * *

Dad stayed another two days, worried that somehow Kineally would bust out of jail or that she had an accomplice the police hadn't detected who would emerge from the bushes in front of my house to seek revenge. When no one did, he admitted to a desire to get back to his barn and packed up. I'm always sorry to see him go, but it would be nice to have the house back to myself again.

One reason I wanted the solitude was that I'd decided it was time to start dating again, although I was not going to pursue a relationship with Ben Preston. For one thing, he reminded me of being trapped in a toolbox. For another, he'd been a little—no, a *lot*—too dismissive of me when I'd been right about who the killer might be. Any guy who deserved me would have at least pretended to take me seriously.

Paula showed up on Monday, full of energy and unaware of the drama that had taken place over the weekend because no one—not Dad, Duffy, or Ben—had bothered to call her. I told her about it, only because it felt dishonest not to, and she was aghast, despite seeing that I was perfectly all right (I didn't tell her about the nightmare I'd had that I was becoming a socket wrench). But I gave her some more research to do, and she was back to work. I did notice her coming out of her office more often, ostensibly with a question about something I knew she understood.

She called Damien Mosley's mother, only to find that she had moved away and not left a forwarding address. That cut off any possible photographs of Damien that might have been helpful. But now it felt less urgent to look into Duffy's possible past. There were times I actually found myself wanting him to be the character I'd written, sprung from the bounds of his papery existence and existing entirely as the creation I'd envisioned. It was like having a movie made of one of my books, except that the movie followed you around and you could talk to it. And you didn't get any money.

Speaking of having movies made from my books, Adam was somewhat distraught—almost to the point that I thought he'd have to be put on suicide watch—when he found out that the impending offer from Beverly Hills Productions had in fact been a ruse designed to help me be murdered. Mostly it was the loss of the potential deal that was bothering him, but that's his job.

Hugh Ventnor had passed on *Little Boy Lost*, he reported, but vowed to play on until the book found a home with a nice caring producer who would take it for walks and scratch it behind the ears until it fell blissfully to sleep. Or something. I wasn't the greatest listener these days; my mind tended to wander a bit.

When Brian Coltrane called me from the Plaza Diner asking where the hell I was on our regular lunch day, I told him I hadn't forgotten about the commitment so much as I'd thought it was on hiatus.

"You told me Cathy was upset about how we were friends and you couldn't hang out for a while," I reminded him.

"Cathy moved out," Brian reported. "I told her it was unfair to try to alienate me from my closest friend, and she threw a fit and packed up her stuff."

"I feel awful. Your girlfriend moved out on you because of me." I didn't feel *that* bad, but it's what you're supposed to say.

"Tell you the truth, it's a relief," Brian said. "She was driving me nuts, and the fact is, we hadn't actually had sex in weeks."

"TMI," I told him. "We're friends. I'm not your shrink."

"Come to lunch. I'll let you steal my French fries. I feel bad that I put Cathy ahead of you. How could I do that with what you were going through?"

"Yeah, I'm thinking of breaking up with you as a friend."

"It would serve me right. Come to lunch. You can order a soda and hate it, and I won't even point out that you do that every time."

I considered. "Nah. I appreciate the offer, but I really have to get to these revisions. I'm way behind." It was true; I hadn't done much work since being freed from the dusty confines of Kineally's attic. Or her ex-husband's attic. That guy must have been a piece of work—who marries a woman like that?

Brian made me promise to show up for our next scheduled lunch, and I assured him I would. Now that he was unattached, I'd have to hear about every woman who passed him on the street and whether or not she was "the one." By definition, the vast majority of them were not, and I could tell him that, but why kill the man's dream?

I sincerely, whole-mindedly dug in on the revisions to the new Duffy book. The first step is just to read through the whole manuscript looking for inconsistencies, mistakes, typos, anything (you never know who you're annoying). Just make sure the story makes sense and the characters aren't different in this book or this chapter because I was in an unusual mood or had written myself into a corner. It's a first pass, and it should be simple. One problem is that reading anything off a screen, even something I wrote myself, tends to make me sleepy. Paula has had to wake me up some days when I start snoring at my computer.

I was laboring to stay conscious today (in a less stressful atmosphere than the toolbox) when the doorbell rang, and Paula informed me that Duffy Madison was outside.

The heat had broken a little—it was still in the lower eighties, but much less humid—so I went out and sat with Duffy on the bench next to where there would be a fountain if I had James Patterson's money. He (Duffy, not James) looked a little wild, like he'd been up all night, and when I asked if he was okay, he informed me that he looked like what had indeed happened.

"I couldn't sleep the whole night," he said. He stood up and put his hands behind him, a pacing pose that, when he bent over a little, made him look like Groucho Marx. "What you said to me was haunting me, prodding me. I think it was a call to action."

"What I said to you? What did I say to you?"

"You told me that Damien Mosley was missing and had been missing for four years," Duffy reminded me. It must have been sinking in that there were direct parallels he couldn't explain. Maybe the information coming from me had actually awakened some memory in him and caused a breakthrough.

Wait, maybe this meant he wasn't going to be Duffy Madison anymore.

I had to put my own feelings aside. If I could help the poor man remember his true identity, get back to who he really was, it would be selfish for me to hold him back just because I'd decided it was fun to have my little mind puppet running around in flesh and blood. I should be happy that I could be of so much assistance.

"That's right," I said. "He left just about the time you showed up here in New Jersey."

"Exactly." Duffy's pacing was gaining speed. If he kept going back and forth like that, he would wear a groove in my flagstone. "So I think there's only one thing we can do."

We? It was one thing to be his impetus; it was another to be his guide back to sanity. "I don't think I'm qualified, Duffy," I said.

"Nonsense. You were invaluable on this last case. You'll be invaluable on the new one."

There was clearly a disconnect here, and I was starting to realize it was based squarely in my court. "What new case?" I asked.

"It's clear," Duffy said. "We need to find Damien Mosley."

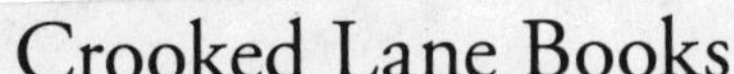
Crooked Lane Books

CROOKED
LANE
NEW YORK

Chapter 1

For Duffy Madison, the period between missing persons cases was never wasted time. Relieved not to be working against an ever-ticking clock to find someone who had been abducted or had simply vanished, Duffy would not let his mind go unoccupied; he'd do research into the latest technologies for evaluating crime scenes or sharpen his observational skills even on short strolls through his own neighborhood.

"That man is lonely and frustrated," he told Angela Mosconi on a walk through Schooley's Mountain Park this Saturday morning. "He looks only at women, but not in a leering fashion. He presses his hands together and flexes his arms whenever he sees a woman he finds attractive, but not to show off any musculature. It's a gesture of anxiety and hopelessness."

"Maybe he's just cold," Angela said. "It can't be more than forty degrees out here today. I should have worn a heavier coat." She hugged herself for warmth, but Duffy, in his intense desire to be more observant, missed the signal that perhaps she would like to have *his* arms around her.

He shook his head. "It is forty-seven degrees today, and the temperature will rise to about sixty later in the morning. That's not weather-related. Look at the way he—"

"Look, we haven't known each other very long," Angela broke in. "But there's something I think you might need to know."

"If this is about your two failed marriages or the childhood bicycle accident that resulted in your left leg being a quarter inch shorter than your right, you have no reason to be concerned," Duffy said, still watching the man he'd deemed lonely as he walked through the park. "I don't believe anyone but I is aware of those things without your knowledge."

Angela stared at him for a moment with a mixture of admiration and annoyance. "I know you well enough not to ask how you know about those things," she said. "But I was getting at something else entirely."

"Interesting," Duffy answered. But his mind was clearly elsewhere. "See that woman in the orange T-shirt? I believe she might once have spent time in county prison."

Angela sighed a little too heavily. Getting through to Duffy Madison when he was trying desperately to focus on something in the absence of an immediate problem to solve was a daunting task she was just beginning to understand.

"Duffy," she began again.

But his face had already frozen in place, and his gait, until now difficult to match, had stopped completely. Duffy looked ahead and stared, so Angela followed his gaze. People were running and gathering at a spot easily two hundred yards ahead.

"Perhaps you'd better stay here," Duffy told her. He began running toward the crowd before she could reply. Angela pursed her lips and followed him.

At the crest of the hill in front of him, Duffy found the crowd gathering. Some women were moaning rather than weeping, and some of the men had to turn away. Duffy shouted, "Morris County Prosecutor's Office," and still had to gently push a couple of people out of the way to get to the edge of the hill and look down.

Off to one side of the hill was a drop of about thirty feet, which had been fenced in to avoid exactly what had happened: A man dressed in bicycle pants and a blue T-shirt was lying faceup, staring blankly at the sky. He was impaled on one of the fence posts that had been poorly maintained and had pierced his chest. The man was dead.

"What a terrible accident," a woman next to Duffy said.

Duffy took in the scene as closely as he could. "This was not an accident," he said, more to himself than to the woman. "That man was murdered."

* * *

I stared at the screen and scowled. I know I scowled because my face was reflected in the screen of my computer, and there was no mistaking the look on my face. It perfectly matched my mood.

Usually, beginning a new Duffy Madison mystery novel was my second favorite part of the writing process. (The favorite part for every writer everywhere is typing the words *The End*, and I also enjoy seeing the name *Rachel Goldman* on the front of the book.) But this one seemed heavy-handed and clumsy. The fact that I just used two terms that mean the same thing might give you an idea of how I felt.

Paula Sessions, my part-time assistant, looked at me from the door to my office, which is in my house in Adamstown, New Jersey, and belongs more to Valley National Bank than to me. "You just started, and you're already unhappy with it?" she asked.

"It's trite and stupid," I said, at least using adjectives that meant separate things. "It's like I'm trying too hard, as if I were writing someone else's character. I used to know Duffy Madison, and now he's a mystery to me."

Paula stifled a chuckle. "Imagine that," she said.

It had been six months since a man had called my house claiming to be the living incarnation of my fictional character. He called himself Duffy Madison, and instead of working for the Morris County Prosecutor's Office as a consultant on missing persons cases, this Duffy had creatively chosen to present himself as a consultant on missing persons cases for the *Bergen* County Prosecutor's Office. See that subtle change there?

The problem was, I'd discovered that he really did work for the Bergen County prosecutor, he really did consult on missing person cases, and everyone he had met knew him as Duffy Madison. They had no idea I wrote a series of mystery novels with a character by that name, so I had both the utter confusion of the situation and the thrill of knowing that no one working one county over from where I lived had ever heard of my books. It's a writer's dream, truly.

I'm being sarcastic. It's a Jersey thing.

The flesh-and-blood Duffy had told me at the time that he believed I had actually created him four years earlier, because he had no memory of anything before that time. He'd said it with a straight face and seemingly in earnest, so after he was out of earshot, I'd asked Paula to do as much research on the supposed Duffy as possible. She came up with very little; he had records stretching back to high school, but no one she contacted could ever remember seeing or talking to him. He seemed to have no family. He existed only on paper. Which somehow seemed appropriate.

"Maybe you need to see Duffy again," Paula suggested now. "You've been ducking him for months."

"I haven't been ducking him," I protested. "I don't want to go off on a pointless crusade with him, but that's not ducking."

In the course of her research on "Duffy," Paula had discovered the wispy trail of a man named Damien Mosley (note the initials), who was the same age as my Duffy, had grown up in the same town, attended the same college, and then vanished at almost the exact moment flesh-and-blood "Duffy" had arrived at the Bergen County Prosecutor's Office and helped with his first missing person.

After our adventure, which had ended in a harrowing fashion for me, Duffy had decided we needed to find Damien

Mosley in an effort to prove to me (!) that he, Duffy, was real and not a literal figment of my imagination. I had resisted that suggestion on the grounds that he was nuts.

I thought that was a pretty strong argument, personally. But Duffy had been calling regularly every three days since then, and now it had been six months. Duffy might be crazy, but you couldn't say he was easily dissuaded.

"It certainly is ducking," Paula said, turning her back as she walked back to her office, across the hall from mine. "If it wasn't ducking, you'd talk to him instead of making me lie every time he calls."

"Duffy knows where I live," I reminded her, loudly now because she was probably behind her desk, which is larger and disturbingly neater than mine. "If he really believed it was necessary, he could come here to persuade me."

"He's been here twelve times," Paula said, not raising her voice at all. She just has an air of confidence that stems from always being right. "You keep pretending you're taking a shower because you know he'll get embarrassed and leave."

"You work for me, you know."

"You don't want to fire me," Paula said, and again, she was correct. "You think your whole life would collapse if I ever left." And it would. Paula thinks it wouldn't, but I barely make it through the days she's not working.

I sat there and stewed for a while. There was obviously no point in trying to debate the point with Paula, especially since she'd continue to insist on being right about everything and taking all the fun out of it. But staring at my computer screen and seeing the fairly turgid prose I'd been turning out, with a deadline pressing in only three months, wasn't helping.

The thing about every writer is that we're sure we're frauds, and sooner or later the world will catch on. Even the midlist types like me—who sell enough books to keep getting published but not enough to live on a tropical island and have young men fetch us drinks in coconut shells—see writing as a gift, and the thing about a gift is that it can be taken back at any moment. Even if you keep the receipt.

What I was seeing in front of me was clear evidence my gift's warranty period had just expired.

This was going to lead to sleepless nights. Clenched stomach. Long hours spent looking at online employment ads. A strong consideration of going back to school to obtain a master's degree in . . . something. And I'd no doubt gain six pounds in the next month, watching my screen stop accumulating words in significant numbers.

I'd watch the calendar and calculate how many words I'd have to write each day to hit my deadline before my editor, Sol Rosterman, started getting impatient. Sol had nurtured me through five Duffy Madison mysteries, the latest of which would be published in four months. He expected number six in three months, and sitting here on the first day I'd begun writing, I saw no clear path to delivering it on time.

The problem was the character. Duffy had always come naturally to me; I'd never really had to think about how he'd react to any situation. I just knew it because the character was part of me.

But now the character could stand in front of me and tell me how he'd react to something, and that was putting a serious damper on my creativity. What if Duffy read the book and thought I'd gotten him wrong? It had already happened once, but I had a completed draft then. This was new territory, and it wasn't friendly.

The rational thing to do, of course, was to banish the living Duffy from my thoughts completely, to not care what he'd think because I'd never see him or talk to him again and therefore didn't have to worry about his reaction. After all, he'd told me more than once that he was simply himself and had never read any of my books in his life. He said he didn't even know there were Duffy Madison novels until he'd had to research a case involving a mystery novelist and stumbled across one of my titles.

Imagine the ego boost: Even the character I wrote almost every day for five years hadn't read any of the books about him. And here I was, despairing over what he might think of the mess I was making of *his* character.

My interior life can be very complicated.

I stared at the screen another few minutes, changed three words that were especially egregious, and then sat back in my deluxe lumbar support swivel chair and sighed. The story in my head was okay, but it needed Duffy to show up and be himself. The way I saw it, there was only one possible solution to this problem, and I didn't like it one bit.

I picked up my phone and called Duffy Madison.

Chapter 2

"The way I see it, we should plan on driving to Poughkeepsie, New York, as soon as possible." Duffy Madison, or the deranged soul believing himself to be Duffy Madison, sat opposite me on the futon I used to use as a sofa but which now was covered in papers, books, folders, one pillow, and a large stuffed dog (not the real kind). And of course one tall, thin, odd man squeezed into the near corner. It was the only seating space in my office aside from my work chair, and that chair is my personal domain.

Duffy had answered on the first ring, seeing my name in his caller ID. He'd been so happy to hear from me that he'd suggested driving to my house in the first six seconds we were on the phone, and I figured that was the quickest way to move forward. But my plans and Duffy's were clearly not in sync, since I had no plan to go to Dutchess County. I had writing to do in New Jersey.

"Poughkeepsie?" I said reflexively.

"Yes." Duffy sat with his left leg crossed over his right. "That is the last known residence of Damien Mosley, so that is the most logical place for us to begin searching for him."

I had realized, of course, that Duffy would expect my call was about Damien Mosley. It was the subject occupying his mind, especially if he did not have an active case he needed to consider, so he would assume I'd be equally obsessed. It's how his mind works. I know. I invented his mind.

But being somewhat self-centered myself, I had failed to look past my own motivations in the moment. I hadn't considered actually searching for Mosley, so Duffy's attitude had startled me just a little.

"We're not searching for Damien Mosley," I informed him.

Duffy's eyebrows rose. "But it's important that you understand my existence," he said. "I can't have you assuming I am delusional. Tracking down Damien Mosley, a matter that appears to be a cold case for the authorities involved anyway, is the logical step to alleviate your concerns. I am Duffy Madison. It's necessary for you to understand that. Finding Damien Mosley should achieve the goal. You'll see he is a separate human being and accept who I am."

Perfect: This was the explanation of a man who admitted he had no memory before five years ago—the problem was all in *my* mind. "Duffy," I said in what I hoped was a gentle tone, "I don't see the issue the same way you do. We've talked about this before." It was true; when Duffy had first broached the subject of searching for the man whose existence seemed to lead directly to his, I'd argued—successfully, I'd clearly been wrong in believing—that there was no upside to going to Poughkeepsie and looking for a man who had vanished there five years before. I urged him to seek some therapy, and he'd said that had not had any positive effect on him in his (limited) memory. In other words, Duffy had tried the talking cure, found it wanting, come to terms with what he saw as the only logical solution, and was now attempting to convince me of the same.

"Then why did you ask me to come here today?" Duffy said. The fact that he'd more or less invited himself over when all I'd done was pick up the phone seemed unimportant even to me.

"I'm having difficulty writing the next book," I said. I couldn't face him as I said it; the inability to conjure my Duffy once I'd met his Duffy was embarrassing, although I didn't really have a handle on why that should be the case. "I've been trying to write Duffy the way I always have, and I keep running into difficulty because your interpretation of the character is blocking mine these days. I think of him, and I see you."

Duffy scowled; I was not accepting his logic when it seemed crystal clear to him. "I have no interpretation of your character. I have never read your books. I am Duffy Madison. Do you want me to become someone else?" The question was meant to be a taunt, but the fact was I thought he *was* someone else and he just didn't want to admit it to himself.

"I don't want you to do anything," I said. "I'm flailing here. I'm confused. There's no reason for you to be who you say you are, and no matter which way we interpret your identity, I should be able to write my original Duffy the way I always have. So I've asked you here today because I want to say good-bye so I can go back to the way things were before."

Duffy sat and squinted at me for a moment; it's what he's always done when confronted with behavior he believes to be irrational. I wrote that for him. This guy who claimed never to have cracked the cover on my novels had my character's mannerisms down cold.

"You are asking me not to contact you again?" he said. "You believe if I absent myself from your life that you'll be able to revert to your old style of writing?"

I turned away from him again. I had to like the guy; I'd written him over and over again. It was very painful to hurt his feelings this way because I was one of the few people on the planet who knew he *had* feelings.

"That's basically it," I mumbled.

Duffy stood up; I could see the movement from the corner of my eye. "You realize this behavior is not rational," he said. I figured he was the expert on irrational behavior, so maybe I should consider what he was suggesting. "Banishing me from your sight will not erase me from your mind."

I hate it when he has a point.

"No, it won't," I told him. "You're a good man, and you literally saved my life, so I'm more than grateful to you. But this is my means of making a living, and you're standing in my eye line when I'm trying to write. You're a distraction."

"I'm not sure I understand the issue," Duffy admitted. "Have I done anything or in any way behaved in a fashion that is inconsistent with your concept of the Duffy character?"

I acknowledged that he hadn't done so without saying aloud that I believed it was because he'd internalized the character from my books so completely that he could do a truly admirable impression. He'd have told me he never read a Duffy Madison book before I gave him my rough draft after we met.

"Then how is the concept of the character at all affected by my presence?" he asked.

It was a good question, and I had been considering it for some time, so I had an answer ready. "The thing is, I like you, Duffy. You're a nice guy, and I don't want to see you come to any harm."

That didn't seem to impact real-life Duffy significantly; he looked puzzled. "Your writing a novel will not cause me any harm," he said.

"No. But in order to make the story work, I have to put Duffy Madison through the wringer. The job of an author is to take the character and create a situation that tests him to his limits. This is the sixth Duffy book, and each one requires me to raise the stakes a little. In my head, I have to come up with more and more trying circumstances for the character to face. And knowing you makes it hard for me to torture the character because I feel like it will be torturing you. Like *I'll* be torturing you."

"I understand there is an artistic process, but I have to say that is not a rational argument," Duffy told me. "Nothing in your books has ever actually happened to me. The cases I've worked with Ben Preston on at the prosecutor's office have never even mildly resembled the ones you've written. You're not going to do me any harm." The nutjob was telling me what was rational. And it was still early in the week.

"Maybe not, but your personal circumstances are almost exactly like the ones I've written for you. Like this: I just started writing Duffy a romantic interest."

The reaction I'd expected and hoped I wouldn't get was exactly what happened. Duffy grimaced a little and stood still. "I have recently started seeing someone," he said quietly.

I pointed at him, acknowledging the coincidence we both noted. "I'm planning on killing Duffy's love interest." (I hadn't actually decided on that yet, but why quibble on the details?) "Do you want me to take that chance?"

"If this magical connection exists as you seem to suggest," Duffy said, "the consequences will occur whether I am a presence in your life or not."

"Maybe, but maybe not. All those times I wrote about Duffy before I met you, I wasn't worried about hurting you, and you were all right as far as we know. Maybe if we're not in contact, that will still be the case. I just don't want to take the chance."

Duffy pursed his lips and nodded slightly; he was thinking. Pretty sure I gave him that move, too.

"I'll make a bargain with you," he said. Duffy's speech tends to lean a little British when he's thinking because I think of Sherlock Holmes when I'm writing those moments. "I think I can help you with your problem."

Well, I hadn't seen that coming.

"You do," I said. It was a placeholder. In a couple of hours, I'd think of what I should have said there and double back in my mind. It's why I'm an author and not, say, a stand-up comedian.

"Yes. As you see it, the impediment to your writing me as a character is that as a three-dimensional man standing in front of you, I change your perspective on the person you're writing; is that correct?"

"More or less, yeah."

"So if you were to prove once and for all that I am *not* Duffy Madison, that I am in fact someone else who perhaps suffered a trauma and took on this personality after reading your novels, despite the fact that you hadn't published them at that time, you could go on writing your fictional Duffy without any further difficulty. Does that make sense to you?" Duffy was pacing in front of me, slightly stooped and with his hands clasped behind his back. If Groucho Marx was a tall, thin, serious man and gave up the greasepaint mustache and eyebrows, he'd be Duffy.

I thought through what he was saying, feeling like it was going in a direction I didn't like but not actually understanding how it was getting there. If we could prove this Duffy wasn't my Duffy, would that help me write him—my Duffy, for those keeping score at home—again?

"Yes, I guess it makes sense," I said.

"So then we have a common purpose, even if we are approaching it from opposite viewpoints." Duffy stopped pacing and looked down at me, as I hadn't moved from my swivel chair. "If we find evidence that I am actually Damien Mosley, I can stop being Duffy Madison in your mind and perhaps heal some hideous memory I have been repressing. You will be relieved of the notion that I am your character and can go back to writing him as you always have."

The trap was springing around me, and there was pretty much nothing I could do about it, but I gave it the old college try. "Suppose we find no evidence of Damien Mosley and you continue to insist I made you up and you sprang to life five years ago? That's what you believe we'll find. How does that help me?" The best defense, I felt, was a good get-Duffy-out-of-here ploy.

He spoke quietly and with serious gravitas. "If that is the case, perhaps we can both find some peace of mind, no?"

My immediate thought was *no*, but somehow three days later, I found myself in a car with Duffy Madison, heading to Poughkeepsie, New York.